TEASE MY DESIRES LACHLAN & HALEY PART II

STEELE INTERNATIONAL, INC. - JACKSON CORPORATION A BILLIONAIRES ROMANCE SERIES CROSSOVER BOOK 2

CHARMAINE LOUISE SHELTON

CONTENTS

FREE BOOK

Get the start of the STEELE International, Inc. A Billionaires Romance Series with *Discover My Desires Sebastian & Lola Prequel* FREE!

Click Cover Below or visit **bit.ly/CLBooksNewsletter** to subscribe to my newsletter for latest news and launches, books from my author friends, and sizzling reads in book promotions. Plus, start reading the steamy billionaire romance *Series Prequel* of Sebastian Steele and Lola Lewis.

Their stories. Their discovery of unknown desires…

FREE BOOK!

EXCLUSIVE FOR SUBSCRIBERS!

STEELE INTERNATIONAL, INC. - JACKSON CORPORATION

A BILLIONAIRES ROMANCE SERIES CROSSOVER

ABOUT STEELE INTERNATIONAL, INC. - JACKSON CORPORATION A BILLIONAIRES ROMANCE SERIES CROSSOVER

Welcome to the titillating world of the multibillion-dollar global companies and the love affairs of the families that controls them.

STEELE International, Inc.- Jackson Corporation is a series of interconnecting Billionaire romance. Follow the Steele and Jackson families as they fly around the world chasing the women they love and their happily ever afters. Get ready for glitz, glamour, and steamy romance books. What's better than that? The Jet-set Lifestyle has never been hotter...

The Desires Series is not for the tea set; it's for the top-shelf vodka straight up in a pretty crystal glass coterie!

Don't miss any of the sizzling romance books in the STEELE International, Inc. - Jackson Corporation A Billionaires Romance Series Crossover:

Tempt My Desires Lachlan & Haley Part I

Tease My Desires Lachlan & Haley Part II

Grant My Desires Lachlan & Haley Part III

Intrigue My Desires Harris & Kat Part I

Decode My Desires Harris & Kat Part II

Honor My Desires Harris & Kat Patt III

A Trilogy of Desires Lachlan & Haley Parts I-III

A Trilogy of Desires Harris & Kat Parts I-III

Series Extras

Series Playlist

Visit CharmaineLouiseBooks.com for the complete list.

ABOUT TEASE MY DESIRES LACHLAN & HALEY PART II

Tease My Desires Lachlan & Haley Part II

Welcome to the titillating world of the multibillion-dollar global companies and the love affairs of the families that control them.

Lachlan gave in to the temptation of his best friend's kid sister Haley. But not enough to give her what she wants—her happily ever after. Now another male wants to make her his.

Can a certain violet-eyed Scottish lass in Lachlan's life make up for his loss of Haley? Or will their irresistible magnetism draw them together again?

Travel with Lachlan as Haley teases him with a life he shouldn't want with the off-limits temptress. Aberdeen,

New York City, St. Lucia, and more await in their too-hot-for-words love triangle billionaire romance.

Anthem: "Would You Mind" Janet Jackson
https://www.youtube.com/watch?v=Y8JGTS56nVU&
list=PLXwYvn0e218Ak-4oI6AHV7tBXs2yQA2vG&
index=6

Playlist:
https://www.youtube.com/playlist?list=
PLXwYvn0e218BrcVnQ_jFx_04NREhVfozt

Visit CharmaineLouiseBooks.com

LACHLAN

"*O*h, come on, bro! I *cannot* believe you've been moping around for the past two months like your favorite puppy ran away. What the bloody hell is wrong with you, Lachlan? And do not give me any more of your bullshit excuses either."

My youngest brother Laurent throws his hands up in the air, then slaps them on top of my desk as he leans over to scowl at me. His bottle green eyes—so like my emerald ones, a Jackson family trait—blaze.

When I don't answer, Laurent growls as he stands to his full height of six feet, three inches and runs his hands through his collar-length sable brown hair. Frustrated, he paces my office in Aberdeen, Scotland at Jackson Town House, the headquarters for Jackson Corporation—our family's multigenerational, multibillion-dollar company.

Its repertoire comprises fine dining, distilleries, and

vineyards worldwide. Our Irish and Scottish family created the finest single malt Scotch Whiskey and became billionaires years ago in the Granite City. King James VI titled the Jackson family as Marquess of Huntly with our family seat—Jackson Castle—in Banff, Aberdeenshire. Our father Connor and mother Lucinda—aka Lucie—use their titles. Even though I'm the heir apparent, my siblings— Lydie, a year older at thirty-five, Lucien thirty-two, and Laurent thirty—and I prefer less formality and use our titles rarely.

Each sibling works at Jackson Corporation: Lydie, Overall Vice President and Vice President of the Board; me, President of Liquor and Second Vice President of the Board; Lucien, *The Sexy Chef*, President of Restaurants/Bars/Lounges and Third Vice President of the Board; Laurent, Director of Jackson Corporation Cigars Division and member of the Board.

Our mother runs the Jackson Foundation. It operates alcohol treatment centers for lower-income individuals and support for their family members. The annual fundraising gala is the highlight of Aberdeen's social calendar. Patrons from across the United Kingdom and the world attend.

Connor holds the head position as CEO and Chairman of the Board and expects to retire in a year. Our father also expects me—as the eldest son—to take over despite Lydie being the firstborn and busting her ass for years. Lydie's sole goal to prove herself worthy to follow in the steps of our forefathers to lead Jackson Corporation.

Unfortunately, her gender proves the problem for Connor…

If I don't use my title of Earl of Aboyne as the heir, I really avoid the role of CEO to the vexation of our father. My allegiance is to my sister. I will do nothing to hurt her. It would crush her very soul to lose the position she's compelled to get since our father gave us a tour of Jackson's first distillery at eight and seven, respectively. Lydie deserves CEO, and I won't stand in her way. For anyone.

To my vexation, my father's insistence on me bearing the next Jackson heir has increased over the last year and a half. Especially since my best friend Sebastian Steele—who's two years older than me—finally tied the knot. Like me, Baz is the eldest son and an Alpha Dom whose time focused on STEELE International, Inc. as recently promoted CEO and president of the Retail Properties Division.

STEELE is his family's luxury real estate development and management corporation based in New York City. One-night trysts to satisfy his sexual and Dom needs supplemented his work. Marriage? Yeah, to STEELE until he met Lola Lewis, and the rest, as they say, is history.

Thanks to the Matriarchs, the Jacksons and Steeles are as close as cousins. My mother and her best friend Michelle *Shelley* Steele spent most of their adult lives together in New York City after my mother ran away from her home in New Orleans. The duo formed a closer bond than they have with their blood siblings and relatives.

As fate would have it, our mothers met our fathers

while working as a bartender in one of the Jackson pubs and as a shopgirl in a STEELE retail space. Both families became close even without sharing DNA. Hence our cousin relationship and Aunt Shelley and Uncle Morgan.

Aside from Baz, the rest of the Steele clan includes Malcolm *The Enforcer* thirty-four, Roger *The Responsible* thirty-three, and fraternal twins Harris and Haley the Dynamic Duo thirty. Like Baz, they work at STEELE: Malcolm president of the Entertainment Properties Division; Roger, president of the Residential Properties Division; Harris and Haley, co-founders of the subsidiary STEELE Technology and Cyber Security.

Although the Steeles call New York City home and the Jacksons have Aberdeen, our families spend a lot of time together. Summers at our Southampton Village beachfront compound in New York near to theirs. Our mother insisted we not loll around the pool, so my siblings and I interned at Jackson's New York City offices. We alternate Thanksgiving between Jackson Castle and The STEELE Tower and Christmas at a STEELE resort. Lucien and Malcolm, Laurent and Harris are best friends, like Baz and me.

Everything was great growing up with our American cousins. Until that summer fourteen years ago, when I was on break from Pembroke College at the University of Oxford. Little Haley—who tagged behind Baz and me as we went about our escapades as kids and teens—at sixteen no longer reminded me of a little sister.

The night Haley fell and hurt herself as she followed us

through their darkened beachfront mansion and looked up at me with soulful platinum gray eyes that shimmered with tears behind her glasses, my heart stuttered. As I tucked a long lock of silky ebony waves behind her ear, then stroked tears from her heart-shaped face, a tingle passed throughout my body.

It was at that moment, I realized Little Haley was no longer just my cousin I regarded as a little sister. She was more. Her behavior towards me changed that summer, too. She was more shy; averted her eyes when our gazes met; lingered near me with a faraway look on her face. It made me wonder if Haley felt the same connection.

But the enormous problem? The obstacle that could keep us apart forever?

Haley was Baz's little sister—*my best friend's* little sister. Completely off-limits to me. Taboo.

Despite the deep part of me she ignited unexpectedly. What I sensed from her didn't matter one bit. Not to mention, she was only a sixteen-year-old girl, and I was a twenty-year-old man. Not happening. Or so I thought…

Thirteen years later and countless trysts with nameless women I fucked who were the direct opposite of Haley with their blonde hair, slim figures, and not stellar brains, I have no choice but to come to terms with my desire for her. My Baby Girl was a fully grown, curvy, brainiac of a woman who came to me to express her desire for more. A desire born from a teenage crush that simmered with a slow burn, despite being held back for years.

We began a forbidden love affair secret from her

brothers—The Big Four—and from our families, except for our mothers who gave their absolute approval. I made Haley Steele mine when she gave me the greatest gifts—her innocence and her innate submission. For a beautiful year of unimaginable bliss, our relationship flourished; our love grew.

Sure, we had bumps along the way. Fiona Ridel the twenty-nine-year-old Scottish heiress my father wants me to marry to seal a merger with her family's oil business. Harris figuring My Baby Girl and me out; Lydie the same situation. And, of course, the ever-present shadow of Baz hanging about the periphery. The tolls of keeping our relationship secret, along with the long distance between Haley in New York City and me in Aberdeen.

We reached the edge more than once—not only the erotic one.

But it was during our one-year anniversary trip to Punta del Este where My Baby Girl realized I hadn't spoken to Baz about our relationship that drove her from my arms. To make it up to her, I asked her to marry me. However, it was too late and not the fairy-tale ending she wanted.

My Baby Girl left me.

No matter the amount of pleas or requests for her to come to my flat one floor below hers at The STEELE Tower, Haley refuses to see me, let alone rekindle our love. Two fucking months of sheer hell. My head and heart ache —not to mention my cock and fist.

So excuse the *fuck* out of me, little brother, if I've *been moping around for the past two months like your favorite puppy ran away.* In a way, she did.

I sigh aloud and roll my eyes inwardly as I rise to my full height of six feet, four inches. The muscles of my sizable frame—honed from decades of Scottish martial arts just like Laurent's body—tighten from stress. One of my hands runs through my slicked-back, sable brown hair while the other swipes over my three-day stubble. Who cares to shave?

Thank fuck it's after working hours.

I stride to the bar on the side wall and pour two fingers of Jackson Special Blend Scotch into Waterford Crystal snifters.

"Shit, Lach, you look a mess, bro," Laurent says as he takes the proffered glass. "What happened to the movie star Cary Grant lookalike all the women adore?"

Now, I roll my eyes blatantly as I grunt into my snifter. What a way to drive in the last nail, little brother, I muse to myself.

"Earth to Lachlan. Have you lost your tongue, *dhuine?*" Laurent asks.

"No, but if you keep bugging the shit out of me, you'll wish I had," I threaten with a cocked eyebrow as I drop onto the tufted leather sofa.

He lowers himself into a club chair across from me and places his snifter on the coffee table.

"No, seriously, Lach. Is everything okay with you? Lydie called me concerned, too," he adds.

I haven't told Lydie. Only our mother knows about the

breakup. The advice I received was to give Haley some time. Even Aunt Shelley voiced the same opinion. So a month ago, I flew back to Aberdeen. But how much more can a man take?

And I know Haley can't feel any better.

I miss My Baby Girl. My urge to care for her grows stronger every day. But what the fuck more can I do?

"Fine, don't tell me," Laurent says exasperated. "However, your ass will be on my jet in the morning. Even if I have to spend the night in your penthouse to get you to the airport, bro."

I stare at him blankly.

"Oh, for fuck's sake, Lach!" He says once again throwing his hands into the air. "The Young 3's 3-0 Birthday Party?! Hello… my thirtieth birthday celebration with Harris and Haley. How could you forget, bro?!"

I blink. Then a slow smile spreads across my face.

The answer I've been seeking. Thank fuck!

My Baby Girl won't be able to avoid me at their party. And it won't appear odd for us to be together.

So hell yeah, I'll be on Laurent's GulfStream G650, ready to get my woman back in my arms. Where she belongs. Forever.

"Happy Birthday, Baby Girl."

She startles, then spins around to gaze up at me. Her wide platinum gray eyes peek out from behind an elaborate mask made of pearls against a cream silk backing with strands that twine up into her hair piled high atop her head.

The length of her swan-like neck emphasized by the turtleneck of her cream-colored stretch-PVC mini dress. The tight fit of the long-sleeves and bodice that flares out to a pleated skater skirt shows off her full tits. It would be demure except for the cut-out back. Her mile-long toned legs end in clear PVC mules. As always, the contrast of My Baby Girl's sinfulness and sweetness tantalizes me. The sexy look fits in with their party's masquerade theme and venue they closed to members for their private birthday celebration.

LEVELS New York the flagship location of the global, luxury, members-only BDSM/dance clubs in Manhattan's Meatpacking District. It caters to the crème de la crème of society and the über-wealthy—politicians, titans of industry, celebrities, and royalty—who prefer to keep their consensual sexual proclivities private with rigorous background checks and nondisclosure agreements. They choose between Global All Access or Dine/Dance memberships.

Lucien and Malcolm selected the historic location as a play on the area's name. Put a club where men pack their meat into willing women and willing men allow women to pack them with their toys. The theme is minimal and industrial. The fixtures and furniture that appear well worn are high-end, modern replicas used to add authenticity without the grime of old pieces.

All Access members can choose from any of the seven levels. While the Dine/Dance members only have access to the party levels—Sky Lounge, Dance Club, and Level 4 Restaurant. For consistency and members' comfort, locations share the same layout with varying views:

Seven levels: 7th Sky Lounge that offers for the Meatpacking location a stunning, 360-degree view of Manhattan and across the Hudson River to New Jersey's shoreline, a bar, restaurant by day dance club by night, a coverable pool that's open during the warmer months, and a glass-retractable roof; 6th and 5th multilevel dance club with two bars and a lounge for food and drinks; 4th Level 4 Restaurant and bar open for breakfast, lunch, and dinner; 3rd has twelve private suites for members to continue their pleasure apart from the BDSM levels; 2nd Peepshow for BDSM with seating alcoves, primary stage, mini-stages, performance rooms, and a bar that serves non-alcoholic mocktails; below ground the Cellar, a BDSM dungeon with mocktails bar.

The wild ones of our families cooked up the idea while Lucien finished his hospitality and culinary training at Le Cordon Bleu in Paris.

When they came to Baz and Lydie with the idea, I agreed with them when they questioned: who the hell goes through that prestigious training to come up with a titty bar? Well, years later Lucien's idea proves it's bigger than that and has a high profit margin with more locations in Paris and London.

The LEVELS clubs are one of many business partnerships that STEELE has with Jackson Corporation. Our products pair well within STEELE's casinos, hotels, resorts, and residential and retail properties.

Right now, the partnership that's my top priority stands before me.

My hands itch to run over her lush curves; my fingers want to trail along her inner thigh before they slip beneath the flirty hemline of her mini dress; my arms flex to pull her to my chest tight.

It takes all of my will to not cover her mouth O-shaped in surprise with mine and kiss her breathless until she melts against me. Then carry her to a private suite to make up for all the days we've been apart.

But most of all, I want My Baby Girl to tell me she still loves me and wants to marry like I asked weeks ago. I send up a silent prayer for a positive reaction from her.

"Lachlan? Wh—what are you doing here?" She asks as her eyes skitter everywhere around the room except my face.

Not quite the response I hoped for. My heart slams in my chest. This won't be as easy as I thought. Damn.

"Baby Gir—"

"Don't! Do *not* call me that, Lachlan," she whisper yells, platinum grays flash like lightning. "I *cannot* believe you're here and calling me what I am not to you anymore! Please…

Please leave me be. What we had ended when you failed to uphold your promise to me. I will *not* get back on that merry-go-round with you again, Lachlan Jackson. Move on. I did."

With a shattered heart, I stare after the love of my life as she stalks away without a backwards glance.

HALEY

The enormous five story, twelve bedroom, sixteen bathroom chalet sits quietly with everyone out enjoying the sunny winter day in Verbier. It's a comfy and chic custom-built chalet with all the top amenities and accoutrements a chi-chi family expects.

Roger gifted the property to Leonie as one of his wedding presents when they married a little over a week ago. He proclaimed it the winter retreat for their new little family of him, Leonie, and their three-month-old identical twin boys—Rodolphe and Gaspard, the first Steele grandchildren. Since her favorite holiday is Christmas and it's the time of year most filled with joy, Leonie named their winter residence *Chalet de le Joie.*

Verbs, as the in-the-know jet-set call Verbier, is a town in the Swiss Alps. A part of the Valais canton in the southwest of Switzerland, France borders Verbier to the west with Italy to the south. It's the most exclusive ski destination in the world.

It's the winter version of Monaco, with the difference being people who go to Monaco want to watch or be watched. Whereas Verbier has an understated style where wealth is glamorous, stylish and tasteful. People are here for the reasons one goes to a ski resort—the superb skiing. Not to mention the phenomenal bars and restaurants; the après-ski is perfect for party lovers. Verbier is a glamorous winter playground.

Roger and Leonie's luxury chalet occupies the area south of the Médran lift. They're slightly away from town along Rue de Médran, where the extra space means they are rarely overlooked and have a private, exclusive vibe. The residential compound is opposite to the STEELE Verbier Hotel & Resort that's closer to the heart of the village square. The concept is for the STEELE Verbier Chalets to access the resort for its five-star amenities. The most important include the luxury thermal bath spa and the three Jackson Corporation restaurants headed by our cousin Lucien *The Sexy Chef,* as he's known by his millions of followers.

The STEELE Verbier had its grand opening during last year's ski season. They planned the Residential Properties Division's completion of the by-application-only compound of ten state-of-the-art chalets and private clubhouse to take occupancy for this year's season. As always, both top-notch properties deserve the STEELE stamp. Both projects have proven successful.

The entire Steele clan, along with Leonie's parents Guy and Josy Beaulieu with The Twins, arrived after Roger and Leonie had the chalet to themselves for their honeymoon. It's been so much fun skiing and going to the clubs. But a sizable piece of me is still missing.

Wistfully, I make my way to the nursery to spend time with my adorable nephews. The thought of them and having seen Lachlan at the wedding makes my sadness increase. I wish we could have had the same as Roger and Leonie. Hell, Sebastian and Lola, and now Malcolm and Starr, too. Even after six months of being apart from Lachlan and *living my life* supposedly, I miss him and what we shared.

The other day, I had to fess up to Lola, Leonie, and Starr about Lachlan and me. Not so much detail. I merely admitted my attraction to him and my wish we could have more. Leonie burst out in laughter, "Thinking about your overbearing brothers. Better you than me!"

Yeah, tell me…

I put on a brave face and knock on the nursery door and open it when Leonie calls for me to enter.

"Bonjour! How are my darling nephews?" I ask brightly as I swoop Rodolphe from Nanny Grace and cuddle him to my chest. Then stride over to Leonie and kiss Gaspard on his chubby cheek.

And the winner for best performance is… Haley Steele!

"Where are you going?" I ask noting their outerwear as I bounce Rodolphe, who laughs. "Bouncy, bouncy, baby!"

"Into the village for some family time."

Roger's booming voice makes us turn around. He greets Nanny Grace and takes Rodolphe from me.

Oh, well, there goes the idea of boosting my depression with some baby loving. I nod and head for the door.

"Hey! Why don't you come with us? We can have breakfast and see what's going on," Leonie asks.

"No, that's okay. Have fun!" I respond. But Leonie will have none of it.

So in the end, we climb into one of the Mercedes-Benz G-Wagens and head to Place Centrale. We drop the SUV with the STEELE Verbier valet, then walk along the main street, checking out the options.

The delicious scent of cinnamon and nutmeg escapes the warm confines of a restaurant as a couple with a toddler exit. Once inside, Roger slips his beanie off, and his ebony hair falls around his stubble-covered cheeks. The light streaming through the oversized windows makes his dove gray eyes sparkle as he smiles at the hostesses.

They nearly swoon.

Oh, for heaven's sake! A baby in his hand and two women with him don't deter women. My brothers attract them like magnets… Leonie and I glance at each other and roll our eyes with a huff.

One of them seats us and grins at Roger the entire time. Shortly after we settle The Twins, a server takes our orders.

"So, you're the new DILF on the scene?" Leonie teases Roger with a broad grin. My sister-in-law is a megamodel whose Tunisian and Parisian heritage make her a stunning woman. Few can compare to *The Lion*'s beauty. Super confident in herself and in their love, she can joke easily.

I throw my head back and crack up and add another joke about hot dads until Roger growls at us annoyed by our teasing. Which only makes us laugh louder.

"Haley?"

We turn to find a handsome Scotsman towering over my chair. His emerald green eyes darken when I smile up at him. Long blonde hair curls around the collar of his down jacket.

"Oh, Callum Graham! What a surprise!" I exclaim as I stand to give him a hug.

He pulls me into his powerful embrace as I rise on the balls of my feet to reach my arms around his neck. At six feet, five inches, he's nine inches taller than me. A brawny lad, as I teased him before.

It's a shock to see the Duke of Montrose, whom I met while attending Harvard Business School. He's four years older than me at thirty-four. A delightful fellow I studied with many a night and went for a jog with around campus to relieve the stress.

"Good to see you, lass! You look amazing! No glasses, huh? Although I must say I thought you were cute in them," Callum says with a grin. Then he pulls back to stare into my eyes and adds, "Regardless, you have always been a beauty, Haley Steele."

My cheeks heat from his intense gaze. I bite the corner of my lower lip and avert my eyes.

Whoa! Why the hell does my heart flutter? It has to be

the dominant personality and the Scottish accent—albeit thicker—that reminds me of another brawny lad.

A male cough sounds behind me.

Roger and Leonie, right. Callum—and the thought of the other one—sort of blanked my mind for a minute.

I slip from Callum's arms and turn to my brother and sister-in-law to make the introductions.

He explains he was just leaving since his friend never showed up because of a hangover.

I look to Roger for his approval for another disruption of his *family time*, and he offers Callum to join us.

He accepts happily and helps me into my chair before he lowers his massive frame into the seat next to mine. His eyes never leave my face while in my periphery I notice Roger's eyes never leave Callum. *The Responsible One's* signature intense stare on full alert. Undoubtedly, he'll arrange a comprehensive background check. Not even a duke is good enough for The Big Four's—Sebastian, Malcolm, Roger, and Harris'—baby sister.

We enjoy a tasty breakfast, during which Callum regales us with royal tales. He's as personable as he was in school. With ease, he even gets Roger chuckling about some escapades. Leonie grins like the Cheshire Cat as her amber eyes flick between Callum and me. I can hear her brain working on a matchmaking scheme and sharing it with Lola and Starr when she gets back to the chalet. Especially since Leonie knows things aren't solidified with Lachlan.

I let it all go and enjoy our time together as my sadness takes a backseat.

After the meal ends, Callum asks me to go for a stroll around the village. I agree, and we leave Roger and Leonie with a promise by Callum to return me to the chalet.

"So tell me, Haley, what have you been up to? You ghosted me after graduation, even though I reached out many times. You almost gave me a complex," he says with a smile that makes his eyes sparkle.

Damn, was it that obvious? I didn't give Callum a chance because I set my mind on Lachlan and only Lachlan. Any other man was only a friend. Nothing more.

I push my mirrored Ray-Ban Aviators up the bridge of my nose.

Callum chuckles and asks, "Aha, so you still have that cute little habit, lass?"

I frown up at him, and he stops to face me.

He slips a glove off and uses his index finger to touch the tip of my nose, then glides it up to my sunglasses. His fingers dance down the side of my face to hold my chin between his thumb and forefinger as he leans down to peer at the lenses.

"Haley, I know we've only reconnected. But I don't want years to pass before I see you again," Callum says with a cocked eyebrow before he continues. "Since I'm working between Aberdeen and New York City now, I'd like to spend more time with you. Would you mind?"

I knew he was at HBS in preparation to take over as the

CEO of Graham Energy, Oil & Gas Company from his father. When he asked Roger how STEELE Residential Properties Division handled heating, Callum told us he's the president of GEOGC. I hadn't realized he moved to the City.

Even more importantly, I hadn't realized he still wanted more than a friendship with me.

I swallow to moisten my suddenly dry mouth. It takes every bit of my willpower to not adjust my sunglasses. I refuse to let my nerves get the best of me.

Not to mention the fact, I *did* tell Lachlan I moved on with my life. So it's about time I did just that. And what better time than now with someone I know and trust?

I close my eyes behind my sunglasses and take a deep, cleansing breath. Then release it slowly as my eyes reopen. In with the new; out with the old.

"No, Callum, I wouldn't mind at all," I respond confidently as a sense of peace settles over me.

A beatific smile spreads over his already gorgeous face.

"Excellent, Little Lass," Callum purrs.

I shudder.

"Don't you look stunning, Little Lass."

At Callum's words, I startle at his unexpected gruff voice in my ear as I stand in the chalet's wine cellar. He chuckles and strokes the five o'clock stubble on his square chin and firm jaw. His eyes rove up and down my body appreciatively.

We're gathered for New Year's Eve pre-dinner cocktails

with family and friends, including some we met up with on holiday, Callum included. The bartender and sommelier for STEELE Verbier crafted a selection of drinks and wines for dinner and the party.

For the 70s disco era theme, I chose a style similar to one worn by Bianca Jagger at Studio 54. The leopard-print silk mini dress with spaghetti straps inspired by delicate lingerie highlights my full D-cup breasts with the vee-neck and long, toned legs trimmed in black scalloped lace. Sheer black silk stockings with seams and black stilettos, along with oversized gold hoops, are the only accessories needed. I swept my hair atop my head in a messy updo and kept my makeup minimal with red matte lipstick.

I smile and give a twirl.

"Why thank you, sir," I respond. Then blink when Callum's eyes flash.

Oh, dear, that was a slip of the tongue…

To skip past my faux pas, I loop my arm through his and lead him to the bar for one of the signature cocktails. We chat with other guests until the butler enters the wine cellar to announce dinner served upstairs in the dining room.

Callum offers his arm with a bow of his head, "My lady, shall we?"

I giggle and curtsey as I respond, "Yes, we shall."

We join others at a table to feast on the scrumptious meal prepared by Roger and Leonie's new chef. Again Callum's charm enthralls the guests while he keeps his attention on me evenly. After dessert, I excuse myself for the ladies' room.

"Haley, sweetheart, Roger tells me that's Callum Graham, a young man you were friends with at Harvard. You seem pretty cozy. Anything you want to share with your mother?"

I glance up to the mirror to find Shelley behind me, an elegant eyebrow arched in question.

A flash of guilt hits me. Then I remember how Lachlan didn't put us first. His best-friend relationship with Baz ranked higher than our relationship. Lachlan's refusal to stand up for us was the end. So while I'd rather be celebrating the New Year with Lachlan, I won't let the past keep me from my future.

With a deep breath, I turn to face my mother—a fan of Lachlan and me as a couple.

"Mom, you know why I broke up with Lachlan. As much as I miss him, I cannot spend the rest of my life waiting for him like I did before. I'm not ready for a relationship. Callum is someone I know and feel comfortable with. Okay?" I say.

She studies me for a moment, then nods and pulls me into her embrace.

"Haley, you have my support for whatever path you choose. Just be sure you're doing what *you* want. *Okay?*" She responds.

"Okay!" I say, then squeeze her tight.

. . .

THE DJ from Farm Club Verbier spins a variety of music.

We party it up in the disco next to the wine cellar. The set up works well with people moving seamlessly from the bar to the dance floor or the banquettes along the walls. A gigantic screen shows scenes of countries around the world celebrating the start of the New Year with Sydney, Australia first.

Callum spins me out, then pulls me back into his muscular chest. We move in sync as the beat guides us. It's so nice to let loose and be carefree after months of sadness.

A piercing whistle blasts, and we turn to find Sebastian on a raised platform with one arm around Lola and the other beckoning to Roger and Leonie. Then he raises his Champagne flute.

"Before midnight strikes, I want to congratulate my brother on his new bride and darling Twins, my new sister and nephews. We love you all. Steeles for life!"

Everyone claps and stomps with more wolf whistles.

The DJ calls for more Champagne with five minutes to go.

Earlier, Harris angled the exterior cameras toward Verbier Village and relayed the footage to the screen. Now, he switches the feed, and the live view appears for the countdown clock and fireworks display.

Callum hands me a flute from a passing server, then slips his arm around my waist, melding me to his side. I smile up and thank him.

The lights dim as the countdown begins.

The screen is so large, we might as well be front row in the village.

We chant the countdown, then cheer as midnight strikes and glittery silver, gold, and white balloons fall from the ceiling.

"Happy New Year, Little Lass," Callum murmurs before he leans down and kisses my lips softly.

"Happy New Year, Callum," I whisper.

Well, here's to a fresh start. One I deserve. At last.

LACHLAN

"*O*h, Lachlan, don't you look oh so debonair! The other women will be so envious you're on my arm, my lord!"

Although I want to cringe every single time at the nickname Fiona uses since Haley called me My Lord, I smile graciously.

Over the past five months, Fiona acts as my go-to partner for events. Occasionally, we have dinner, or I'll visit her art gallery in Aberdeen for an opening. It's easy to spend time with her since I've made it clear I'm not in the market for a relationship, and she's agreed to friendship only. At first, I thought she'd push for more. But so far, she's kept it platonic. Thank fuck.

Meanwhile, I've caught wind of Haley gallivanting around the world with Callum Graham. Besides being a part of Scottish royalty and nobility circles, I know Graham from our gentleman's club, The Royal Northern &

University Club Aberdeen. The forefathers of the Jacksons and of the Grahams share the same status as founding members.

He's also an Alpha Dom.

The thought of Graham doing anything with Haley—let alone Dominant/submissive related—makes me want to rip his fucking face off.

A veil of red descends over my vision as my fists form at my sides.

"Lachlan? Are you all right?"

Fiona's questions in her soft Scottish lilt reach through the haze to draw me back to the present.

I shake my head to clear it and take a deep breath, then glance down. Fiona's striking violet eyes—wide in her porcelain face—peer up at me.

She's a beautiful woman with ash blonde hair that hangs like a curtain to her narrow waist. A willowy figure at five feet, nine inches, the top of her head meets my shoulder in her heels. She may resemble the women I fucked prior to Haley to keep my desire for her out of my mind, but Fiona is smart, like her.

Before Fiona opened her successful art gallery, she attended Gordonstoun School with Laurent and graduated with honors from the University of St. Andrews with a degree in Art History. Not only a socialite from one of the oldest families in Scotland, but Fiona is also a philanthropist who supports the arts in schools. She's the epitome of the woman my father wants me to wed and with whom to have Jackson heirs.

If not for the facts I still love Haley with all of my heart and hope we can reconnect at some point, I could marry Fiona. But oh, well…

Instead, I smile down at her.

"All's good, Fiona. And thank you, but *you* will be the belle of the ball and every man will want to dance with you," I respond as I gesture at her gown.

Her elegantly simple white satin floor-length dress skims her lithe body from the strapless neckline to her knees, where it flows to the tips of her matching heels in the front and a train in the back. It's in a flattering silhouette. Somewhat bridal in appearance.

I shake my head again to rid it of that unexpected comparison.

Fiona beams and loops her arm through mine. We head out of her suite at STEELE Montaigne in Paris for the rooftop ballroom. I drove over moments ago from my *seizième* penthouse to meet her.

The *huitième* arrondissement five-star hotel has extraordinary views of the Champs-Élysées, Arc de Triomphe, and the Place de la Concorde, not to mention the Seine. At night, with the lights of Paris shining brightly, will prove a spectacular venue for the gala.

Roger asked Jackson Corporation to sponsor Leonie's charity gala for the girls and teens center she mentors at regularly. Lucien and I—being the closest of our clan based in Paris and Aberdeen, respectively—came to represent our company and to support our cousins. In addition, I crafted signature libations using the Jackson portfolio for the cocktail hour and *The Sexy Chef* created tantalizing hors d'oeuvres and the dinner.

However, my chief hope is Haley will attend. It's been too long since we've seen each other in person. The last time, my eyes were on her back as she strode away from me at her birthday party...

My mobile vibrates in the trousers pocket of my bespoke classic tuxedo. I slip it out as Fiona and I enter the elevator with other well-dressed guests going to the gala undoubtedly. We exchange nods in greeting.

Hey, bro. I'm already here. Where the bloody hell are you?

With a grunt, I unthread my arm from Fiona to type a quick response:

Ash, dhuine! On the elevator, man.

She peeks up at me with another concerned expression. Before she can speak, I shake my head and smile.

The doors ping open. We queue up for the step and repeat highlighting the event sponsors, including Jackson Corporation, STEELE International, Inc., Lola's Coterie, Banque Montaigne, Elie Saab, Van Cleef & Arpels, and other high-profile companies. Ahead of us, I spot Lucien with his date. I shoot him a text to let him know Fiona and I are in line behind him. He waves us forward for group shots.

"About time!" He says as he claps me on the shoulder. "Busy getting it on with the fine Fiona?"

"No, wanker!" I grumble with a scowl while he chuckles.

The women smile at one another before we pose for the photographers.

Once inside, I spot Sebastian and Lola close to Roger and Leonie. My heart beats faster. Perhaps Haley came after all.

As though sensing my thoughts, Baz glances up and waves. I return the greeting and lead Fiona to them. Lucien follows with his date.

"Good to see you, guys!" Baz exclaims as he bro hugs Lucien and me. Then he glances over my shoulder. "Ah, hello, Fiona. How are you?"

She smiles and shakes his proffered hand.

"Hello, Sebastian. Well, thank you. How are you? And you, Lola?" Fiona replies as her violet eyes flick from Baz to his wife.

While he responds, Lola eyes Fiona and glances at me with pursed lips.

"Hi, Lola, you look lovely," I say as I lean down to double kiss her cheeks.

She huffs and nods.

"Thank you, Lachlan. You're obviously doing well. Hello, Fiona," Lola says and turns away. "Oh, hi, Lucien! So good to see you. The hors d'oeuvres are delish. As always, *you* rock!"

Fiona blinks, and Lucien pulls Lola into an embrace, much to Baz's chagrin.

"Oh, hello, Lachlan."

I glance around to find Leonie and Roger approached.

She arches an elegant eyebrow at me. Her feline amber eyes glitter dangerously.

"Hi, Leonie, how stunning you are tonight. Congratulations on your gala!" I say. Perhaps *The Lion* will be less inclined to eat me alive if I pepper her with compliments.

She gives an arrogant Gallic shrug: sticks out her full lower lip; raises her eyebrows and slim shoulders simultaneously; followed by a patronizing, *"Bof."*

Roger watches our exchange with his characteristic intense stare.

Damn.

"Hello, Leonie, Roger."

Fiona cuts into the awkward exchange with grace as she extends her hand.

Her signature megawatt smile spreads across Leonie's beautiful face.

"Hello. And you are?" She asks.

In my periphery, Lola smiles. The petite spitfire's hazel eyes shine with devilment.

Oh, these two besties are up to no good. Both more than likely remember Fiona from Thanksgiving at Jackson Castle all those months ago…

"Fiona Ridel, we met before—"

"Hmmm. I meet so many fans, it's hard to recall. Well, thank you for coming to my gala. Enjoy!" Leonie says breezily as she loops her arm through Lola's and sashays away.

Another woman gives me her back…

Fiona glances at Baz and Roger, then at me.

I offer her a smile.

"Come, let's get a cocktail," I say, gesturing to a bar. "I hear they're *delish*, too."

A dazzling smile appears as her violet eyes twinkle at my dig.

I return her smile with a chuckle.

We select our drinks and peruse the silent auction. Jackson Corporation offered two lots: a day at one of our distilleries in Scotland with a weekend stay at our inn and a seven-day getaway to Jackson Château and Winery in Médoc, France.

"Jackson Château seems so romantic!" Fiona exclaims as she stares at the colorful marketing brochures and framed images on the table.

My heart clenches when I remember the week Haley and I spent there.

As I open my mouth to respond, the hairs on the back of my neck rise. I glance around the alcove with the auction. A flash of yellow catches my eye.

Across the room, Haley stands. No glasses cover her flashing platinum gray eyes. They lock on me with an intensity greater than Roger. Even from this distance, I sense she's upset, despite how gorgeous she appears.

An alluring plunging neckline and thigh-grazing split meet in a twist at her slim waist cinched by a chunky gold chain. The soft jersey material allows for the long sleeves and the bodice to have a blousy fit in contrast with the sexiness of the floor-grazing gown. Ultra-high strappy gold sandals wind around her toned calves. Another Haleyism—bright and seductive.

My jaw drops.

Fuck. Me. She looks so good.

Then, to ruin the whole situation, that wanker Graham slips his arm around her waist possessively and leans over to whisper in her ear.

At first, she continues to glare at me. Then her face softens before she turns her body to his and smiles up at him. His sizable hand slides beneath the fabric of the cutout at her back to graze her bare skin.

The red veil descends and all sound fades. My vision tunnels on the lovey-dovey pair.

I step forward, but a hand on my forearm stops me. I snatch away, but the grip tightens. A growl rumbles in my chest as my head swivels to the offender.

"What?!" I bark through clenched teeth.

"Lachlan, what's up?" Baz asks with a cocked eyebrow. "I called you a moment ago."

Double fuck me.

A ragged breath flows from my mouth. A deep inhalation clears the thick haze.

"Nothing. What's up?" I ask, blanking my face and forcing my eyes to stay on his and not stray to Haley. However, my periphery picks up her movement from the alcove to the primary room as servers announce dinner.

"We're at the head table with Leonie. She wants us seated now," Baz says as he studies my face.

I nod and glance around for Fiona. I forgot about her

completely. She's a few feet away chatting with Lola. Baz and I walk over to them and head for the table.

My mind races as I process seeing Haley finally, and she's with Graham. It's one thing to hear about them through the Jackson-Steele grapevine. But it's a whole other thing to witness them. Together.

Fortunately, they're seated at another table out of my line of sight. Thank fuck!

I go on autopilot and converse with the others at the table. Fiona proves she's a great social partner by chatting with everyone and making witty comments. She's even managed to warm Leonie and Lola up to her. A bit.

Me?

I still get an occasional side-eye from the besties. But I guess it has to do with my status of persona non grata with Haley. Well, better to be hated than not thought of at all.

The evening continues through dinner to the announcement of the silent auction winners. When the emcee rewards a couple for the Jackson Château trip, as the sponsor, I shift in my chair to find them in the crowd.

My gaze meets Haley's instead. For a moment, her eyes shine as though she holds tears back. Then she blinks and rises from her chair.

Before I realize I've moved, I'm striding past tables to reach her. My urge to comfort her crests.

I catch a glimpse of yellow to my left as I exit the ballroom and follow. She goes into the ladies' room. Again, I follow without hesitation.

Haley stops at the vanity in the anteroom and places

her hands on the surface with her head hanging. A sob slips from her lips.

"Haley?" I call out softly.

She startles and swings around to face me. One hand braced on the vanity behind her, the other swipes a tear from her cheek.

"Baby Girl—"

"Lach—"

The door opens.

"Lachlan?" Fiona asks.

Haley's face hardens, and her back goes ramrod straight. With her head held high, she sweeps past me and Fiona out the door. Again, without a backwards glance.

My molars grind as I bite back her name.

Fuck!!!

"Sorry, I didn't mean to interrupt," Fiona says. "Would you mind if I returned to my suite? My head bothers me."

I blink and shift my gaze from the door to Fiona.

"Oh, of course not. I'll escort you—"

"No! Uh, no need for you to ruin your evening on my account. I only came to let you know, so you didn't think *I* up and disappeared on *you*," she says.

Surprised by her tone, I cock my head to gauge her mind-set.

Fiona waves her hand and smiles.

"Oh, don't worry about me. I'll be just fine!" She says, overly bright.

Did I imagine her clipped response?

Regardless, as a gentleman, I will not leave her to return

to her hotel suite unattended, even in the posh STEELE Montaigne.

"I'm sure, Fiona. But I'd rather see you to your suite. And no, you're not ruining my evening. We came together, and we leave together," I declare with a smile I hope settles her.

Fiona doesn't deserve to suffer from my craziness with Haley.

The upside, she must still feel something for me. Why else would My Baby Girl cry?

HALEY

"*How* I love my job!" I profess with a giggle as Starr Knight and I stretch out on oversized chaise lounges on the white sand of Palmilla Beach.

She giggles as she takes a sip of her mojito. As much as mine in my cheeks, her dimples pop in her angelic, chestnut-colored face when she joins in.

Almost three years ago, Starr helped to put Lola back together after her breakup with Baz. The fitness retreat on the Fijian private island of Laucala Starr hosted rejuvenated Lola, and they became fast friends.

Like Lola with Lola's Coterie, Leonie with her modeling and work at STEELE, and me with my subsidiary, Starr is an Independent Woman who took her passion and made it into a successful business. Starr Light Fitness & Wellness Center Beverly Hills grew from an idea and her love of helping others to achieve their best lives to a world renown, multimillion-dollar international company.

Lola paid it forward by introducing Starr to Malcolm, since he runs STEELE Entertainment Properties Division that encompasses our resorts. The partnership developed will expand SLFW to STEELE properties as standalone centers and locales for luxury fitness retreats.

Now, the partnership extends to Malcolm and Starr's love life. The two are inseparable. More than likely, I expect to have a third sister-in-law shortly. And I couldn't be happier! It's time for less testosterone in the Steele family…

We're on a construction site visit for the first international center—Starr Light Fitness & Wellness Resorts at STEELE Cabo San Lucas.

The beach features a one-mile-long stretch of gorgeous, soft golden desert sands and blue-green swimmable waters. The five-diamond SCSL is the only resort with direct access. It's nestled near the southern tip of Palmilla Beach and commands stunning views over the turquoise water. Guests enjoy complimentary activities, including snorkeling, stand-up paddleboarding, and kayaking at SCSL's very own Pelican Beach.

SLFW Resorts sits back from the shoreline behind lush foliage of palm trees and hibiscus bushes. Close to the primary hotel, the center has beachfront footage for our activities without interfering with guests of the hotel. The structure mimics the Spanish-style property with white stucco walls, red tile roof, arches, and blue accents. A rooftop terrace takes advantage of the panoramic view—miles of turquoise water dotted by mounds of earth breaking its surface.

I joined Starr to oversee the installation of the center's technology systems.

Since Harris and I are the youngest of the Steele clan and a double surprise for our parents, who had not planned on having more children, we wanted to make our impact on STEELE undeniable.

Although fraternal twins, we share a similar love of technology, with Harris a coder and me a hacker. Our brothers tease us for being nerds, but we know our stuff. So much so, Baz and our father approved for Harris and me to create our subsidiary. As co-heads, we're responsible for all of STEELE and external clients from around the globe, including SLWF—and Jackson Corporation. Ugh! Despite Harris and me being the babies of the bunch, we're super smart, and our brothers have grown to depend upon our tech skills.

"Harris wanted your project, but he lost out. My paper beat his rock. I always tell him brawny doesn't always win!" I giggle, then take a sip of my tasty mojito.

Our antics crack everyone up. If we weren't so smart, people would think we're crazy to do business based on a random game of chance!

"I'm glad you won, too! Now we can hang out when the workday ends and sip mojitos!" Starr declares as she clinks my glass with hers.

We lean back against our chaise lounges to catch up on

our lives. Other than my brief conversation with the girls in Verbier, I haven't spoken with them about the status of my love life. If it even exists.

CALLUM:
+ Makes me laugh
+ Makes me feel special
+ Not afraid to be seen with me
+ Alpha Dom
+ Gorgeous, smart
- Not Lachlan…

THEN THERE'S LACHLAN:
+ My teenage crush, my heart
+ Knows me so well
+ Completes me
+ Alpha Dom
+ Cary Grant/movie star gorgeous, smart
- Won't stand up for *us*!
- With Princess Fiona the Fair!

A COUPLE OF WEEKS AGO, when I saw him at Leonie's gala, I could not believe he was with the violet-eyed princess—of all people. But I knew she was angling for him since Thanksgiving. So of course Lachlan would turn to her as soon as we broke up. How convenient?

Seeing how joyful that couple who won the week at Jackson Château acted reminded me of the incredible time Lachlan and I spent there. My stomach churned. I had to get out of the ballroom. Pronto.

I almost ran into his arms when he followed me all the way into the ladies' room. The sight of him so dashing in his tuxedo with eyes so full of love and need nearly broke down my shields.

Then whammo!

Here comes the ethereal fairy princess floating in from the Scottish moors to dispel the wisp of a connection Lachlan and I made in that moment. Hell, she even dressed like a fairytale bride in her white mermaid gown! Only doves flying into the cloudless blue sky and the gentle sounds of harps were missing from the tableau.

I refused to allow Fiona to see the level of pain I was experiencing. Not to mention getting any idea Lachlan meant more to me than a cousin—a close relation of the entire Steele family. So as quickly as I left the ballroom, I returned to it. Determination hardened my heart.

Callum voiced concern for my abrupt departure. But I blamed an eyelash on my contact lens since I knew my eyes were red from my tears of heartbreak. An expression of skepticism crossed his face as he studied me, but he let it go. Thankfully.

Our evening continued uninterrupted by glimpses of Lachlan and Princess Fiona the Fair since neither reappeared. However, my heart ached wondering if they were off somewhere fucking. Whether in his penthouse where he took my virginity or in a suite at my family's hotel makes it even worse.

Not much beyond Leonie's speech did I tell Callum I needed to return to the President's Suite. He obliged, and we bid everyone good night.

Of course, Baz and Roger told Callum to return me to my suite and to go to his. Despite Lola and Leonie's attempts to laugh off my brothers' command, Callum got the hint. Big time since neither Baz nor Roger cracked a smile.

My face flushed scarlet.

Callum heeded their command. But he gave me a scorching kiss. For a moment, I allowed myself to meld to his brawny frame to drive the pain from my heart. Despite how good it felt, he still wasn't Lachlan.

The next morning, after Callum and I ate breakfast with Baz and Lola, I flew back to New York City. I had to check on the final systems for SLFW Resorts at STEELE Cabo San Lucas ahead of our site visit. My team implemented some new technology that needed tweaks before the systems go live. Then Harris and I ran the programs. With all set, I flew to the resort to meet Starr.

As she tips her head back to sip her mojito, the sun reflects off the gems at her throat. The diamond-pavé letter S in its platinum mesh center sparkles like fire.

They remind me of questions I've been meaning to ask Starr.

"How do you feel about your collar?" I ask, as I trace my finger over my bare neck.

Starr chokes on her drink. I reach across to her chaise lounge to pat her on the back as her wide sorrel brown eyes fill with water. She gasps for air.

My question caught Starr off guard completely. But it's more than surprise that has her sputtering. I'm sure she's thinking about Malcolm and his reaction to my inquisitiveness.

I'm no fool and recognize my brothers dabble in domination and submission. Hell, Malcolm and Lucien started LEVELS. How obvious can they be with memberships and their frequent visits to the sex clubs? Sure, Roger and Harris aren't Alpha Doms like Baz and Malcolm—even our Dad. But like them, they're Alpha males through and through.

And I understand firsthand Lachlan is an Alpha Dom since we touched upon aspects of BDSM. Silk ties and masks, spreader bars, orgasm control, spanking. But as they say, mostly vanilla. And I want more.

Callum appears to be a dominant too. Although we haven't gone that far…

I'm curious.

Starr sits back on her chaise lounge and squints at me.

"Why do you ask?" She asks after a while.

I sigh and stare towards the horizon as though the sparkling turquoise waters of the Sea of Cortez and of the Pacific Ocean hold the answers.

"I want to be dominated," I respond confidently. Happy at last to share my desires with one of my sister friends.

Silence.

I bring my gaze back to Starr, who stares at me in consideration. Okay, I've gotta get her to talk, despite Malcolm.

"Lola told me how you helped her after she broke up with Baz. She says you offered really excellent advice"—I shift in my chaise lounge to gaze at Starr—"I'm torn between Lachlan and Callum. You know the Scottish duke I was with in Verbier. They're both dominants. But I don't know how to make things right with Lachlan and wonder if I even should and instead focus on Callum."

Starr nods in encouragement when I pause to gather my thoughts.

"I told you, Lola, and Leonie how I've always had an attraction to Lachlan. What I didn't tell you was... I need you to promise not to tell anyone. Especially not Malcolm," I say.

"Absolutely I promise, Haley. I will never betray your confidence. No more than I did Lola's. Trust me," Starr responds fervently. Tendrils of her long curly hair slip into her face. She pushes them behind her ears and with a nod clasps her hands palms together before her heart center.

I take a deep breath.

"Lachlan and I were lovers for a year before I ended our relationship since he refused to tell Sebastian about us. He's more concerned with not upsetting his best friend than me," I end on a sob. Tears fill my eyes, and I turn to the tranquil waters again.

I sob harder when Starr slips her arms around my shoulders and hugs me close.

"Oh, Haley, honey! Just let it out," she croons.

When the fountain dries, I squeeze Starr and settle back on my chaise lounge with my legs tucked beneath me. She sits in front of me in lotus position. I stare into her eyes and see the trust. Relieved, I continue.

"It broke my heart to have my teenage crush at long last, only to have him not man up enough to face my brothers. When I told him I couldn't take it anymore and was leaving, he asked me to marry him," I say and roll my eyes at the less than stellar proposal. I want a genuine marriage, not one forced on my lover.

Starr nods but doesn't interrupt. Her peacefulness bests the waters before us, and I continue to reveal more secrets with ease.

"But Callum. He's just as much a dominant as Lachlan. The difference is, he won't allow my brothers to interfere. At least he hasn't so far. Despite their veiled threats…" I shake my head. "If not for Lachlan, I wouldn't hesitate to take things further with Callum. We knew each other at Harvard. But I confined him to the friend realm out of loyalty to my love for Lachlan. And look at where that got me, huh? Nowhere!"

Even Starr can't stop a huff at that revelation.

"I know, right?! I also refuse to let my brothers control my life. I am determined to live, live, live as Leonie says! The Big Four *cannot* control me. But I'd welcome it from my prospective Alpha Doms without hesitation!" I admit to Starr.

We laugh and sip the last of our mojitos. A server

appears as though in the wings for refills. Starr looks at me, I look at her, and we burst out in giggles as we nod our approval for another round. We need liquid courage after all!

"Well, Haley, that's incredible you've kept this all to yourself. Thank you for sharing with me. I judge you not," Starr says once the server leaves us. "For me, submission is the giving up of control to a man who is powerful, cares for me, and focuses on my needs. His dominance doesn't supersede my Independent Woman. Rather, she allows him to take over in the bedroom, not in the boardroom—or any other area of my life. His possessive caveman provides us with great pleasure."

She touches her hand to her collar. A satisfied smile spreads across her face.

"I wear Malcolm's collar not just as a symbol of our D/s relationship, but as a sign of our commitment to one another. The collar may not be a wedding band, but it declares our connection to those in the lifestyle. I'm his and Malcolm is mine," Starr finishes with a nod.

I nod back.

"See! I knew you'd help me figure things out," I exclaim with a grin. "You do not know what it's like having four brothers and two male cousins in my business! Of course I exclude Lachlan from our Jackson cousins."

I raise my freshly topped off mojito to Starr's.

"Here's to my sisters. First Lola, then Leonie, now you! At least Baz, Roger, and Malcolm are worth something.

Harris... Well..." I giggle, then tip my cocktail to my smiling lips.

The tears subside with my determination to live my life as I want with whomever I want, however I want.

Take that The Big Four!

HALEY

"So, missy, what's the latest with you and your bonny Scotsmen since we spoke a few months ago. Things must have swung in Callum's direction now he's here for your Mom's event. Mmm hmmm…"

Starr says with glittering sorrel brown eyes as she steeples her fingers and taps them together in front of her smirking face.

I can't help but to laugh at her pseudo-villain cackle.

She's stayed true to her word since I haven't heard a peep from Malcolm. Not even Leonie and Lola have mentioned anything to me. Starr is the best!

So I loop my arm through Starr's as we stroll along the private beach of my parents' Southampton Village mansion on the Atlantic Ocean. It's within our family compound, with three other mansions for Baz, Malcolm, and Roger. Harris and I stay in the primary home. Our wing is on the opposite end of our parents'.

I suppose at some point we'll buy the houses next to our compound to expand it as our brothers did. For now, we don't mind hanging with Morgan and Shelley. Our parents are way beyond cool. Not to mention the home is ginormous, with plenty of room. Even room for a certain bonny Scotsman in the guest wing.

Things have gone well and enough, so he's here for my mother's annual STEELE White Party for STEELE Foundation over Labor Day weekend in the Hamptons. Shelley runs our family's foundation that builds and manages attractive, affordable housing for urban, lower-income families. The name is a play on the house foundation, being strong and supportive like steel.

Besides Callum, Starr, and me at the compound, my parents, Malcolm, and Harris left New York City to arrive early. We're prepping for tonight's sunset dinner on the beach—a traditional New England Clambake. My fave!

Sebastian, Lola, Roger, Leonie, The Twins, Nanny Grace, and Blair Thomas—Lola's assistant and a close friend of ours—are on board the STEELE Sikorsky helicopter heading to the Southampton Village Heliport. Billie Chandler—Lola's West Coast assistant and another member of our Girls' Crew—will fly in with her Scottish billionaire beau Patrick Rockett on his helicopter later this afternoon and stay at his beachfront property.

Leonie's parents and Luc Montaigne—the billionaire Parisian banker and her and Lola's mentor—will arrive from France to the private airport for the Hamptons.

Our entire gang will be present. And of course the Jacksons, who also have a compound nearby.

But never mind all of that...

"Let's say things are splendid with the Duke!" I respond with a Cheshire Cat grin. "We're spending a lot of time together going to dinner, hanging out with his friends for billiards... Yeah, I know! We've even been out here a few weekends. It's been—"

"Good of you to join us, Haley..." Harris says as he slaps his gloved hands free of sand from the wood for the bonfire. "Care to help us?"

"Do not worry, Haley. I'll help Harris," Callum responds in that sinful Scottish accent of his.

I grin and rise to my toes to give him a kiss on his cheek.

"Thanks so much, Callum!"

As expected, Malcolm and Harris exchange glances. Despite the glowing report Sebastian's guy gave after he conducted an extensive background check on Callum as soon as they met him while we were in Verbier for Christmas. Apparently, nothing in it caused concern. So The Big Four are happier I'm with Callum and not with Lachlan.

And so am I! Princess Fiona the Fair can have him. And she does since paparazzi have photographed them together more times than I can count...

We finish with the setup for the clambake just in time to drive to the heliport to pick up Sebastian and the rest of the clan. Billie sent a text message to let us know she's on her way. Leonie's parents and Luc should have landed by now, and my parents went to get them.

When I return, I go in search of Callum. He stands by the water's edge.

"Hey!" I call out and wave when he faces me with a grin.

"Hey there, Little Lass! Glad you're back. Everyone good?" He asks as he scoops me from the sand and spins in a circle.

I giggle and push on his chest to release me.

He sighs and puts me on my feet, then holds me steady when I stumble.

"Yes, they're settling in before the clambake," I respond. "Do you want to go for a walk?"

Callum nods, and we stroll through the surf. The water splashes our legs as the waves break on the shore. We chat about nothing in particular, just enjoy each other's company.

The sun begins to set, so we go to the tables for our delicious seafood feast. The perfectly steamed clams, lobsters, potatoes, and corn on the cob topped with melted butter and paired with local beer and white wine make for a scrumptious meal. Dessert options include warm blueberry and apple pies with vanilla ice cream.

During the meal, Billie elbows me and grins.

"This is tasty, even to a Southern gal like me! But it appears as though Haley and my tastebuds have expanded to include bangers and mash. Right, Haley, girl?" Billie says in her Savannah accent with a Scottish twist in the end.

The visual of the double entendre made me blush and Callum sputter his ale.

Not one of The Big Four found Billie's joke amusing. Naturally.

As it so happens, Callum and Patrick know each other. With around ten Scottish multibillionaires, it's no wonder they're familiar with one another. The über-wealthy flock together.

"Well done, mate!" Patrick guffaws. The former rugby player now head of Rockett Construction—STEELE International's biggest competitor—reaches around Billie to clap Callum on the back.

He raises his ale in salute and grins.

Did I say he's not afraid of the big bad four?

I smirk inwardly.

Afterwards, we sit around the bonfire chatting.

"Don't forget beach yoga at seven tomorrow morning!" Starr calls out to Leonie as she and Roger leave the beach with The Twins.

I lean back on the log and trace circles in the sand with my toes. Wistful thoughts of Lachlan seep into my head at the sight of everyone cuddled up with their significant others. Sure, Callum and I are closer, but we're not on the level of the couples.

"Penny for your thoughts, Little Lass," Callum murmurs in my ear.

Busted thinking about another man in the presence of Callum. My face flames red from embarrassment. Fortunately, the warmth of the fire can be the cause.

"Only a penny?" I ask teasingly. "Aren't I worth more than that?"

Callum's emerald green eyes spark in the firelight.

"Oh, Little Lass, you are worth a gazillion times more. If only you would allow me to show you," he responds gruffly.

I shudder and bite the corner of my lower lip. Oh my…

THE NEXT FEW days prove relaxing. We do more yoga, lounge around the pool, swim in the ocean, or hang out on the entertainment level of the primary house to bowl, play in the arcade, or watch movies.

It's good to unwind with everyone since it's the first time we've all been together in a few weeks.

Now we're gathered on the beach for a rowdy game of touch football. Callum and Patrick told my brothers American football sucks and isn't even football, since the ball stays in the players' hands more often than not. They insisted on a round of rugby—"the real man's sport."

Ever the competitors, The Big Four accepted the challenge.

Between drooling over the gleaming muscles, the girls and I cheered them on. We couldn't care less, as long as the guys remained sweaty. Morgan, Shelley, Guy, Josy, Luc, and The Twins watched from the sidelines.

"Come, take a dip with me, Little Lass!" Callum called out. "The victor wants his spoils!"

I giggled and trotted down to meet him. He swooped me up and charged into the water as I squealed in delight.

I MAKE my way down one side of the double staircase. Callum talks with Harris below the chandelier in the entry.

He glances up at me and grins wolfishly.

The lightweight silk crepe de chine sleeveless playsuit embellished with delicate crystals along the vee neckline with a ruffled hem shows off my full bust and long legs. Its white color stands out against my olive-toned skin, kissed by the summer sun. Ties from the white thong sandals wrap around my calves. I left my ebony waves loose to cascade down my back. Thin extra-large diamond hoops dangle from my ears and glimmer alongside my dewy skin bare of makeup.

A whistle rings out.

"Hot damn! Get a look at my twin!"

My eyes flick from Callum's hungry ones to my brother's playful platinum grays.

Both men look just as dashing in white linen shirts, trousers, and slides. Callum four inches taller than Harris, but equally muscular builds. The Scotsman's long blond hair shimmers with natural streaks of gold from the sun contrasts with my twin's short jet black hair.

"Well, boys, let's get this party started, shall we?" I ask saucily as I saunter down the remaining stairs.

"Hell yeah!"

"But of course, Little Lass!"

The giant side lawn, aglow by thousands of fairy lights and lanterns, has two sumptuous pavilions, one for dinner and the other for dessert and dancing. Beyond it, on the beach, several bonfires burn. Waitstaff mill about with trays of champagne and wines or hors d'oeuvres. To one side a band plays lively music piped through speakers, also out on the sand.

Guests mingle, sipping drinks in the different areas, all dressed in the theme of the annual STEELE White Party.

It's already bustling since it's the party of the season and everyone wants a ticket for a chance to see and be seen amongst the world's elite. Not to mention raising funds for STEELE Foundation.

We make our way through the crowd, stopping to speak with guests along the way. Everyone wants a chance to speak to a Steele: a business opportunity; a photo-op; a marriage… Soon Mrs. Steele hopefuls swamp Harris. The cad that he is relishes the attention and leaves us with two on his arms and one trails behind.

Callum made it clear to Mr. Steele potentials by keeping his hand possessively on my lower back or tucking me closer to his side when they neared us. I can swear I heard a low growl rumble deep in his chest when a former Harvard classmate greeted me with a kiss on the cheek.

From a distance, I spy Leonie, Roger, Blair, and Luc chatting. As my gaze drifts around the lawn, Lachlan appears. My breath stutters.

Damn.

Quickly, I pivot to avoid him, then move in the opposite direction.

"Hello, Haley, darling!"

I glance over my shoulder to find Aunt Lucie and Uncle Connor behind me. She sweeps me into her arms for a tight squeeze. Then steps back to glance at Callum.

"Graham, how are you?" Uncle Connor says in a thicker Scottish accent. "What brings you to a STEELE event?"

Callum slips his arm around my waist as he shakes my uncle's proffered hand.

"This lovely lass and the opportunity to raise money for a good cause. So I'm very well. And you?" He responds before he faces Aunt Lucie. "Marchioness, a pleasure to see you."

She schools her face—only I can tell she's not pleased to see me with Callum.

"Your Grace," she replies, then turns to me. "Kindly excuse Haley and me."

Without awaiting a response, she bustles me from Callum's side.

"Honey, I don't mean to intrude, but how are things with Lachlan? It's been quite some time since you parted ways. Have you given any thought to a reunion?" Aunt Lucie says rapidly as we glide past the guests for a less busy space.

As I open my mouth to speak, the hairs on my neck rise. "Haley."

My mouth dries.

Suddenly, Aunt Lucie disappears, and Lachlan stands beside me.

"La—Lachlan," I say through sand.

His emerald green eyes scan my face before he places a hand on my lower back and guides me further from the crowd.

"How are you?" He asks.

I shrug and push at my non-existent glasses. Then roll my eyes, annoyed at picking up my old habit out of nerves. Get over it, Haley Steele! I admonish myself. What does he care? He's with Fiona.

"Fine, thank you," I respond. As much as my Independent Woman wants to propel me away from Lachlan, my heart and soul beg me to stay and hear him out. I wait.

He sucks his lush lower lip into his mouth and blows out a breath.

"Haley, I miss you," he blurts.

The ice around my heart beads with condensation. I rub my chest.

"Can we talk tomorrow? I want to know where you stand," Lachlan continues in my silence. "We can't let our relationship end the way it did. You mean more to me than you can ever know. Talk to me, Haley. Please."

I swallow past the lump in my throat. How can I believe he misses me when he's been with Fiona all this time? What is he getting at? Aargh!

"I'm seeing someone," I say aloud.

Lachlan's emerald eyes darken to seaweed in turbulent waters as they narrow. He glances over the top of my head at the guests behind me. Undoubtedly, he seeks Callum. Knowing the Steele-Jackson grapevine, Lachlan knows about him.

A frustrated growl slips past my lips.

"Listen, Lachlan, I don't have time to wait for you to get your shit together. Now, you want to talk?! Gee, I'm surprised your Fiona let you loose!" I snap.

He returns his irate gaze to my face and opens his mouth to speak.

The gong rings to announce dinner.

Saved by the fucking bell!

I huff and storm away.

LACHLAN

"I'm so glad you could meet me for breakfast, Lachlan, sweetheart. I want a chance to speak with you before the gala tonight."

Aunt Shelley sits across from me at a table in one restaurant at STEELE Aberdeen. A slight furrow forms between her elegantly shaped eyebrows as her soulful chocolate brown eyes fill with concern. She's a stunning woman in her late fifties who passed her independent and feisty traits to her daughter, along with her curvy figure. I also sense she's a sub like Haley…

The Steele clan—so far not Haley—arrived last night for the Jackson Foundation annual gala. I had hoped she would show, but I rather doubt it. She would have flown in on the private jet with her parents, Sebastian, and Lola.

Despite my request we speak a few weeks ago, Haley hasn't responded to my phone calls or text messages. I stopped, not wanting to cause an even bigger rift between us. She knows I want to talk. Now it's up to her.

Especially since I put it on the line with Sebastian during their Labor Day fundraiser.

"Lachlan, what the fuck, bro?!"

Still in a daze from Haley's pronouncement about being with Graham, I'm slow to react to Baz. Instead, I keep walking away from the crowd in the tents.

"Hey! I'm talking to you!" Baz says as he grabs my shoulder.

His aggression triggers my defense mechanism borne from years of Scottish martial arts training. I swing my elbow and catch him on the chin.

"Fucker!" He grunts and follows with a hook to my jaw.

We face off.

"What the fuck are you on?!" I snarl.

His gray eyes flare like molten platinum as they narrow on me.

"Seriously? You tell me! What the fuck's going on with you and my little sister? You've been acting shady for some time, and now you're arguing? What. The. Fuck. Bro." He responds.

Just what I need...

Well to hell with it. What do I have to lose?!

"Haley is a grown woman, not your little sister anymore! Shady? Nah, bro! I love her and she love—"

CRACK!

My head snaps back, and I stumble.

Before I hit the ground, Sebastian lands on my chest and gets in a punch to my left eye.

Instinctively, I block his rapid blows—the wanker trains in

MMA with a former world champion—before I raise my bent knees to knock him in the back.

He falls to the side, and we roll apart leaping to our feet in fighter stances.

"Cut this shit out!"

"What the bloody hell?!"

Without taking my eyes from Sebastian, I recognize Malcolm and Lucien's voices. They step between us. Glares all around.

"Did you fuck my little sister???" Baz demands, chest heaving, eyes bulging.

Malcolm lets loose a string of curses as he pivots on me.

"Hold the fuck up!" Lucien growls. "Back down! All of you! This is not the place or the time. Lachlan, go home. Sebastian, go inside and clean up. Now, dammit!"

We grumble. But part albeit begrudgingly.

Neither of us have spoken since.

Apparently, Aunt Shelley has something to say.

And I'm eager to hear.

"Of course, Aunt Shelley. I always have time for you," I respond with a genuine smile. I love her like my own mother.

A smile brightens Aunt Shelley's face, momentarily replacing the worry.

"Oh, Lachlan, sweetheart, you're such the charmer!" She laughs, then turns serious. "But not enough to keep my Haley happy. It's been too long since you've parted. If you truly love her, you need to do something about it. I'm afraid you have competition."

A chill grips my heart.

My worse fear comes to life.

Haley with another man.

Fuck. Me.

Memories of us together flick through my mind like a reel of our love affair. A drunk Haley attempting to strip and demanding I fuck her after Baz's wedding; her expression of shock and carnal bliss when I took her virginity; us grinding on the dance floor at a club in Las Vegas; sunlight filtering through the sheer curtains onto her gorgeous sleeping face; the way my heart soared whenever she smiled at me with pure love.

Then her rejections.

I run my fingers through my hair and tug on the strands. The sting rouses me.

"I've tried. Just last month, I finally got her alone for a moment and told her I miss her. She didn't give a f—. I mean, she didn't care," I shake my head. "Callum Graham, huh?"

Aunt Shelley purses her lips and nods.

Fuck. Me.

Now the reel shifts to visions of the Alpha Dom with my sub taking what's mine. Instead of happy thoughts filled with bright images, I see red. That bloody wanker!

"But you can't blame her, Lachlan. It's not as though you've been single."

Aunt Shelley's words cut through the haze.

I blink to clear my head.

"What?" I ask, confused.

She arches her eyebrow and cocks her head. The side

eye she gives me rivals Haley's famous one. Like mother, like daughter, again.

"Oh come now, Lachlan, do not play dumb with me," Aunt Shelley says, more like a Domme than a sub.

Did I say feisty?

"Aunt Shelley, I don't know what you mean. I'm single," I respond. And boy am I. My poor cock aches for more than my fist. It demands Haley's tight, wet heat. Mouth, pussy, ass…

"Fiona Ridel," Aunt Shelley states with pursed lips.

Oh.

I shake my head vehemently.

"No, you're mistaken. Fiona and I have a platonic relationship. She understands I'm not interested in more than her attending events with me or hanging out a bit. My work at Jackson Corporation is my only mistress," I respond.

Aunt Shelley searches my face for any sign of guile. None found she nods.

"Very well," she concedes. "But you still haven't said what you'll do to make Haley happy and reunite before you lose her to Callum."

My first thought is to fly to New York City and demand she speak with me. But I can't. The event tonight and a full schedule of meetings throughout Asia, Australia, and South America over the next two months. I'm even missing Thanksgiving. I didn't want to sit at the table and not see Haley, or worse, have that wanker Graham there with her.

Aunt Shelley must sense my inner turmoil. She reaches across the table and cups my cheek.

"Lachlan, sweetheart, I nor your mother wish to pressure you. We only want our babies happy. If you don't want to be with Ha—"

"Oh, no, Aunt Shelley! That's not it at all!" I exclaim, then rush on. "I have a ton of business meetings set for the next few weeks. All the way to Christmas."

I duck my head sheepishly and add, "Honestly, I need to keep busy, or I'll lose it. I love Haley with all of my heart, body, and soul. She completes me. So I leave little room for idle time. It's necessary social functions—like tonight—and work."

Aunt Shelley nods with a sympathetic look in her warm gaze.

"I understand," she says. "I'll let you know if something should come up before you have time to speak with Haley."

Then winks conspiratorially.

"So you know, I'm Team Lachlan!" Aunt Shelley adds.

We laugh, then enjoy our breakfast.

"ANOTHER SUCCESSFUL GALA for your mother! She outdid herself this year, what with the spectacular transformation of the ballroom into an enchanted forest! It felt as though we stepped into a fairytale! The Marchioness amazes me!"

I smile at Fiona's exuberance.

The event was a tremendous success, raising over £29 million—the most in the foundation's history. My mother certainly outdid herself. The combined Jackson and Steele clans whooped and hollered when she made the announcement a couple of hours ago.

As expected, Haley didn't show.

However, Graham did. He was alone—not a good sign. He must be more serious about Haley than I thought. I noticed him but chose not to approach him. As soon as Fiona saw him, she made a beeline to greet him. I was obliged to shake his proffered hand.

What I envisioned was a duel with Highland broadswords where I ended the competition and reclaimed my woman…

"—hear me?"

For a minute, I tuned out Fiona. Now she stands before me in her suite at STEELE Aberdeen staring up at me with questioning violet eyes.

"My apologies. What did you say?" I ask.

A scowl flits across her face before she smiles.

"You've disappeared all night long! What's bothering you? Perhaps I can help?" Fiona asks as she strokes the silk lapels of my bespoke tuxedo.

Her head tilts.

I step back and shake my head.

"Excuse my behavior," I start.

Her fingers tighten on the material, halting me. I glance from her hands to her face. Her eyes sparkle.

"Um, Fiona?" I ask.

A breathless sigh slips from between her seashell pink lips.

"Lachlan, tonight… Well, not just tonight… My friends and parents question our relationship," she says.

Alarm bells ring in my head. I attempt another step backwards. The lapels lift from the jacket held firm in her grip.

"I do too… It's been over a year. I know I said I was fine with only a friendship. But I—I developed feelings for you, Lachlan. It's impossible not to. I—I want more…"

The Alpha Dom in me rises to the forefront.

"Fiona," I say in an unyielding tone. "I never intended to cause you to expect more than I will give. Yes, we discussed it some time ago, but my stance has not changed."

I cover her hands with mine to extricate myself from her clutches. She whimpers and drops her head to my chest.

"Oh, Lachlan, please! Please don't be angry with me! I—I—I love you!" Fiona wails.

She rises to the balls of her feet and throws her arms around my neck. Color pinkens the delicate cheekbones of her porcelain face. Wide eyes beseech me.

"Your father told me he'll speak with you. But I told him you would listen to me. I will be the perfect wife for you. I'll give you your Jackson heirs. Our families will blend seamlessly both personally and business-wise. I promise!" Fiona states in a rush.

Her fingers lock behind my head in an effort to pull my face down to hers for a kiss.

Damn.

I thread my fingers with hers and pull her hands apart.

Startled, she lets go easily. But gathers my hands to her mouth to brush her lips over my knuckles.

"Lachlan, I know this may be a surprise to you. But I'll make it right. I won't pressure you for a wedding date. We can get engaged now and—"

"Fiona! Enough!" I roar.

She drops my hands and covers her mouth, shaped in a perfect O.

"Listen to me," I continue less ferociously. No need to yell now that I have her full attention. "Let me be very clear, Fiona. We will never marry. Apparently, my father misled you as I gave no sign you and I were more than friends. I apologize and will speak with him."

She stands mute.

I finish, "It is best we end our friendship. I wish you nothing but the best. Goodbye, Fiona."

Her soft sobs follow me out the door.

"The view is incredible! You can see for miles. The Faraglioni are majestic even from this height!"

"Not as incredible as you, Little Lass," Callum says.

I glance over my shoulder and smile at him. We stand in the Gardens of Augustus on Capri where he met me while here for Thanksgiving with my family. Callum happened to be in Sorrento and wanted to take me to dinner. Roger suggested he come over and stay.

This is the first time we haven't celebrated the holiday with the Jacksons. I wonder if it's because of Lachlan and me, despite my mother's assurances that's not the case. In a way, I prefer not to spend another holiday with Fiona at the table. I don't want to lose my appetite. Ugh!

Instead, along with Leonie's parents, we're at Villa dei Fiori. It's where she and Roger had their babymoon. She fell in love with Lucien's former home the moment she set eyes on it. So, of course, Roger bought it for her. The villa has fast become one of their most cherished homes.

The salmon-colored stucco exterior with white trim around the windows, columns, and roof lines blend beautifully with the lush greenery and stunning sea views from all sides. The sea-edge gardens, bountiful with camellias, magnolias, and palm trees, prove as captivating as the impressive views of Mount Vesuvius, the Peninsula of Sorrento, the entire Gulf of Naples, and Anacapri. Its private swimming pool set in the side garden's grass and its exclusive sea access with a second plunge pool below makes it a unique property.

After Verbier and Labor Day, everyone welcomes Callum with open arms. The Big Four expressed he's an excellent match for their little sister. A guy who's worthy of me, has his own fortune, and blends well with our family. Baz still can't get past his best friend with me and said it's best I'm with Callum. When he told me, Baz gave me an appraising look. But I shrugged it off. Only my mother remains aloof to Callum. Oh, she's polite, but only cordial. And I'm sure I know why…

Starr hasn't breathed a word to the others. She only asked after she led us through a vigorous vinyasa session and kicked the guys out of the sunroom. By that time, it was obvious Callum and I were a bit more than friends. The kisses gave us away.

I admitted only to the last couple of months since I saw Lachlan at the fundraiser. The girls claimed the drama of my love triangle with one man who's her brother's best friend and one man who's had his eye on her since Harvard proves more intriguing than any telenovela they've seen. I agreed wholeheartedly, with a giggle.

Now, I turn to Callum and wonder what will come next with us.

While we sat on the deck of Leonie's vintage steam yacht where we had Thanksgiving dinner, Callum invited me to spend Christmas with his family at Montrose Castle in Turriff, Aberdeenshire. Funnily enough, it's near to Jackson Castle.

I told him I'll be with my family in Verbier. Not just because it's the truth, but because I have a feeling he wants to *introduce* me to his family. And I'm not sure I'm ready.

Damn Lachlan!

No matter how much I try, he draws me to him like a magnet. What he told me keeps buzzing in my head. It makes me wonder and second guess a relationship with Callum.

I give it a shake to clear my thoughts and grin at the man.

"Oh, you're too sweet!" I tease. "Let's head back to the villa, it's time to get ready for dinner."

Callum turns and stoops to lift me onto his back.

I giggle and grab his sturdy shoulders as he traipses down the hill. The brawny Scotsman has no problem carrying me all the way to the bottom. I note how his muscles ripple beneath his white t-shirt. Hmmm...

We hop into a Mercedes-Benz G-Wagen for the return to Villa dei Fiori. Our laughter floats out the windows to mingle with the sounds of the Mediterranean Sea.

* * *

"Well, Little Lass, it'll be a while until I see you for New Year's Eve. Will you miss me?"

Callum's question reminds me of Lachlan.

Damn him!

"Oh, don't worry, the time will pass quickly," Callum says, mistaking my sour face as a reaction to our time apart.

I don't correct him. Instead, I flash a smile as much to dispel the negative thoughts as to assuage his concerns.

"I can't wait! It'll be a year since we reconnected, you know," I respond brightly.

He smirks and says, "Oh, I know, Little Lass. I know."

We turn at the sound of Roger's Sikorsky S-92 Executive Helicopter. It touches down on the helipad at the rear of their villa. The wind ruffles my hair, and Callum sweeps it behind my ears before he cups my face and kisses me breathless.

"Be good, Little Lass," he says against my lips. "We'll be together again soon. I promise."

I sigh when he slips away, then wave as the helicopter lifts off.

LACHLAN

"Hi, Aunt Shelley."

"Lachlan, sweetheart, you made it just in time! We're gathered in the great room. Come."

I follow her into the chalet.

As soon as my Gulfstream G650 landed at Sion Airport, my driver stopped me off here. I didn't bother going to STEELE Verbier to check into my suite. When I read the text message from Aunt Shelley last night, I didn't hesitate to change my flight plan from Buenos Aires. It's late. But time is of the essence to get My Baby Girl back.

As Aunt Shelley walks through the grand chalet's entry to the great room, I hear laughter and the sounds of Christmas carols. Once we step into the room, Aunt Shelley glances at Haley, then at Sebastian.

Fuck that!

I stride right in.

Haley's eyes go wide, and her mouth drops open. She

blinks up at me when I stop in front of her and clasp her hands in mine.

Without my emerald green eyes leaving her dove gray ones, I address Uncle Morgan and Sebastian.

"No disrespect, Uncle Morgan. We're like brothers, Sebastian. But Haley is mine, and I won't go another day without her for anyone."

Silence descends.

"What the fuck, Lachlan?!" Sebastian growls as he advances on me. "What do you mean Haley is yours?"

I ignore him and continue to stare at Haley.

Tears fill her eyes as she bites her plump lower lip. A lip I ache to suck.

"Baz, babe, let them be. It's Haley's decision, not yours," Lola says calmly.

"*Oui*, give them some privacy," Leonie adds. "Haley, go to the library. No one will disturb you, *Chérie*."

"Leonie—" Roger growls.

"*Non!* Enough of the big brother meddling! Let Haley live her life," Leonie demands with a roar of her own. *The Lion* is not playing with her mate.

Haley nods, and she squeezes my hands before we leave the great room.

I can sense lethal glares from Sebastian, Malcolm, Roger, and Harris burning my back. I even swear I hear Harris growl. He's the most easygoing of The Big Four. But he's extremely protective of his twin. Especially since he knows our whole secret story.

Can I blame them? No.

Do I give a fuck? Hell. No.

My Baby Girl ranks above all. Where I should have placed her from the start.

This past year taught me to value her and us more than my friendship with Sebastian. Add in the element of another man with my woman makes my blood scorch my veins, setting me ablaze with caveman possessiveness.

Haley Steele is mine. All mine. From this day forth.

Even she won't stand in my way.

Once inside the library, she faces me expectantly. A tear slips down her cheek.

I catch it with the pad of my thumb and bring it to my lips as I watch her reaction.

She shudders when I lick her tear into my mouth along with the tip of my digit. When I place it against her lips, she moans and parts them to allow my thumb to slip inside. She sucks it.

My cock hardens. It's been way too long.

"Baby Girl," I breathe.

Her eyes sharpen, and she jerks her head back.

My thumb pops from her mouth.

"No! You won't mesmerize me so easily, Lachlan Jackson!" She says feisty as ever. "What do you mean? And be very clear."

I take her hand and lead her to the window seat. The inky blue sky sparkles with a million stars while the ski lifts and lights of the village glow in the distance. Even at night, it's a beautiful view.

But nothing compares to the beauty of My Baby Girl seated beside me.

"I mean what I said. You are mine, and I won't go another day without you for anyone. Not your father. Not Sebastian. No one," I respond as I lace our fingers together. "I told you before, I miss you, Baby Girl. I love you more than anything. We belong together."

I lift our entwined hands to my mouth and kiss her knuckles as I stare into her eyes.

"Do you understand, Baby Girl?" I ask.

She stares back at me. Her eyes flit across my face to uncover the truth of my words. Whether or not I mean them.

The breath I didn't realize I held releases slowly when she nods, and a dazzling smile replaces the scowl.

"Really?" She asks clutching my hands as she sits forward.

I can't hold back any longer and crush my mouth over hers. The tip of my tongue sweeps across the seam of her full lips, demanding entry. They part on a sigh.

My cock twitches against the zipper of my jeans.

Our tongues tangle in a familiar dance. I dominate hers and suck it into my mouth, then swallow her sweet moans.

"Tell me I'm yours. Tell me you belong to me, Baby Girl," I groan against her kiss-swollen lips.

She clambers onto my lap and wraps her arms and legs around me.

The heat of her pussy seeps through her leggings to ignite my turgid cock. With a growl, I grip her lush ass and drag her against my sizable bulge. It throbs from the erotic contact and punches against the zipper at her mewls.

"Lachlan, you're mine and I belong to you," My Baby Girl cries. "I missed you so much. I love you."

She tugs on my hair to deepen the angle of our kiss.

I nip the corner of her mouth as a low growl rumbles from my chest.

The sub remembers her Dom, and she relaxes her grip to meld against me.

Our passionate kisses continue building in intensity as My Baby Girl grinds down as I thrust up. We're like horny teenagers. So bad, my heavy balls tighten as a zing zips along my spine.

Fuck!

I cannot cum like this.

"Baby Girl, I want to be inside of you. But not here. Come to my suite," I say as I lift her from my lap onto the seat. My fingers slip the hair from her flushed face as I continue. "Go pack your bag and meet me here. We'll tell everyone together."

She bites her lower lip and glances from me to the door.

"Haley," I warn as I draw on my Alpha Dom.

Her eyes snap to mine.

"Yes, Sir," she whispers.

I damn near cum.

Instead, I slap her ass when she rises. Her yelp makes me grin wickedly. Oh, the things we'll do. And we have all the time to do them.

By her return, my erection eases up enough to not be obvious. I take her duffle bag, surprised it's only one.

"I just packed a few things. I'll get the rest tomorrow," My Baby Girl answers my unasked question.

Good, girl, I think as I nod and take her hand.

Every head turns when we step into the great room.

"Haley and I are going to my suite at the hotel. We'll return tomorrow for breakfast," I announce.

"Wonderful, sweethearts!" Aunt Shelley says as she claps. "We'll see you then."

"Very well," Uncle Morgan adds. "I expect you to share your intentions, Lachlan."

"Yes, sir," I respond respectfully.

"Good night," Haley says with a wave.

Smiles from her girls and more glares and grumblings from The Big Four precede our departure.

I bite back a smirk and nod.

The ride to STEELE Verbier can't happen fast enough or the elevator ride to my floor. Once inside the suite, I drop the bag and sweep My Baby Girl off of her feet to carry her into the bedroom. Where I toss her onto the king-size bed covered in sumptuous white linens. She bounces amongst the pillows with a giggle.

Without hesitation, I grab the back of my cashmere sweater and yank it over my head. My biceps and pecs flex as my eight-pack abs ripple. I drop to one knee to remove my boot, then switch to the other. As I stand to unfasten my jeans, I catch My Baby Girl licking her lips in anticipation, and I smirk.

"Missed me much?" I quip.

She leans back on her hands and scissors her long legs open and close.

"Missed me much?" She parrots with a smirk of her own.

My jeans drop with my black silk boxer briefs.

She gasps as my ten-inch cock bobs and smacks my happy trail.

"I see you did," she purrs as she rips her turtleneck sweater over her head. Her long ebony waves drop to her waist, framing her D-cup tits covered by black lace.

I stalk to the foot of the bed and grab her legs to pull her to the edge.

She falls to her back as she glides along the duvet, arms raised overhead, a smile on her gorgeous face.

"Mmmm," she purrs. "Manhandle me."

I chuckle and slip my fingers beneath the waistband of her leggings and hook her thong. A few tugs as she wiggles her curvy hips, and the clothes drop to the floor.

"Open," I command as I tip my chin towards her bra. "Show me those juicy tits."

My mouth waters when they bounce free. Plump pink nipples stand at attention. Now it's my turn to lick my lips.

The scent of her arousal wafts into the air, adding to the tantalizing temptation.

I pounce.

And feast.

First on her slick pussy.

Her sweet nectar covers my nose and dribbles down my

chin. My day-old stubble bristles against her swollen, sensitive folds. Her carnal cries like a red cape spur me on.

All the while, my turgid cock rubs along the silky duvet beneath me. Stroking me like my lover. Heightening the intensity.

Her bountiful tits call for me, and I reach up to knead them, pinching the hardened nipples between my fingers. A trail of open-mouthed kisses from her bare mound, across the flat expanse of her belly, up to the tender undersides of her tits. I lave, nip, and suckle until she writhes beneath me, begging for my weeping cock.

But first. I must know.

"Did he take what's mine, Baby Girl? Did you give him what's always been mine only?" I ask.

She places her palms on the sides of my face and brushes her thumbs over my lips.

"Lachlan, you are the only man I have ever known. The only man I ever want to know," she responds.

Thank bloody fuck!

I hook her knees over my shoulders, then bracket her head with my forearms and hands to hold her in place. One snap of my hips and I impale her with my hungry cock. It drives her into the mattress as it fills her sopping wet pussy to the hilt.

"MINE! MINE! MINE!" I roar with each thrust as I reclaim My Baby Girl.

"OH! OH! OH!" She cries from the burn of my massive cock stretching and filling her tight, little pussy.

It flutters along my shaft as I compel toe-curling

orgasm after orgasm from her core. No matter how much I want to cream inside of her, her pleasure comes first. Each clench of her inner muscles threatens to end me. But it's not until she's pleading for me to cum, do I give in.

I sit back on my haunches as I lift her to my lap. Gripping her hips, I pound up into her wrecked pussy, chasing my release. With a gut-tightening roar, I spurt like a geyser held back for far too long. Unending ropes of semen fill her pussy and leak to my flexed thighs.

Blind from lust, I bury my face in her neck and suck on the sweaty skin. She mewls and digs her nails into my shoulders. Only once I'm sure to leave my mark do I let go and lick the heated flesh.

"You are forever mine, Haley Steele," I rasp through ragged breaths.

"And you are mine, Lachlan Jackson," her sultry voice thrums in my ear.

The caveman in me purrs in satisfaction.

HALEY

My pussy moistens at the sight of Lachlan asleep on his back with one arm thrown over his face and the sheets bunched around his v cuts. The outline of his ginormous dick stands out in bas-relief, calling to me.

I crawl over the bed and lift the sheet from his narrow hips. He shifts but doesn't wake. A sly smile plays at my lips that ache to wrap around his thick length. Every. Single. Vein. And. Ridge.

My butt meets my calves as I bow to worship his bonny cock.

The bulbous tip glides onto my tongue as I swirl it around from the slit to the sensitive underside. I take a breath and swallow him to the back of my throat until my gag reflex kicks in, and I pull back with a gasp.

He groans and lifts his hips. The muscles tighten

beneath the feathery trail of hair on his lower belly, and he clenches his right fist.

I dive back in until my throat swells with his girth.

"Oh, fuuuck…" Lachlan groans, still asleep.

I moan.

The vibrations tease his dick, and his eyes pop open. Emerald fire showers down at me.

"Baby Girl," he breathes as I pull back to his head and flick the slit. "Fuck!"

He clasps the sides of my head and guides my movements until I feel him swell and thump against my palate.

"I'm gonna cum," he groans, pulling my head back.

I shake it and hollow my cheeks to suction his shaft with a hum of erotic bliss.

"FUCK!" Lachlan roars as his hips piston to fuck my face. His cum shoots down my throat, and I swallow through my tears.

"Yum…" I say as I swipe an errant string from the corner of my mouth with my finger and lick it clean.

Lachlan groans and flops back on the bed.

"You'll be the death of me, Baby Girl…" he groans.

I giggle and drape myself over his heated body.

"Haley and I were a couple for a year and broke up for a year. I was a wanker who allowed my friendship with Sebastian to take precedence over Haley. However, I learned my lesson and intend to rebuild our relationship. I love her, and she loves me."

I glance around the table. Like my mother, Lola, Leonie, and Starr grin as they nod. My father and Roger stare at him intently as though peering into his very soul. Malcolm grunts and cracks his knuckles—*The Enforcer* to the end. Harris cocks his head at me, then nods when I smile reassuringly. Guy and Josy watch in silence, a smile on her face.

Baz, well… He explodes.

"Fuck you, Lachlan! How the hell did you mess around with *my little sister* right under my nose? I asked you years ago what was going on with you and Haley. You said nothing! Now, you tell us you were in a secret relationship? For. A. Fucking. Year."

"Sebastian! Please! It's Haley's life!" Lola cries out as she pulls on his arm to sit back down.

I start to speak. But Lachlan squeezes my hand to stop me.

"You're right. Years ago, I said nothing was going on between Haley and me. And it wasn't. You asked again during the weekend of your engagement, and I told you to fuck off. Nothing was happening then either. However, I cannot deny my attraction to Haley once she graduated from Harvard. But I backed off. Until years later, she let me know her attraction to me, too. Then we became a couple. And we are again. This time not in secret."

Lachlan turns to me.

"I will never put another before you or us again. That I vow," he finishes.

Tears fill my eyes, and he kisses my lips gently.

"Uncle Morgan, I hope my intentions are clear," he says a moment later.

My father shifts his platinum gray gaze to me.

"Haley, do you want a relationship with Lachlan?" He asks.

"Yes, Dad. I love Lachlan. I always have," I respond confidently. "So know his passion is not one-sided. It never was and never will be."

My father looks at Lachlan and nods. Then says, "Your intentions are very clear. You have my blessing. I realize you already had Shelley's."

He turns to her with a cocked eyebrow. She grins.

"Absolutely! Team Lachlan all the way!"

"Team Lachlan!"

"*Oui!* Team Lachlan!"

"Team Lachlan in the house!"

"*Félicitations!*"

Giggles burst from my mouth as Shelley, Josy, and my girls cheer and whoop.

The Big Four roll their eyes and grumble.

But our parents grant their approval. No further discussion required.

I'm beyond thrilled! At last, Lachlan and I can be free to be a couple in love!

"Ahem."

Oh boy, here we go.

All heads swivel to Sebastian.

He stands and rounds the table.

Lachlan stands with a frown. His body coiled, ready to strike.

"Listen, Sebastian, we're not fighting again. Get over it," Lachlan states.

I frown.

Fight again? What?!

I don't realize I spoke aloud until Sebastian responds.

"Yeah, well, that won't happen. Unless you hurt Haley," he says and turns to me. "We sort of got into it at the Labor Day fundraiser when he told me he loves you. It was totally his fault, the fucker."

Shocked, I sit with my mouth agape. Why didn't Lachlan tell me he spoke to Baz? That was months ago! When I reflect on that period, I remember Lachlan's many voicemails and text messages I ignored. He must've wanted to tell me. And I was an ass...

I jump to my feet as the two men face off.

"Sebastian! Lachlan! Enough!" I shout as I put my hands on their chests and push. They're walls of muscle and don't budge, but I make my point. "You're best friends, for fuck's sake! I love you both. You better cut this out. Right. Now!"

Their eyebrows raise over their widened eyes.

Yeah, shy Haley put her foot down. My Independent Woman comes to the forefront and demands respect.

Baz is the first to speak.

"Wow... Haley," he says as he runs his fingers over his signature five o'clock shadow. "I agree. I was only coming over to apologize to you and Lachlan. You'll always be my baby sister. But I respect you're a grown woman, too. As

Lola told me, I have to let you live your life. Even with my best friend."

He turns to a shocked Lachlan and continues.

"Listen, cuz, you're a fucker for not being honest with me all along. But I get it. And I respect your decision to keep your relationship private. Let's move forward as we were before, just with more trust. Okay?"

Lachlan grins and accepts the bro hug Baz offers with gusto.

"Sounds good, cuz!" He responds.

"Well, thank fuck for that! Now, can we hit the slopes for our Christmas Run already, or what?"

Everyone laughs at Harris' typical jokester behavior, even in a serious situation.

"And enough with the dramatics, Haley!" My twin says as he grabs me and noogies my head. We tussle as usual, while everyone laughs.

Shelley's mobile rings.

"Oh! It's Lucie! We have to tell her," our mother says gleefully. "She'll be so relieved… Lucie! Yes… Yes, they just finished telling everyone… I know! Tell Connor to hold his britches. Okay, okay! I'll put you on speaker."

"Finally, we'll have a more permanent alliance between the Jackson and Steele families!" Uncle Connor's voice booms out in the room.

"Connor Jackson! Don't you dare start with that again!" Aunt Lucie admonishes him.

Lachlan shouts, "Dad!"

"Well, it's even better than Sebastian and Lydie, since

the children will bear the Jackson name!" Connor continues triumphantly.

My father takes the mobile and leaves the room as he mutters.

"Seriously?!" Lola asks.

Baz shakes his head.

"Kindly disregard my father, Lola. He's out of line, and I apologize," Lachlan says.

Lola waves her left hand and laughs.

"I couldn't care less! I've got the rings, baby!"

We join in her laughter as Baz kisses her silly.

"That's our hint to gear up!" Malcolm says as he claps and rises. "Come on, My Angel, let's get going."

Starr takes his proffered hand, and we follow them out of the breakfast room to the oversized ski room.

Lachlan slips his arm around my waist and kisses the spot on my head Harris knuckled.

I sigh contentedly.

Our world is right again.

* * *

LITTLE LASS, just landed. Can't wait to see you!

Fuck!

I forgot about Callum coming for New Year's Eve! I glance over to where Lachlan plays billiards with Baz in the chalet's game room. What am I going to do?

I pivot to head for the door to think and bounce backwards. Lifting my gaze, I meet Roger's intense one. He raises his eyebrow.

"What's got you so upset, little sis?" He asks flicking his dove gray eyes to my mobile.

My mouth opens and closes like a fish out of water. Where the hell is my Independent Woman when I need her most?

Roger narrows his eyes, glances behind me to Lachlan, and takes me by the elbow to lead me from the room.

"Spill it," Roger demands.

Remembering Baz's request for trust and honesty, I tell Roger *The Responsible*. He looks thoughtful, then nods.

"It takes forty-five minutes to get from the airport. You could tell Callum over the phone. But after dating him for a year, he deserves a face-to-face conversation," he starts, then continues. "Text him back you have to tell him something, so he doesn't come here all gung ho to see you. He'll know it must be serious. Most importantly, you have to tell Lachlan now."

"Tell Lachlan what?"

Roger and I spin around to find Lachlan and Baz behind us.

Oh boy…

"Um… With how busy we've been, I forgot Callum was coming for New Year's Eve—"

"What?!" Lachlan shouts. "That bloody wanker is on his way here?"

"I know. I know. But I have to tell him I can't see him anymore"—I raise my hand to stop Lachlan's next words—

"Let me send him a text I have to speak with him. We can finish when I'm done."

Callum shoots a text back right away.

But I don't answer. I have to calm my man down.

"Lachlan, it's okay. We planned this last month. I just forgot. When he arrives, I'll tell him we can't date anymore, and you and I are a couple. Okay?" I say as I rub Lachlan's arm, the muscles tense beneath his turtleneck.

He fusses some more. But Baz and Roger agree it's best this way. He relents on the condition he's in the room. I agree.

No more secrets.

"ROGER, Merry Christmas and early Happy New Year! Good to see you, mate!"

Callum's greeting reaches from the entry into the great room where I wait with Lachlan on a sofa. We rise when he enters the room behind Roger.

"I'll leave you," he says with a nod. "I'll be in the den with Baz, Malcolm, and Harris."

Callum glances from Lachlan to Roger, then me. A frown mars his handsome face.

"Haley, what am I missing?" He asks. "Jackson, what are you doing here?"

I gesture to the sofa across from us. We sit.

"Callum, I know we dated for a while—"

"Dated? Past tense?" He asks as his emerald green eyes flick to Lachlan. "What do you mean?"

"I'm sorry, but Lachlan and I reconnected. You and I can't date anymore," I respond and rush on. "I'm so sorry I didn't tell you sooner! It just happened over Christmas."

Callum sits back as though punched in the chest. A myriad of emotions flash across his face—shock, suspicion, anger. He closes his eyes, then reopens them. His expression blanks as he regains control.

"Well, I suppose my surprise marriage proposal is a bust, huh?" He says as he pulls a little black velvet box from his coat pocket and twirls it in his fingers. "I'd give it to you, mate. But it's a family heirloom, and my Da would be mighty pissed."

Callum returns the engagement ring to his pocket as he stands. He extends his hand to Lachlan.

"I guess you're the best man who won in this case, Jackson," Callum says as they shake. "But I tell you this, mate. Hurt Haley, and I'll kick your bloody ass, then take her from you before you can blink."

Lachlan snorts.

"Good luck with that, *mate*," he rejoins.

Callum winces, and I glance down at their clasped hands, noticing the white-knuckle grip Lachlan has on Callum.

Oh boy, here we go with the caveman pissing match…

Callum concedes with a nod.

"Haley Steele, you are an absolute treasure," he says with a smile that doesn't ease the sadness in his eyes as he searches my face. "I wish you the best, Little Lass."

As if on cue, The Big Four appear. Roger nods at Callum, then leads him from the great room.

"It's been real, lads," he says as he passes my brothers. "I assume our business deals will continue as planned?"

"Of course," Baz responds as his STEELE International CEO takes over from big brother. "Business as planned."

The others respond in the affirmative as they shake hands.

"See you at our club and on the social scene, Jackson," Callum adds before he turns to leave.

"Naturally, Graham," Lachlan responds, as he slips his arm around my waist and eases me against his side.

I wrap my arms around his muscular torso and lean my cheek against him.

Now we can start the New Year on a fresh note.

"THREE... TWO... ONE... HAPPY NEW YEAR!"

Glittery gold stars, sun disks, and streamers float from the ceiling of the disco in the chalet as we ring in the start of a new year. The DJ pumps up "Jungle Love" by Morris Day and The Time in honor of Leonie's theme, and the party guests go wild.

Delighted, I shimmy in my one-shoulder leopard-print mini dress. The stretch-jersey clings to my curves, and the side cutout adds to the sex appeal. I toss my head back and roar.

Nearby, my parents dance along with Uncle Connor and Aunt Lucie. They flew in to celebrate Lachlan and me as a couple. Lucien and Laurent need no excuse to party, so they came, too. Lydie had plans she couldn't switch. Fortunately, Uncle Connor apologized to Lola, who ribbed him until she had him wrapped around her little finger. The one next to her engagement and wedding rings.

Three of The Big Four bump and grind with their women. Meanwhile, Harris dances sandwiched between two women he met at L'Etoile Club last night…

"Happy New Year, My Baby Girl," Lachlan rumbles against the shell of my ear as he grips my hips, swaying us to the beat. His massive cock rubs against my mound, and my roar turns into a needy moan.

I hold the Champagne flute we shared in the air with one hand while the other grips the back of his neck. My fingers tangle in his silky sable brown locks.

"Happy New Year, My Lord," I purr, a contented kitty. "Here's to many, many more we'll share."

LACHLAN

"**W**ell, look who made it minutes before the lights dim for the opening. What? Do we frighten you, Little Lord Fauntleroy?"

Malcolm snarks as I walk into the STEELE International luxury suite high above the basketball court at Madison Square Garden.

It's been a month since we left Verbier and the first time I've been with The Big Four. Baz invited us to a Guys' Night Out for the New York Knicks versus the Los Angeles Lakers game. He thought it would be a pleasant bonding experience without the girls. They're back at his and Lola's duplex penthouse at The STEELE Tower. We'll meet them for dinner at Per Se later.

I flew in from Aberdeen and came to the Garden directly. So Malcolm can suck it.

"Oh, yeah, I'm so scared..." I respond with a fake tremble, hands raised. "*The Enforcer...* Oh no!"

He smirks and tips his head and raises his Waterford Crystal snifter filled with two fingers of amber liquid at me.

"Well, at least you're worth something," Malcolm says. "This new Scotch blend of yours is extra smooth."

I clap him on the back as I move further into their spacious suite.

The seating area with brown leather chairs and a sofa have Knicks jerseys and pennants on the coffee table. I grab a flag, twirling it between my fingers, and saunter through the center section. The STEELE logo displayed on one wall with an extra-large flat screen TV on the opposite one. Below both stand marble-topped sideboards loaded with food beneath silver domes on one and fruits and desserts on the other. A marble-topped bar stands in the middle with the suite attendant beside it.

"Would you care for a cocktail and hors d'oeuvres, Mr. Jackson?" He asks. "As requested, the chef prepared your shrimp tostados bites. I can pour your preferred ale to go along with them."

"Lachlan, son. Good to see you!" Uncle Morgan says, drawing me in for a hug.

"You're just in time for the team intros. Grab a drink, and let's sit up front," Baz adds as he approaches us with his snifter raised. Undoubtedly filled with his favorite Jackson Special Blend Scotch and not my new one.

Malcolm follows us to the two rows of black leather stadium chairs in the outer portion of the suite. Positioned in the middle of the Garden, it gives us the best view of center court below. On either side of the suite, other guests enjoy their private rooms. A few guests glance across the glass partition as we stride down the step and nod. Some wear Lakers jerseys. This will prove an interesting night.

Roger, Harris, and Luc greet me as I near them in the first of the two rows.

"Hey, hey! The gang's all here!" Harris chuckles as he stands and pulls me in for a bro hug. Low, so only I hear he adds, "You're lucky my twin is still happy with you. And she better stay that way, or your ass is mine."

He steps back with dove gray eyes glittering dangerously before he claps me on the shoulder. A touch harder than necessary.

But, hell, I'll take it. My Baby Girl is more than happy, and that's what matters the most.

The past few weeks have been the best we've ever shared. After Verbier, she went to work out of STEELE London. I moved to Jackson's offices there so we could be closer. We stayed in my One Hyde Park penthouse flat in Knightsbridge. She left a few days ago. While I had meetings to attend and couldn't get to New York City until now.

"Hey, Jackson! That is you, mate. I was in the suite's loo and thought I recognized your voice."

I glance over my shoulder to find Patrick Rockett striding over.

"I hear you bested ole boy for wee Ms. Steele. Well, isn't that something," he adds.

The fuck.

My blood boils.

Rockett extends his hand with a Cheshire Cat grin.

"*Whit's fur ye'll no go by ye! Aye?*" He says with a chuckle.

I relax and grip his hand firmly, "*Aye*, mate."

"Okay, so what the hell does that mean about our little sister?" Roger asks as he stands to face us. Patrick raises his hands in surrender and responds, "Hold on now, mate. It's a Scottish saying for *what is for you will not go by you*. Or as you Yanks say, *what will be, will be*."

Everyone laughs heartily, then takes seats as the arena lights dim and the spotlights zoom across the court.

"Ladies and gentlemen, entering the court for the game of the season… The Los Angeles Lakers led by LeBron *King* James!!!"

The Garden rocks from tip-off to an incredible last second three-pointer by LeBron that broke the tie and stole the game. Even die-hard Knicks fans have to give respect to the *King* for the unbelievable play.

We hop into a STEELE Mercedes-Benz Sprinter for the ride to the restaurant. Still hyped from the rush of the game, we josh around until the driver pulls up to Columbus Circle.

We make our way through Per Se's main dining room to the private East Room. Patrons turn to watch our advance. Eight six-foot-plus Alpha males stride by emanating power and wealth proves irresistible. Women—even those with men at their tables—stare eagerly. *Nae!*

As we near the private room, a server opens the door in the glass divider covered by silk drapes for privacy. My gaze skips past the impressive views of the Manhattan skyline and Central Park clear across Columbus Circle to Fifth Avenue. I only have eyes for My Baby Girl.

She wears a long-sleeve knit dress that skims her curves to the middle of her calves. The crimson color makes her olive-colored skin glow. Red strappy fuck-me sandals adorn her feet. As she laughs at something Billie says, My Baby Girl tosses her head back. Glossy ebony waves cascade down her back, past her waist.

It reminds me of how long her hair has grown in the year we've been apart. I find it's the perfect length to wrap around my fist as I fuck her from behind.

As though sensing my carnal thoughts, she glances over her shoulder. A long lock falls over her eye, and her eyes widen, then narrow with desire.

"Hi," she says as she saunters over. "I missed you."

I slip my arms around her narrow waist and pull her close as I bury my face in her silky hair.

"I missed you, too, Baby Girl," I murmur as I inhale the delicate yet intense floral scent of her elegant perfume. Jasmine, orange flower, and musk blend harmoniously. The contrast again, like my lover—sensuous yet innocent still.

We spend the rest of the time catching up and enjoying one another. Starr brings up the basketball game, and Billie jokes about her date with a basketball superstar.

I chuckle to myself when Patrick whispers in her ear, and her eyes widen as she turns bright pink. He sits back with a satisfied smirk.

Ah, yes, another Alpha Dom. The guys know since he's a Global All Access member of LEVELS. I have yet to take My Baby Girl to one. But we'll remedy that soon enough. I have other plans for her.

"Guess what?" I whisper in her ear as my hand rests on her thigh.

She tilts her head to glance at me with an arched eyebrow.

"Tomorrow morning, we fly out of town," I continue, then squeeze her leg when she starts to protest. "Harris agreed to handle your projects for the next week. So no worries."

She opens her mouth and closes it as she bites the corner of her bottom lip. I can hear the gears moving in her head. My Baby Girl loves her work and undoubtedly considers her schedule. Before she can make an excuse, I seal the deal.

"It's our first Valentine's Day together since we broke up. Would you rather stay here on your laptop or cum with me..." I state suggestively, well aware of my word inflection.

She flushes a pretty pink and flicks her eyes around the table to check if anyone heard our private conversation.

I chuckle wickedly and squeeze her thigh once more before I turn to Leonie to ask after The Twins.

* * *

"Oh, Lachlan! This is absolutely stunning! So lush and tropical! Thank you for such a wonderful surprise!"

Haley squeals as she leaps onto my torso and wraps her arms around my neck. She smothers me with delicious kisses.

I would die a fortunate man with My Baby Girl clinging to me in this paradise. As the mini dress bunches at her thighs, her bare pussy—she's no longer allowed to wear panties with me—heats my abs through the thin cotton of my t-shirt.

We arrived at the beachfront villa in St. Lucia moments ago.

The white sand of Sugar Beach sparkles in the sun as dazzling as the crystal-clear turquoise waters of the Caribbean Sea glittering beyond our river rock seawall. The saltwater infinity pool blends into the horizon as though bringing the sea to us. A set of stairs from the deck made from teak in varying shades of brown leads to the beach below.

Beneath white umbrellas, oversized teak chaise lounges with white deep-seat cushions invite you to relax all day long to the sound of the waves and the scent of the bougainvillea. An eating area with a dining table and chairs sits beside an outdoor kitchen beneath a pergola draped with sun shades. The exterior of the villa rivals the sump-tuous interior.

Two one-bedroom bungalows flank the ten-bedroom,

two-story primary villa. Made of the same teak wood with immense floor-to-ceiling picture windows and disappearing sliding doors, the structures blend seamlessly with the nature surrounding the eight-acre private property. Nestled between St. Lucia's iconic Gros Piton and Petit Piton, they set the opulent villa in one of the most extraordinary spots in the entire Caribbean.

But not one thing compares to My Baby Girl.

I carry her to the nearest chaise lounge and sit with her on my lap. My erection tents the gray joggers and stands tall between us. It twitches greedily when she reaches for it.

"Oh, my… Still not satisfied after the Mile High Club action?" She croons to my cock lovingly. "What should we do about it, Sir?"

Swiftly, I yank her mini dress over her head. Bountiful D-cups bounce in my face. I lean in and capture a plump rosy nipple between my teeth. Her yelp makes my cock harden into a steel rod and weep. Bared before me, I make a meal out of her tits as I lavish them with my tongue.

By the time I'm done, wet patches from My Baby Girl's soaking wet pussy drench the front of my joggers. I inhale the tantalizing fragrance of her arousal and groan. The need to be balls deep within her makes my cock ache and my sac heavy.

Warm from the sun and inner heat, I grip the t-shirt at my neck and yank it off. I smirk as her hooded gaze caresses the flexing muscles of my chest and abs. Lifting my hips, I push the joggers down, and she scurries to pull them below my knees.

My fingers grasp her round ass as she fists my cock to align it with her seam. One brutal thrust, and I impale My Little Temptress. Her entire body judders as she keens from the carnal invasion. Inner thighs tighten around my hips when I sink deep. My groin cradles her ass.

"Oh… Fuuuck… Siiir…" she wails.

I grunt as her inner walls clench on my ten-inch girth. Her tight little pussy molds around my cock like a custom sleeve. As she pants, I give her a moment to adjust. My mouth covers hers for a toe-curling kiss.

Her fingers rake along my back when I begin a tempo of fast thrust followed by slow drag. Every vein and ridge of my dick strokes her quivering slippery pussy.

"You like how my gigantic cock claims every inch of your pussy," I growl when she shivers as I stroke her G-spot with my tip.

"Y—yes, Sir… Oh fuuuck yes…" she says. When I smack her ass three times in quick succession, she adds, "Sir!"

I reach between us to pinch and tug on her distended clit with my thumb and index finger.

She yowls and shudders as another orgasm rips through her.

"Or do you like that better, Little Temptress?" I purr against the shell of her ear. "A touch of erotic pain?"

She nods fervently.

THWACK. THWACK. THWACK.

"Words, Baby Girl. I will have your words," I demand in full Alpha Dom mode.

"Yes, Sir!" She squeaks.

I smirk and tweak her nipple.

"Good, girl," I purr. "Now, cum for me again."

On cue, My Little Temptress explodes. Her eyes squeeze shut as her head falls back and her mouth opens to unleash a long, low moan that ends in a wail. Her spasming pussy flutters along my cock, making it thicken impossibly harder.

"Fuck!" I growl.

Without breaking our carnal contact, I stand and lay My Little Temptress on the chaise lounge. One hand braces against the back while the other grips her hip, holding our groins together. A knee between her thighs with the other foot on the floor gives me the traction I need to pound that pussy raw as I chase my release.

"Uh… Uh… Uh… Uh…" she cries with each snap of my hips. Arms thrown overhead, her fingers grip the top of the chaise lounge. Back arched, her head tosses side to side.

"Or do you like my balls slapping the crack of your ass as I make your pussy mine?!" I growl.

Sweat drips from my forehead to land between her bouncing tits. I drop my head to lap it up and suckle on a pebble nipple.

She breaks beautifully for me again.

Her climax triggers my own. With a guttural roar, I spurt a torrent of seed deep in her throbbing womb.

"Haley!" I rasp.

"Lachlan!" She replies with a strangled cry.

My legs give out from the intensity, and I collapse onto her sweat-drenched body. Her trembling thighs wrap around my hips as she threads her finger through my damp hair. Our bodies quake while we ride out our erotic ecstasy.

Moments pass before our heartbeats return to normal. A kiss to her throat, and I roll to my feet.

A sated Haley lies on her back, skin glistens in the tropical sun; luscious tits rise and fall as she breathes deeply; legs splayed, coated with our combined juices; her swollen pussy folds slick.

Yeah, absolutely nothing compares to the beauty of My Baby Girl.

* * *

"Happy Valentine's Day, Baby Girl. I love you, Haley Steele."

"Happy Valentine's Day, My Lord. I love you more, Lachlan Jackson."

It's been six days of bliss. Hours of lovemaking until neither of us could move. Early morning skinny dipping on the private beach. Followed by couple massages beneath a gauzy canopy made of bamboo. Sunset dinners on the deck with fresh seafood and grilled vegetables prepared by the chef. Second to cuddling with My Baby Girl were the hours of sailing and of snorkeling in the Caribbean. It reminded me of my excursions on my full-rigged sailing yacht—*Gorm Domhainn*—on the North Sea.

Now on our last morning, we float in the infinity pool sipping Mimosas.

My Baby Girl surprised me with herself naked covered in succulent fruit as she laid on the outdoor dining table. As she giggled *bon appétit*, a slice of kiwi slipped from her peaked nipple.

I gobbled it up, along with the rest of the fruit and her sweet pussy. The juices mixed as they dribbled down my chin. My Baby Girl licked from the cleft to my lips before she made my heart race with a passionate kiss. After deliciously messy lovemaking, we cleaned up in the outdoor shower and dove into the cool pool.

"Did you enjoy your getaway?" I ask.

A beatific smile spreads across her face. Dove gray eyes sparkle brighter than the turquoise waters. Her cheeks—flushed from the tropical heat—glow.

So fucking gorgeous. So fucking mine!

"Oh, My Lord! It's phenomenal! I never want to leave!" She responds, arms wide as she spins. The water splashes around us, and she giggles. "Let's run away forever!"

The Cartier Love bracelet—diamond-paved in platinum on her wrist—glints in the sunlight. The timeless elegance of the piece is stunning. Its symbolism of a chastity belt that locks the loved one from any, but the lover who has the key is powerful. One day she'll wear my collar and wedding rings, too.

I slip my arms around her waist and pull her close. My heart swells with love for my woman. Burying my face in her hair, I inhale her scent to imprint it on my mind for all time.

"I'll run away with you anywhere in the universe, My Baby Girl," I murmur.

Her sigh of contentment as she slips her arms around my neck is the best part of our tryst.

HALEY

"*Oh chérie*! You're glowing with love! How is your sexy Cary Grant? How was St. Lucia? It's one of my favorite islands in the Caribbean. So lush and enchanting! I did one of my *Sports Illustrated Swimsuit Issue* shoots there. It was my best-selling cover for them."

Leonie rattles on exuberantly as we sit in her and Roger's triplex penthouse in The STEELE Tower Paris with Lola. The Twins play with their Bichon Frises. Their laughter makes me smile. And my womb ache.

Their residence is on the thirtieth through thirty-second floors in the Front de Seine district of Beaugrenelle in the *quinzième*. My parents and Baz and Lola have penthouses here, too. Normally, I'd take a suite at the STEELE Place Vendôme. But now I stay with Lachlan at his penthouse.

The STEELE Tower Paris, like New York, is mixed-use with commercial and residential space plus the largest mall in Paris. The views of the Seine and of the Eiffel Tower are incredible, especially at night when the spectacular light display flits across the monumental iron structure.

"You do look amazing, Haley! What the freedom to love whom you please can do to a woman..." Lola adds with a Cheshire Cat grin. "Baz still grumbles a bit about you and Lachlan. But he knows better than to bother you if he still wants me to give him—"

"La-di-da-dee-dee," I sing with my hands over my ears. "TMI, Lola! TMI!"

Leonie snorts with laughter as she holds her pregnant belly. Then adds, "*Oui, Oui!* Roger does the same, and I tell him he won't get—"

"Enough! For goodness' sake, Leonie!" I whine. "No! I do not want to hear about my brothers' sex lives. At. All. Thank you!"

Lola clutches her lower back with one hand and the other rubs her pregnant belly as she joins in with Leonie's giggles.

They're so cute, I can't help but to laugh, too.

"Okay, so what's got you girls hysterical?"

We glance around to find Roger and Lachlan standing in the doorway of Leonie's study. The two of them search our faces for a clue.

Leonie looks at me and cracks up while Lola titters.

My face flames red. If I don't want to hear about my brothers, it's guaranteed they don't want to hear about Lachlan fucking me! Can a hole open up and swallow me, or what?!

"Roger, something tells me we don't want to know, really," Lachlan says with a smirk, as he notes my discomfort. His emerald eyes glitter with mischief.

"Yeah, I agree," Roger replies as he leans down and kisses Leonie, then rubs her belly. "How's my Hot *Maman* and baby?"

She giggles and nuzzles against his side.

I smile wistfully. That's what I want. The marriage, the carriage, the happily ever after with Lachlan. I startle when I feel a hand on the back of my neck. My eyes lift to see him smiling down at me as though he senses my wish. I smile in return.

"Hi, Baby Girl, I have a surprise for you later," he murmurs as he bends over to brush his lips over mine. He turns to Leonie and Lola and adds, "We just dropped in on our way to train with The Champ. So you girls can get back to your chitchatting uninterrupted."

I had a yoga session earlier this morning with Anita—Norman Green aka The Champ's wife—at his eponymous Elite Training Facility. A friend of Roger's for years, Norman switched from being the Heavyweight World Champion to a boxing instructor and personal trainer. STEELE partnered with him to open global locations of his Facility for some for the über-wealthy and athletes and others for underprivileged youth. The one in Paris is my favorite.

"Yeah, we'll be on our way," Roger says as they stride towards the door. "Don't forget dinner later tonight. I reserved Épicure as requested."

"Fantastique, Mon Cœur, merci!" Leonie says as she shimmies and claps.

Roger chuckles as he and Lachlan wave.

Immediately, Lola turns to me with a wicked grin.

"Don't think you're off the hook, Haley. Time for you to dish," she says as she rubs her hands together.

"Absolument, chérie," Leonie adds.

Gleefully, I tell them all about our fabulous trip to St. Lucia and how thrilled we are to be back together. We raise our wrists with our Cartier Love bracelets—Baz and Roger gave them ones as wedding presents—in solidarity. The diamonds sparkle brighter than our ear-to-ear smiles.

"I KNEW it would look incredible on you, Baby Girl."

I preen under Lachlan's wolfish gaze as I step out of my dressing room in his penthouse. When I returned from Leonie's, he had laid a gorgeous hot pink sequined Tom Ford dress on the bed, along with Manolo Blahnik silver strappy sandals. No lingerie, of course.

The close fit of the embellished satin combined with the plunging neckline and open halter back with a cutout just above my derrière makes me feel like a sensuous siren. I pulled my ebony waves up in a messy updo with a diamond hair clip, holding it in place. Dewy makeup and soft pink lip gloss finish my look.

I lick my lips and twirl for Lachlan.

He growls.

"We better go now before I tie you to our bed and fuck

that luscious mouth," he rumbles. "A vision of the stain from your pink gloss on my cock makes me hard, Baby Girl."

I shudder.

Our ride to Épicure is fraught with sexual tension. I play into it by smoothing the sequins on my lap. When Lachlan joins me on the sidewalk outside of Le Bristol, he places his hand possessively on my hip.

"Later you will pay for teasing me, Little Temptress," he warns as he squeezes.

"Ooh!" I yelp at the jarring sensation.

He chuckles wickedly and guides me into the hotel to reach the restaurant.

As we make our way through the lobby, I note several women watch our progress. Their hungry eyes practically eat up my sexy as sin boyfriend. He looks handsome in a Tom Ford suit with a shirt unbuttoned at the neck. The black-on-black attire on his six-foot-four-inch frame makes him appear like a male model. Sable brown hair slicked back from his chiseled face emphasizes his cleft chin and powerful jaw. Gorgeous!

So I don't blame the wannabes for gaping at my man.

We spot Roger, Leonie, and Lola by the bar. The Hot Mamas stun in a sapphire blue ribbed knit mini and a bronze knit knee-length dresses, respectively. Roger—just as debonair as Lachlan—wears a navy blue suit with a white shirt also open at the neck. Despite standing beside his pregnant wife and wearing his platinum wedding band, a woman behind Leonie eyes him.

Purposefully, I saunter up to her and glare until her eyes widen. With a huff, I put my back to the wannabee and hug Leonie.

"Hey, Hot *Maman*! Don't you look oh so sexy. Roger better watch out!" I say loud enough for the woman to hear. Take that, hussy!

"I wish a fucker would," he responds with narrowed eyes. The Alpha male does not play when it comes to his wife!

I grin.

He and Lachlan usher us to the maître d'. He smiles in recognition of *The Lion* and bows. Roger growls. I giggle.

While we eat a delicious dinner of creative dishes expected of a three star Michelin restaurant, I grin to myself. It's our first couples' dinner, except Baz is on a business trip to Australia.

Roger jokes with Lachlan like he always did. Not eyeing him as some villain once Roger found out we dated for a year and were in love for even longer.

Lola and Leonie—more my sisters than sisters-in-law—laugh and chatter on. Even though they're best friends, they never alienate me. I love them as much as the rest of my family, including Lachlan.

"What are you cheesing about, Haley?" Roger asks. "Private jokes or something?"

I giggle and respond, "Or something!"

Roger cocks his head.

I bite my lower lip and confess.

"Well, it's just really nice to sit here and have dinner

with you, with Lachlan, without having to hide. That's all…" I trail off as my cheeks heat.

Roger studies my face with his signature intense stare while I try my best not to squirm. He nods and reaches across the table.

I place my hand in his sizable one.

"Haley, you do not need to be embarrassed. Our brothers and I have learned to give you the space you need to live your life. It's a tough adjustment being you're the baby and our little sister. But we're working through it," Roger says as he squeezes my hand. "We love you very much and want nothing but happiness for you."

My eyes well up with tears. I give a silent prayer of thanks and squeeze his hand back.

Lachlan wraps his arm around my shoulders and kisses my temple.

"I feel the very same, Roger. Trust I will not hurt Haley," Lachlan says sincerely.

"YES, SIR!"

My cry echoes in the scene room at LEVELS Paris. I guess Lachlan meant he won't hurt my feelings, not my ass.

The surprise he mentioned turns out to be my first visit to a LEVELS club as a member. He bought me a Global All Access membership. Sure, STEELE International and Jackson Corporation invested in Malcolm and Lucien's pet project. But all of them paid for their memberships and private suites. Even Leonie and Lola have memberships. Now I have one, too.

I've been inside of the New York club for my birthday, but none of the others.

In the 7th Arrondissement Palais-Bourbon Le Faubourg, LEVELS Paris inhabits the former Parisian home of a pampered courtesan to a French king. The magnificent *maison* on a tree-lined street sits behind duplicates of the original double carriage doors and features a spacious interior courtyard. They host grand soirees during the warm-weather months under the stars and strings of fairy lights.

The layout—the same as the other locations in New York, Paris, London, and Beverly Hills—spreads across seven levels. As with each club, the Sky Lounge offers a view of a nearby landmark. For Paris, it's the impressive Eiffel Tower resplendent in lights at night. The beauty and history of the property make it special.

On the way back to his penthouse, Lachlan pulled his Aston Martin DB7 Vantage into a side street and stopped the engine. I raised my eyebrow in question, and he reached into the glove compartment to withdraw a flat, black velvet box. He sat back and glanced from it to me, then took a deep breath.

I stared at him quizzically.

"Haley, you know I am a Dominant, and that I never had a permanent submissive in my life before you," he said. Then paused and with his fingertip traced a circle on the box. "In a D/s relationship, a Dom and sub can make a commitment to one another and let those in the lifestyle know. The Dom will ask the sub to wear a collar as a symbol of their commitment."

He pinned me with his emerald green gaze, more like a dark forest in the dim interior of the car.

"Haley, will you wear my collar?" Lachlan asked in a voice deepened with emotion. He pressed the sapphire cabochon closure. The top opened.

My mouth dropped.

A spectacular diamond collar rested on the black silk. Six rows of different cut diamonds form a circle with a giant diamond in the center, surrounded by two rows of smaller diamonds to create the collar. The delicate piece took my breath away.

Tentatively, I reached out to touch it. Then I hesitated and glanced up at Lachlan through the fringe of my eyelashes.

He watched me in silence.

Trained by my father in the art of negotiation, I knew Lachlan wouldn't say another word. The proverbial ball was in my court.

I ran with it.

"Yes, Sir, I will wear your collar as a symbol of our commitment to one another. I want all to know I am yours, Sir," I responded confidently.

His eyes flashed with possessive dominance.

Silently, Lachlan lifted the collar from the box and opened the clasp. He lifted the piece between us. I leaned forward with my neck extended.

"You are my submissive, and I am your Dominant. You

will wear it whenever we are in a setting with those in the lifestyle," he said as he closed the clasp.

The collar fits in the middle of my neck snugly, as though crafted for me. My fingertips brushed over it as I blinked back tears. It's not quite an engagement ring. But I know from my conversation with Starr and my follow-up research the significance of a collar.

"Yes, Sir," I whispered.

Lachlan cupped my face and slanted his mouth over mine for a kiss that ramped up from tender to scorching. His tongue dominated mine, and I moaned into his mouth. He groaned and kissed me deeper.

"Now, we go to LEVELS Paris," he said. "Ready for your punishment, Little Temptress?"

I shuddered then, as I shudder now.

"YES, SIR!" I wail again.

He chuckles wickedly as another strike from the crop on my bare ass makes me jerk.

Bound by red silks to the vamp red leather spanking bench, I buck. It's a fruitless gesture since I'm tied down tight. My ass and the backs of my thighs sting from his marks. But I refuse to give my new safeword—mercy as in *mercy, My Lord*. Instead, I grind my molars.

"So beautifully red with marks of the leather," he purrs. "My marks on my sub. And you are dripping wet for me, Little Temptress."

A low moan slips from my lips when he glides the tip of his thumb along my wet seam up to my puckered hole. He rims it before he applies enough pressure to slip the digit inside. I groan from the burn as the ring of muscles gives way for his naughty entrance.

"Mmmmmm, so tight. Let us stretch you with a butt plug. Shall we?" My Alpha Dom asks rhetorically. He will do to me as he wishes as long as I don't safeword to end our play.

And I have no desire to stop anytime soon. It's too damn good. Erotic pain morphs to carnal pleasure? Count me in.

Liquid drips onto the crack of my ass. I shiver at the contrast of my heated skin and the cool lube. My Alpha Dom murmurs words of encouragement as he presses the tip of a plug to my bottom hole.

A mewl of pleasure turns into a sob at the burn and stretch of my bottom hole. With a pop, he seats it fully within me, all the way to the flared base where my muscles clamp down on the neck. The cool stainless steel warms within my tight ass.

He taps the base a few times, then squeezes my flaming butt cheeks.

I whimper at the pressure on my sensitized skin. I buck again when the flat of his tongue laves from the plug down along my slick seam to circle and suck on my engorged clit. Hard.

An orgasm threatens to overtake me. But I await my Alpha Dom's permission. To my dismay, he brings me to the edge repeatedly until I beg.

Abruptly, he stops. The sound of his zipper loud in the

absence of my passionate cries. He plunges his ginormous cock into my pussy. Once. Twice.

I wince and groan when he pulls out his cock and the plug at the same time. Both empty holes gape greedily. Immediately, he breaches my bottom hole with the bulbous head of his dick. I squeak.

"Open for me, sub!" He commands as he swats my butt cheek. "Let your Alpha Dom into your body!"

I gulp for air as I try to relax the ring of muscles. Tilting my pelvis, I push back against him.

He takes advantage of the angle to slip deeper inside. The lube eases his passage. He grunts as I tighten around his girth. His arm snakes around my hip to my bare mound. A tug to my clit makes me cry out and beg once again.

"Cum for me, sub! Now!" He commands with a pinch and a thrust.

I keen until all breath leaves my lungs. My body convulses. The muscles in my pussy and ass clench repeatedly as the orgasm of life rips through me.

My Alpha Dom rides my ass like a stallion. He groans in my ear as he leans over me. The weight of his muscular body a comfort as he presses me into the buttery leather of the padded bench.

Another orgasm takes hold of me. Lights flash before my eyes and sound fades. His roar and the sensation of his dick expanding as it pumps his semen deep in my ass are the last of my consciousness.

I float in sub space.

. . .

"How do you feel, Baby Girl?"

My eyes flutter open, and I glance around the candle - lit room. We're no longer in the Cellar. This is a plush suite, and I'm lying on my belly on a king-size bed. Cool silk sheets caress my skin, especially nice on my still sore bottom.

"Here, drink this," Lachlan adds.

I guzzle the refreshing water and wipe my wet lips with the back of my hand.

"More?" He asks with a chuckle.

I nod. My throat raw from my passionate cries. After another full glass, I smile at Lachlan.

"Wonderful," I respond hoarsely.

"Good. You did well for your first time in a BDSM club scene. Did you like it?" He asks.

I pause to reflect on our play. It was even hotter than I expected. My loopy grin widens, not quite to my full mental capacity.

"Oh, most definitely," I murmur dreamily.

He chuckles and pulls me onto his lap. Then coos in my ear to soothe me when I whimper from the hardness of his muscular thighs beneath my sore ass.

"I cleaned you up and put some salve on your butt and thighs. You won't have any permanent marks. They'll fade by the morning or the afternoon," Lachlan says. "We'll stay the night here. No need to rush home."

He rocks me on his lap for a while. When I yawn, he

carries me to the bathroom. After I relieve myself, he carries me to the bed where he spoons me.

"Sweet dreams, Baby Girl," he says. "I love you."

As I drift off to sleep, I finger my beautiful collar and smile. One day soon, I hope to wear Lachlan's rings, too.

"I'm truly happy for you, Haley. Lachlan didn't have to tell me how he felt about you. As his older sister, I sensed he was in love with you and struggled to suppress it. Thankfully, Sebastian seems to have let it go."

Lydie winks at me. Her emerald eyes flash as she giggles. A lock of her waist-length sable brown hair falls across her cheek, and she slips it behind a delicate ear.

I've always admired Lydie. She's a stunningly gorgeous, intelligent woman. Never one to back down from a challenge. She runs Jackson Corporation like a boss.

Five years older than me, we rarely spent time together one-on-one. She and Baz were confidantes, and she was too busy making her mark on her family's company. Her principal focus has always been to impress Uncle Connor and claim the top spot after he retires.

It surprised me when Lachlan told me Lydie wanted to

take me to lunch when I arrived in Aberdeen. It's my first official visit as his girlfriend and not as a cousin. So she wanted to be my welcoming party.

I giggle along with her as we sit by the window in her favorite eatery on Union Street.

"Absolutely! Baz was breathing fire hot enough to melt the Swiss Alps by the time Lachlan finished professing his love," I add.

"Lydie! Hello!"

We shift in our seats.

Isn't this just great…

"Oh… Hello, Fiona. How are you?" Lydie responds.

Fiona flicks her violet-eyed gaze towards me. The smile she had for Lydie falters as Fiona's eyes widen slightly in recognition of me. Undoubtedly, she remembers our last encounter ten months ago at Leonie's charity gala.

Again, I use a lesson taught by my Dad: the one who speaks first loses. I wait.

So does Lydie. A twinkle lights in her eyes. This time knowing the situation of the Lachlan-Fiona-Haley-Callum drama. Talk about a love square…

"Haley Steele?" Fiona asks, feigning ignorance.

"Yes?" I respond.

Her eyes flick back to Lydie, who sits silently.

"Hello to you, too! Is your family in town for a visit?" Fiona asks. "I hear through the grapevine a lot of events are happening at Jackson Castle."

I have to hold back a giggle when Lydie bites her lower lip to stop her laughter. Her cheeks redden with the effort.

She picks up her cup of tea and sits back, eager to watch this scene play out.

"Hello and no," I respond. I don't give information unasked directly, yet another lesson.

She glances at Lydie, unsure of what to do next.

Lydie gives in and says, "Are you meeting someone for lunch?"

Fiona nods and responds, "Yes, my brother Heath. Speaking of brothers, how's yours?"

"Which one?" Lydie asks innocently.

A flush creeps up Fiona's chest. Her perfect porcelain skin mottles as her eyes dart to mine.

I blank my face.

"Um… Lachlan. It's been a while since we last saw one another. Is he okay?" She blathers on.

Lydie eyes her coolly. Emeralds appraise Fiona for a moment. Lydie turns to me.

"Well, Haley, how is Lachlan? You've been with him more often than I have. He barely spares his sister a minute of his time these days," she deadpans.

I nearly choke on my tea. After a quick recovery, I glance up at Fiona.

"He's quite well, thank you. Tonight, I'll tell him you said hello," I respond. "Do give my regards to Heath. He just walked in."

Her mouth opens and closes. A myriad of emotions flit across her enchanting face.

"Yes, do tell Heath hello. Good day, Fiona," Lydie adds before she sips more of her tea.

Fiona nods again and pivots on her heel.

Once she's out of hearing distance, Lydie lets a giggle bubble from behind her cup. I join in, covering my mouth with the linen napkin. Lydie and I will get along famously.

Take that Princess Fiona the Fair! No Princess Bride for you!

"So how was lunch, ladies?"

Lachlan asks after the flight attendant returns to his area behind the cockpit.

The pilot flies us—along with Lydie and Lucien—in Lachlan's Sikorsky S-92 Executive Helicopter for the half-hour ride to Banff for Jackson Castle north of Aberdeen. My parents, Harris, and Laurent flew there from New York City together yesterday.

We're spending an extended weekend at their family seat. Aunt Lucie organized activities to introduce me to their U.K. friends and society as Lachlan's girlfriend formally—at Uncle Connor's insistence, of course.

She told me she invited Fiona's parents to avoid an awkward situation. But the invitation didn't extend to Fiona and her siblings. The weekend is an intimate affair with a few guests, Aunt Lucie said. She assured me it's not a faux pas. And she should know, since she's learned all there is to know about social expectations and norms. Particularly since she's American and doesn't want to appear ignorant in the eyes of royalty and nobility.

Despite Lachlan not using his title of Earl of Aboyne

normally, he is the heir apparent and will step into the position of Marquess of Huntly after Uncle Connor. Should Lachlan and I marry—my happily ever after wish—it will style me countess, then marchioness.

Aunt Lucie wants to be sure people recognize and respect me not only as Haley, but as my future positions warrant.

And I'm all for it! What a fairytale come true!

So a Cheshire Cat grin spreads across my face at Lachlan's question. Fiona thought she would be the guest of honor as his girlfriend. Ha!

"It was lovely. Oh, and Fiona asked about you," I respond.

In my periphery, I notice Lydie titter and struggle to maintain a blasé attitude. Lachlan, on the other hand, snaps his head back as though jolted by electricity. His eyes widen, then narrow.

"What did she say?" He asks.

I cock my head and frown. What could she say that would bother him so?

"Nothing, besides it being a while since she last saw you. Why? Did something happen?" I ask, as a sense of doom threatens to ruin the joy I just experienced. That damn Fiona!

Lachlan shifts in his leather chair and reaches for my hand. His eyes soften as he strokes the pad of his thumb over the back of my hand.

"We agreed to honesty, Haley," he says, staring into my eyes. "I ended my friendship with Fiona six months ago. I remember the date only because it was after my mother's annual gala. Fiona was under the assumption—from my father—she and I were going to get engaged and set a later date to marry when I was ready for that commitment."

I gasp and tug at my hand.

He holds firm and cups the back of my neck with his other one.

"I told her I gave no sign we were more than friends, nor would we ever marry as my father led her to believe. The next morning, I spoke with Connor and told him to no longer meddle in my love life. He agreed."

I sag in relief.

Lachlan smiles and continues, "In fact, Aunt Shelley and I had breakfast the morning of the gala. She told me I had competition, and I deduced it was Callum Graham from the photos I saw of you. She also thought Fiona and I were a couple based on photos of us at various events. I told Aunt Shelley it was a platonic relationship, nothing more. At All. If it weren't for meetings I had scheduled, I would have claimed you as mine earlier than Christmas Eve."

He squeezes the back of my neck and leans his forehead to mine.

"You are my future Haley Steele. And always have been. I love you. Only you," he finishes softly.

A sob escapes my mouth, and he covers it with his. Tenderly, he kisses me.

"Aww... How touching! Lydie, pass a handkerchief to me."

Lucien chuckles and Lydie giggles.

"When it's your turn, let's see who makes jokes!" Lachlan states.

Everyone laughs.

THE HELICOPTER APPROACHES JACKSON CASTLE.

Over five hundred acres along the coast of northeast Scotland comprise the Jackson family seat. Sprawling landscaped grounds dotted with carriage drives and horse trails, walking paths, and a few ornamental buildings, including a chapel.

As we draw closer, the baroque mansion comes into view. Built in the early eighteenth century, it replaced the original fortified castle the Jackson family erected two hundred years earlier. The giant status symbol has a four-story center structure with two grand curved east and west wings of three stories each. Six staircases, elaborate fireplaces, and elegant formal entertainment salons along with an extensive art collection make for a splendid interior.

The entire estate is spectacular.

My parents, Uncle Connor, and Aunt Lucie stand near the helipad hidden in a copse of trees. No need to mar the perfect landscape.

"Hi!" I greet them with hugs and double kisses. My joy restored from Lachlan's declaration.

"Hi, sweetheart! Don't you look like you're about to burst with happiness!" My mother says as she holds me by the shoulders to study my face.

"Oh, Lachlan just had a sappy moment," Lucien says. He

ruffles my hair and kisses Shelley on the cheeks. Then chuckles when Lachlan nudges him out of the way.

"Hi, Aunt Shelley," he says, looping his arm around my waist and kissing her cheeks.

"Ever the charmer, sweetheart," she responds with a laugh.

We hop in Range Rovers and drive to the mansion. Even though we're a couple, Aunt Lucie has my luggage sent to the suite I always stay in. Lachlan grumbles. But I hush him with a promise of midnight trysts.

"I'd like to make a toast."

Uncle Connor stands at the head of the dining table with his Waterford Crystal wine glass raised.

Beside me, Lachlan groans.

"I made a promise to my son to not interfere in his love life," Uncle Connor starts with a raised eyebrow and pursed lips. "But I will say, he could not find a better lass than our Haley. Do well by her, Lachlan. *Slàinte mhath!*"

"*To your good health!*"

"Cheers!"

Lachlan's tension fades after he realizes his father's toast isn't inappropriate. Lachlan leans over and kisses my temple as he squeezes my thigh beneath the table. I smile upon at him.

The rest of our dinner and the digestifs after in the East Salon go smoothly. Later, when everyone settles in their suites to sleep, I go to Lachlan's rooms and make good on my promise for our first midnight tryst. And what a fulfilling promise it turns out to be.

* * *

"HALEY, so nice to see you getting along so well."

I turn around to find Maisie Ridel behind me. Not as ethereal as her daughter, she's a pretty woman in her late fifties with honey blonde hair and pale blue eyes in a heart-shaped face. An inch shorter than me in my four-inch pumps, she's willowy like Fiona. A classic column gown in cream silk accentuates Maisie's lithe form.

"Yes, Baroness. It's been a lovely weekend," I respond. Now, I know more about Fiona's mother and their family than when I met them at Thanksgiving.

Aunt Lucie presented me with a primer of all the guests for their names, titles, bios, tidbits, and photos and another primer with information on Scotland from history to present. Her mother-in-law gave her study guides when she and Uncle Connor got engaged. A tradition, she told me.

The primers proved useful over the weekend. I met so many new people and could recall things about them with ease. Some exclaimed in surprise, impressed by my knowledge. In others—particularly women who had single daughters—I sensed an undercurrent of jealousy.

As I do now with Maisie...

"Now that Lachlan and you are an item, will you move here or remain in the States?" She asks.

If I didn't know better, her question would be inconsequential. But no...

"Fortunately, my division allows me to work anywhere

in the world. That, combined with my family's offices and properties worldwide, I always have a location to work from," I respond.

She tilts her head to the side. Her cool blue eyes appraise me.

I suppress a shudder.

"So, you intend to continue working? Hmmm… How modern of you," Maisie states.

"Haley, sweetheart, there you are! Come, I want to introduce you to the Prince," Aunt Lucie cuts in. "Baroness, do you mind?"

Maisie's face switches from a judgmental sneer to a brilliant smile.

"Oh, of course not, Marchioness! Haley, a pleasure to speak with you," Maisie responds with a bow of her blonde head.

Sycophant. She bows to noble hierarchy since my aunt ranks two levels above her. Second to a duchess, Aunt Lucie has more prestige. When I become a countess, I will outrank Maisie, too.

"An absolute pleasure, Baroness," I say.

Aunt Lucie loops her arm through mine and whispers, "Good grief. That woman…"

We snicker and glide through the entertainment salon.

I catch Lachlan's eye, and he winks at me. I grin at my man. My. Man.

LACHLAN

"Hey, I'm doing a Guys' Getaway Bougainvillea Cay next week before Roger and I become dads for the second and first times in just over a month. It's a private island in the Bahamas I bought for Lola. We had our babymoon there three months ago. Can you make it?"

It's been a month since we introduced Haley as my girl-friend. It pleased Uncle Morgan and Aunt Shelley—not to mention Harris. The Jackson-Steele grapevine reports excellent feedback. Hence, Baz's call.

Fine by me.

I open my calendar app and figure I can shuffle around some meetings and appointments. Nothing major, so I'm good to go.

"Yeah, cuz. That'll work," I respond. "Sounds like a gracious gift, huh?"

He chuckles sheepishly.

"You know I'm a sucker for my woman. Whatever Lola wants and all that. I sent text messages to Lucien and Laurent. Of course, Malcolm, Roger, and Harris will be there. I also invited my boys Borya, Scott, and Porter… Listen, gotta fly," Baz says and rings off.

"Isla, kindly come in. We need to revise my schedule for next week, thanks," I tell my administrative assistant over the intercom.

Then I shoot a text message to My Baby Girl. I'll make a stop in New York City on the way back. Time for LEVELS New York.

MY HEART POUNDS FASTER than the racing yacht I navigate through the crashing waves of the Atlantic Ocean. It's The Others against the United States. Lucien, Roger, Laurent, Porter—based in Paris, Aberdeen, and Dubai—and I make up The Others. Malcolm, Harris, Scott, Borya, and Baz comprise our opponents.

Over the next four days of the getaway, we wanted to have time to test the boys' toys Malcolm ordered for the island retreat. First on the list: racing yachts. Right up my alley! Ahoy, mate!

Exhilaration runs through me as we take to the open water at the top speed of fifteen knots. The balmy weather—clear of any rain—provides the best backdrop for being on the ocean. Salty spray flies back and lands on my face. I laugh as I shake my head to remove the moisture from my hair, not daring to move my hands from the wheel.

"Yeah, baby!! We're gaining on them!!" Malcolm whoops. "Let's get it, boys!"

Lucien chances a quick glance as Baz and his crew come abreast with our sailboat. I shout orders for Porter and Lucien. They rush to adjust their sheets for optimum performance.

Aside from being Alpha males, we're a super competitive group. Not one of us likes to lose. So it's balls to the walls on both yachts.

We round the regatta buoy for the return stretch. We're ahead, naturally. But the US is on our tail! Damn near their bow to our stern.

As Baz overtakes us, Porter gives them the finger and Borya yells back curses in Russian. Both crews hustle to reach the finish line. The winner's buoy beckons to us.

Unfortunately, the wind turns against us. Baz takes advantage and they pass the marker less than a minute ahead of us. The US crew hollers in victory as we head for shore.

"Yeah, yeah, yeah. Whoop it up all you want. Congratulations already..." I say as I clap Baz on the back when I hop onto the dock.

"Tomorrow it's the JetSki relay, so let's see who's bragging then!" Laurent adds as he grabs Harris in a headlock.

Laurent's bottle-green eyes sparkle with mirth as he noogies Harris in the back of his head. Evenly matched in muscle, although Laurent at six feet, three inches has two inches on Harris, they wrestle as they've always done—two wolf cubs angling for dominance.

"Fuck off, Laurent! Sore loser," Harris retorts as he flips him off the dock and into the water.

Everyone laughs. Then Borya hauls Laurent from the water.

"*Davay rybka,*" Borya *The War Defender* Alexeyev—personal trainer and former MMA champion—rumbles as he pulls the little fish back onto the dock. "We'll do a training tomorrow so you can learn to defend yourself!"

Again, we crack up. While Laurent rolls his eyes and shakes his head, slinging water over us.

"Time for celebratory drinks, boys!" Baz chuckles as we stride back to the villa. "The winners will even pay!"

"Aw hell, dude! Pay what? We're at your place!" Porter responds.

Baz chuckles and nods, "True!"

WE SHOWER and change into swim trunks. Then lounge on the beach drinking local favorite Kalik beers. In the outdoor kitchen, the chef grills vegetables, fresh fish, lobster, and steaks to go along with the pigeon peas and rice.

The sun dances on the waves as they lap onto the beach before us. Other yachts dot the horizon, taking advantage of the glorious weather. The Exumas live up to their name as one of the best yachting areas in the world.

"Okay, Pops, how do you feel?" Lucien asks Baz as he lifts his bottle to his mouth.

Baz's grin spreads across his tanned face.

"Oh brother, man. He's grinning like the Cheshire Cat. Sebastian, the Alpha Dom playboy turned faithful married man, soon-to-be father will complete his transition to domesticated chap," laughs Porter. "I can't bloody believe it!"

"Well, my friend, believe it. And I'm thankful for it!" Baz responds as he tips his bottle in Porter's direction. "I pray you'll find a woman who will make an honest man out of you. Although I don't know how lucky she'll be. Bless the poor lass!"

Porter throws his head back and guffaws.

"What about you, Daddy of Three? What're your thoughts on fatherhood?" Laurent asks.

Roger grins wider than Baz did. His usually intense stare softens whenever he thinks of Leonie, The Twins, and now Baby Daphne.

"Enjoy every day with your children. Cherish each moment. They grow up in the blink of an eye," he answers, leaning forward with his elbows on his knees as he glances at each of us. "Don't waste a second of your time with them. And just as important with the woman who gave them to you."

"Amen, brother," Baz says as he strides over to him and taps his bottle to Roger's beer. "And I will add, take the advice of those who have gone through it. Roger has been an invaluable resource for me. Thanks, bro."

Roger grins and inclines his head.

"You're more than welcome, brother. Based on the way you've cared for all of us from childhood to now, you'll be an incredible father," he says sincerely.

Malcolm and Harris, along with Lucien, Laurent, and I nod in agreement.

Their banter makes me think of My Baby Girl. I want the same thing with her: marriage, children, a long life together as one. I say a silent prayer of thanks for everyone accepting our love. It's time to take it a step further.

"Thank you, my brother. Now, let us eat. Team The Others will need their strength for tomorrow's challenge!"

Baz's quip and boisterous claps, whistles, and denials rouse me from my musings.

I grin and raise my pint in salute.

"To everlasting love, boys!"

"THE PERFECT WAY TO end our retreat: pumping music, fine liquor, and, most of all, hot babes! Here's to Harris for the fantastic idea!"

Laurent says with a flourish as he raises his crystal snifter of Jackson Reserve Scotch in salute.

"Hear, hear."

"*Za nashu druzjbu!*"

"Yes, Borya, to our friendship!"

After two more days of testosterone-filled macho challenges, we had a tiebreaker this afternoon for the best water jetpack acrobatics. Malcolm, the biggest daredevil of us all, won. So the US beat The Others with flying colors, literally.

To celebrate and to cap off our Guys' Getaway, we came to STEELE Exumas Hotel and Resort for dinner at the restaurant run by Lucien. Afterwards, the singles—Harris, Lucien, Laurent, Porter, Borya—wanted to party at the resort's nightclub.

Everyone agrees to go.

Harris makes out with a leggy brunette in a micro dress damn near showing her ass cheeks. Borya sandwiched between two fashion models bumps and grinds on the center platform of the dance floor. Lucien has Miss Bahamas in a corner on his lap with his hand between her legs, devouring her mouth.

While they flirt with the more than interested female guests, those of us in relationships hang out in our VIP section, partaking in a rum tasting.

I declined an offer to dance from a Bahamian beauty with long curly hair and doe-shaped eyes in her sepia-colored face. Instead, I stayed seated at one booth in our area.

"You should have seen Scott's face when—"

"Excuse me, aren't you Sebastian Steele?"

A stunning ash blonde woman interrupts our conversation to approach Baz. She stares at him with large turquoise blue eyes before she scans him from his head to his lap, her gaze lingering on his groin.

Oh brother, here we go... I turn to Malcolm and talk about my new blend of Scotch.

After a bit of banter, a member of the security team strides to our section and asks the woman to return to her table. She takes the hint and throws a nasty glare at Baz before she leaves with no further comments.

"Good grief. That was the worse pickup line ever," Scott laughs.

"And equally ridiculous reaction," I add with an eye roll as I sip my rum.

Roger and Malcolm agree and return to our tasting.

Nothing deters these women.

My mind drifts to My Baby Girl. I cannot wait to get to New York City for her. And LEVELS.

"LITTLE TEMPTRESS, tell me what makes your pretty pink pussy cream."

I rumble in her ear.

She squirms on the seat between my muscular thighs as we sit on the dark red leather banquette. Through black leather pants, my rock-hard cock presses against the crack of her ass.

The sheer, ass-skimming, silk georgette negligee hides nothing, including the nipple pasties and pearl thong. Silver, six-inch platform mules adorn her feet. An ornate platinum half-mask with white plumage across the top frame, her widened gray eyes as she glances around the room.

We're at Peepshow in LEVELS New York. It's time to feed her voyeur kink.

The stunning pair of diamond drop earrings I gifted to her glitter in the low light along with her collar as her head swivels, taking in the hedonistic sights surrounding us.

Other seating alcoves filled with members in various stages of sex make it hard to determine what's most arousing. Women and men climax with lusty sounds. A main stage and several smaller platforms showcase demonstrations in flogging and breath control. The atmosphere is all about bacchanalia with the melodic thrum of sensual music.

Too slow to answer, I nip the delicate shell of her ear.

She yelps.

"Tell me, Little Temptress," I command with a growl.

She mewls and presses further into my firm chest. Her nails dig into my taut thighs. My growl deepens. She squirms some more.

"Th… The woman dressed in the red latex catsuit on her knees feasting on her Domme… just over there," she pants, tipping her head towards the right.

A raven-haired Domme sits on a table with her ample thighs spread wide. Her sub kneels between them, eyes blindfolded by a red silk cloth. The Domme snaps the tip of a suede whip onto her sub's ass. Both women moan.

I chuckle against my Little Temptress' neck. Then suck some skin into my mouth. Another mark to claim her.

Since being a member at LEVELS, her sexual appetite has expanded to include unthought of desires and things that never intrigued her before. The women case in point.

She turns her head to the left. I follow her lascivious gaze. A man taunts a woman trussed up on a St. Andrew's Cross with a flogger on her enhanced tits and pierced nipples. The woman cries out in ecstasy as a tail lands on her pierced clit. The diamonds sparkle in the light as she twitches from her climax.

I hook my feet around my Little Temptress' ankles and snap her legs apart.

Surprised, she squeaks.

Two of my thick fingers skim across her toned inner thigh. Then breach her sopping-wet pussy entrance.

She bows her back and tilts her pelvis to give me better access to her slippery core.

My other hand presses down on her hip and the top of her thigh to lock her in place. I finger fuck her and tug on the pearl thong relentlessly. She breaks beautifully for me as her juices gush from her pussy.

My cock jumps and weeps.

"Cum for me again," I command huskily.

She tosses her head back and bucks against my hand as I draw another orgasm from her quivering core. The intensity proves too much. She screams.

"Good, Little Temptress," I croon as I pat her sweet pussy lovingly. "Good, girl."

She purrs her pleasure as she laps my fingers clean.

"Come, let's walk along the piazza here. There's a gelato shop just beyond the square."

I smile down at My Baby Girl as I lead her through the streets of Sorrento.

To celebrate our six-month anniversary, we came to the picture-perfect gem of a town on the Italian coast. Perched atop a cliff facing the Bay of Naples, Sorrento boasts panoramic views over the coast and its marina at the base. Built along the cliff, the town stacks to give it a distinct look: glittering water with bobbing boats topped by rows of colorful buildings. The charm of the old town continues with its warren of tiny streets and alleys lined with pretty historic properties, like the ones around this bustling piazza.

I rented a magnificent stone villa with a pool set in the garden high above the bay on the Sorrentine Peninsula. Each of the six bedrooms has en suite bathrooms and either Juliette balconies or access to the stone terraces. We rode a Vespa into Sorrento for lunch and gelato.

The warm July sun shines bright, making it the perfect time for the frozen treat. Locals mix with tourists as they take in the sights. The laughter of children fills the air. People pose for pictures in front of the fountain.

My Baby Girl beams at me and points to the gelateria up ahead.

"There it is! I can't wait to get some stracciatella. Yummy!" She exclaims as she rubs her belly.

I grin at her in a white cotton crocheted dress. The tiers of lace ruffles flutter in the breeze. Her hair swept atop her head, shows off her swan-like neck. Her face bare of makeup has a dewy appearance. Simply gorgeous.

We weave through the crowd and line up for the tasty treats. My Baby Girl teases a little boy as his parents laugh along with them. The sight of Haley with a child makes me want one with her. She's a natural, and I know she'll be a wonderful mother.

While we eat our gelato, we stroll from one street to the next in no particular order. A store window catches our eyes, and we head there. Lively music from around the corner calls to us. On another street, we follow a line of people dressed in all white.

Fluent in Italian, I understand their animated conversations. I tell My Baby Girl they're headed to Chiostro di San Francesco—Sorrento's famous church, monastery, and cloisters. What I don't tell her is they're having an en masse marriage ceremony. The line of people are couples taking part in it.

I put our empty gelato cups in a trash bin. In Italian, I ask a man if they needed marriage licenses, to make a reservation, and other questions. When he told me the ceremony was open to all and everything would be taken care of at the church, I grinned.

It's serendipitous.

"Let's go with them," I tell My Baby Girl as I take her hand and increase my pace.

The excitement builds all around the closer we get to Piazza Francesco Saverio Gargiulo. The church appears, and my heart races. I glance down at My Baby Girl.

Her eyes widen behind oversized tortoiseshell sunglasses. The rows of couples with women holding bouquets clue her in. She swings her head to me. Her mouth a perfect O.

I drop to one knee and clasp both of her hands between mine.

"Haley, my love, I don't want to go another day without you being mine forever. Let me give you your happily ever after. Marry me and be my wife, the mother of my children."

Her mouth opens, and she bobs her head.

"Words, Baby Girl. I will have your words."

A beatific smile spreads over her face as her cheeks pinken.

"Yes! Oh, yes!"

My heart explodes with love, and I swoop Haley from her feet, kissing her deeply.

People clap and cheer.

"But Lachlan, are you sure? I mean, I love you and want to spend the rest of my life with you. But I don't want our marriage to be a knee-jerk reaction because you got caught up in—"

I silence her with my index finger to her lips and shake my head.

"Haley Steele, this is no 'knee-jerk reaction.' Trust me. And believe I will not allow you to back out. Again," I say with a cocked eyebrow.

Her cheeks deepen to crimson, undoubtedly from the memory of my denied proposal in Punta del Este. She bites the corner of her plump lower lip. A tendril of her hair slips from the updo, and I brush it from her face with my lips. Then cover hers for a tender kiss.

I swallow her moans as she melds her soft curves against my firm body, arms wrapped around my neck.

"I want my fairytale with you, My Lord," she murmurs.

"And you shall have it, My Lady," I respond. "Come, let's complete our paperwork."

Two hours later, we walk through an Arabic portico with interlaced arches interwoven with fragrant flowers, plants, and ornamental trees. The melodic sound of birds and the elated chatter of newly married couples fill the enchanted space.

"I love you, Mrs. Lachlan Jackson."

She holds out her left hand with the band provided by the church on her finger and places it on top of mine with an identical ring. After a moment, she beams up at me and buries her face against my white linen shirt. Her breath warms my skin exposed above the open buttons. The strong fragrance of the white lilies in her bouquet tickles my nose.

"I love you, Mr. Lachlan Jackson."

I wrap her in my embrace and press my lips to the top of her head.

"Ready to consummate our union, Mrs. Jackson?" I ask huskily.

She tips her head back and winks.

"Absolutely, Mr. Jackson!"

We practically sprint through the town, cutting between buildings and narrow streets to reach the Vespa I parked down by the marina. Once there, I hop on and help my wife behind me, careful not to expose her bare pussy as she raises her dress to her thighs. Helmets on, we zip to our villa.

She giggles when I scoop her into my arms to carry my bride over the threshold. Then she gasps at the sight of red rose petals that lead to the primary bedroom suite all the way to the top of the bed like a blanket. There white roses form a heart amongst the red. A bottle of Dom Pérignon Rosé Vintage 2005 chills in a bucket of ice with two flutes. A plate of chocolate-covered strawberries sits beside them on a table near the bed.

"Oh, Lachlan! When did you have this done?" My wife

asks as tears shine in her dove gray eyes. "It's so beautiful. Thank you."

My eyes close briefly as I give a silent thanks myself to the butler for arranging it so flawlessly. I sent a text message to him while Haley selected her bouquet. I tell her, and she clasps my cheeks to kiss me.

Gently, I set her in the middle of the bed and place her bouquet on a night table.

She lays back and glides her palms over the petals. Her pupils dilate with lust as she reaches for me, arms open wide.

"Come to me, my husband. Make sweet love to your wife," she purrs.

My cock leaps to life, thickening and lengthening along the leg of my white linen trousers. I toe off my Gucci loafers and strip out of my shirt and trousers, tossing the garments to the travertine floor with my boxer briefs.

I stalk to the bed as I fist my erection. A bead of pre-cum forms at the tip, and I lift it off with my pinky. Without a word, I lower it to my wife's parted lips.

Her little pink tongue snakes out to flick the cum from my finger. She closes her eyes and hums deep in her throat at the taste.

I growl.

The lace of her delicate dress doesn't stand a chance as I rip it from her body, right down the middle. D-cups jiggle as she pulls her arms free. Her flat belly tightens when she lifts her hips into a bridge. I slide the tattered dress from beneath her and toss it to the floor.

She reaches for me, but I wave her hands away.

My fist pumps over my engorged cock. More pre-cum oozes from the angry red head. I smear across my heated flesh for natural lube.

Haley writhes on the bed, legs spread to show her glistening pussy. Eyes locked on my cock. She licks her lower lip.

The vision proves too much. Pleasure unfurls from the base of my spine. I press my thighs against the side of the bed as I widen my stance. My heavy balls tighten. One tug. Another.

"MINE!!!" I roar as great ropes of my seed shoot from my dick to land on my mate's belly and breasts.

Subsequent pulls draw every single bit of my jizz out until my knees give, and I lean on the bed with my free hand. Planked over my mate, I let go of my still erect cock to smear my seed and scent into her soft skin, flushed red with her arousal.

"Lachlan," she moans as she slips a finger coated with my cum into her mouth and sucks until her cheeks hallow out.

My mouth crashes over hers as she barely has time to remove her finger. Our tongues dance. I nip and suck on her lips to feast. The taste of my salty jizz mixes with her natural sweetness.

Her hands grip my biceps as she wraps one leg around my hip.

"Fill me with your seed, my husband," she demands as her heel presses against my ass.

I growl as my caveman claims his mate with one powerful thrust.

She cries out into my mouth.

My cock hardens to the point of pain.

The need to mark my mate inside as I did out drives me to piston my hips repeatedly. Each orgasm I pull from her quivering pussy grips my cock. Her mewls and the suction as I withdraw from her wetness play erotic music to my barbaric grunts and growls.

I ride her tight pussy through a veil of red lust. Once again, the coil grips my spine and whips through my balls and out of my cock. The tip hits her cervix, and she keens. Copious amounts of my seed fill her womb until it overflows to puddle beneath her ass.

My vision darkens, and I collapse atop her body. My sweaty chests slips on her heaving tits. Peaked nipples rub against me. I drop my head to suckle one as my hips make lazy circles. My cock commands a final orgasm from her pussy. I groan as it flutters along my girth.

Fingertips slide along my back to tangle in my damp hair.

The nipple pops from my mouth when Haley tugs my head to bring my lips to hers. I let her take control. A toe-curling kiss full of emotion rocks my world as much as my back-to-back releases. I sigh, content.

Haley Jackson is mine forever.

HALEY

The sun filters in through white gauzy curtains that flutter in the breeze from the balcony outside of our bedroom. Patterns play across my husband's face—handsome even as he sleeps. A smile spreads across mine as I watch him.

When I awoke, it took a moment for me to realize our wedding wasn't a dream. The soreness at the apex of my thighs, marked breasts, and kiss-swollen lips provided proof. Not to mention the wedding band on my left ring finger.

Mrs. Lachlan Jackson, Countess of Aboyne.

I cover my mouth to contain my gleeful laughter.

My fairytale wish finally came true!

It may not have been the ceremony of my dreams with all the pomp and circumstance surrounded by our families at Jackson Castle. But it was amazing and most importantly with the man I've always wanted as my husband.

Lachlan Jackson.

Mine! Forever mine.

Gently, so as not to wake him, I bring his left hand to my lips and kiss his wedding band. I close my eyes as happy tears fill them.

"Baby Girl… Why the tears?"

Lachlan—in a voice thick from his slumber—adjusts his hand to cup my face and swipes an errant tear from my cheek. He sits up on his right elbow to study my face.

"What's the matter, babe?" He asks.

I turn my head to kiss his palm and smile.

"My dream came true," I whisper.

"Baby Girl," he groans as he covers me with his body.

I widen my thighs to cradle his groin to mine. The thickness of his giant dick grows from the heat of my already wet pussy. It clenches in need for my man. I purr into his ear as I tangle my fingers in his mussed hair.

"Already nice and wet for me, Mrs. Jackson?" My husband murmurs against my breast as he strokes his length along my seam.

I purr in erotic delight. My hips lift to meet his movements, and he chuckles.

"Eager, too," he adds.

Not giving in to my demands, my husband makes a meal of my breasts—laving the pebbled nipples, nipping the sensitive undersides, sucking the fullness into his mouth for more possessive marks. He hums his pleasure.

I growl with impatience. Then whimper.

"Oh, and ready for punishment, too, Naughty Girl," he says as he smacks my swollen nipples.

He rolls off and reaches into the nightstand. His back to me, I can't see what he fiddles with. Instead, I admire the ripples in his muscles as they flex beneath his tanned skin. I trace a fingernail along his flank. He shudders.

"Don't try to play nice now, Naughty Girl," he says over his shoulder. He closes the drawer and faces me. "I have a present for you."

My husband morphs into my Alpha Dom. He dangles three jeweled clamps connected by a platinum chain before me.

Instinctively, I cup my breasts and squeeze my thighs shut.

He chuckles darkly.

"But first a bit of pleasure," he says as he nudges my thighs apart to bury his face between my thighs.

My eyes close in carnal bliss at his ministrations. Each lick of my clit and stroke of my G-spot amps my arousal. My lower belly tightens, and I pinch my nipples before I explode with a strangled cry. Then hiss.

Damn! My Alpha Dom binds my clit with the clamp.

Open-mouthed kisses leave a fiery trail as he makes his way to my breasts. He repeats the process for one, then the other, taking me from the height of pleasure to the pit of pain. He sits back on his haunches to admire his handiwork.

"So beautiful, Mrs. Jackson." My husband makes a brief appearance.

A tug on the chain draws a whimper from me. My Alpha Dom returns with a smirk.

I watch as he takes white silk ties from the top of the nightstand and binds me to the bedposts in a spread-eagle position. A tug at the restraints proves I'm held fast. My pussy fills with my arousal. I arc my back as I mewl with need.

"I will give you what you need, Naughty Girl," my Alpha Dom says. "Close your eyes and open your mouth. If you want to stop, open and close your fists."

A silk mask covers my eyes, followed by a gag in my mouth. Losing my senses combined with the restriction of my movement makes me panic. I stiffen and whimper around the cloth.

"Relax and breath through your nose," he murmurs in my ear.

I turn my head in his direction, and he brushes his lips over mine. At the tender touch, the submissive in me takes over. My mind and body give in to my Alpha Dom.

Strong fingers massage the arches of my feet in firm, steady strokes. The delicate skin between my toes receives the same treatment. Instantly, I calm down.

Full lips brush my inner ankle, send a shudder through my body. Sweet caresses behind my knee make me squirm. I shiver when a silky feather skims up and down my inner thighs. A flick across my exposed clamped clit makes my back bow, and a mewl slips beyond the gag. My pussy pulsates.

Ignored, the feather continues to flick across the thin

membrane of my perineum before it circles my bottom hole. I lift my hips for to deepen the touch. It slips away to tease my mound, followed by gentle sucks and pulls by his mouth on the sensitive skin. The tingling sensations stoke the erotic fire within me.

A single, slow stroke along the platinum chain up the middle of my belly leads to increasingly smaller circles around my heavy breasts to my clamped nipples. A dip back to my slippery seam and the feather comes to my lips coated with my juices. The musky natural scent combined with my pheromones fills my nostrils. I inhale deeply and whimper.

"Ready to give me more?"

I jolt at the sound of my Alpha Dom's voice, rough with carnal desire and his warm breath against my earlobe.

My head bobs.

A thick vibrator slips easily into my creamy pussy. The steady rhythm pulses along with my quivering inner walls. Long and even strokes touch every inch of my greedy core. As much as I want to cum, I don't. My Alpha Dom has yet to give me permission.

"Good girl," he murmurs huskily at my control.

I mewl, happy to please him.

The rhapsody stops abruptly when he plucks the clamp from my swollen clit. As the blood rushes back into the sensitive bud, fire licks at it. I cry out in thanks when his mouth engulfs my aching clit. Once again, I mewl. Hips thrust up to bring his face closer to my pussy.

He chuckles and smacks my lower lips.

"Behave, Naughty Girl," he warns.

Another flash of pain as he slips the clamps from my nipples and blood rushes to the tips. He eases the pain with flicks of his tongue as he massages my breasts. A hand skims back down to my pussy. Two thick digits slip inside while the palm cups my mound.

"Cum for me, good girl!" My Alpha Dom commands.

Repeated thrusts graze my G-spot until I gush into his hand with a scream. My body convulses as stars flash behind my eyelids. Frissons of erotic energy thrum through me. Mind blown, I sag against the mattress.

Whispered words of love soothe me as the silk ties slip from my wrists and ankles. Tender hands massage them to increase the blood flow. Lips replace the gag for a heated kiss. Gently, the mask lifts to reveal the smiling face of my husband. I blink.

"Drink," he says as he holds a glass to my mouth.

With a moan, I relish the cool, refreshing water.

"I'll be right back," he says as he slides off the bed and strides to the en suite bathroom. His ass cheeks flex along with the muscles in his legs that bunch with each step.

When he returns, I lick my lips at the sight of his velvet-covered-steel dick bobbing at full mast against his eight-pack abs lined with his happy trail.

My man is an Adonis sculpture come to life.

So distracted by his masculine beauty, I gasp when he scoops me from the bed and retraces his steps. The soothing scent of lavender and ylang ylang essential oils heated by the warm water in the sunken marble tub surrounds us. I inhale deeply and nuzzle against his corded neck.

Gently, my husband bathes me from shampooing and conditioning my hair to the tips of my toes. I lift the sponge to wash him. But he waves my hand away, saying it's all about his wife today. He cleans himself and dries us with warm, fluffy towels.

Wrapped in equally sumptuous robes, we return to the bedroom.

My stomach rumbles at the sight of a hearty breakfast on the table. The tantalizing aromas of bacon and sausages, fresh-baked scones, jams, orange juice, and chamomile tea make my mouth water.

But first…

"Sit," I tell my husband.

His emerald green eyes widen, but he listens.

I kneel between his thick thighs and slide my fingers up the insides to reach his erect cock. He plants his feet further apart and scoots down in the chair.

With a sinful smirk, I take his bulbous tip into my mouth and glide his full length to the back of my throat until my nose rests against his skin. I hum; he groans. My feast ends in an explosion of his salty essence into my belly.

He pulls me to his lap and kisses me breathless.

"I love you, Mrs. Jackson."

"I love you more, Mr. Jackson."

* * *

"Hi! How are you doing? Don't ask about me. Tell me about you, Hot *Maman*. It's almost time… Of course, Roger is going to hover. What do you expect? Ha! Tell me about it… Yes, see you then… Love you and Roger, too… I'll tell him… Ciao!"

I giggle as I end the call with Leonie.

She and Lola are due to give birth in a few days. Our family split to be with both of them. My parents, Malcolm, and Starr are with Lola and Baz in New York City. I'm set to join Leonie, Roger, The Twins, her parents, Harris, and Anita in Paris. Originally, Lachlan was going to New York to support his best friend. But we'll go there after Leonie gives birth.

We have another day here before we leave for Paris.

It's been an incredible week. I hate to leave. But family first, I smile to myself. I'll be an auntie to four munchkins!

I glance down at my flat belly. One day, Lachlan and I will have our first child of many. And I *cannot* wait! My hands rub my pretend baby bump as I giggle.

"Private jokes? Or can you share with your husband?"

Strong arms wrap around me from behind. I lean into Lachlan's broad chest and close my eyes on a contented sigh.

"I just spoke with Leonie—"

"She's all right? The baby?"

I tilt my head and grin at him. I love how he cares as much about my family as I do.

"They're fine. I wanted to check in on her," I respond. Then sheepishly, I lower my head and add quietly, "I was thinking about how I can't wait to be pregnant with your baby…"

Lachlan stiffens.

My heart plummets.

I shift out of his arms to face him.

Wide eyes stare back at me.

"I—we—um… Forget it. Sorry to upset you…" I say as I rise from the chaise lounge and stalk towards the pool. I dive in, mortified.

What the hell?! Didn't he say he wanted me to have his children when he proposed?!

My mind races as I push up to the surface. Before I can catch my breath, a mouth covers mine.

Lachlan!

I push at his chest. But he holds fast. His powerful legs paddle beneath the surface to support us both in the deep water. I bite his tongue, and he hisses. It gives me the opportunity to free myself from his grip. I kick off and reach the side of the pool to hoist myself from the water.

"Hold on, Haley!" Lachlan growls as he grabs my waist. "Do not run from me. Not again. We will talk things out."

I close my eyes to hold back the tears that threaten to fall. I don't want him to see me cry.

"What makes you think you upset me?" Spinning me around, he brackets my body between his arms as he grips the wall.

I look everywhere but at him as I respond, "You froze and looked terrified."

When he doesn't answer, I glance at him.

He bites down on his lower lip as his emerald eyes twinkle.

"True, you took me by surprise. But I want your belly round with my baby, Mrs. Jackson. The sooner, the better!" He chuckles. "How about we practice?"

Now my eyes widen. I wrap my arms around his neck and kiss him silly.

* * *

"Why not?!"

I flinch at Lachlan's angry roar.

He doesn't quite agree with my request we keep our marriage a secret for now. I have my reasons…

For one: I don't want to take away from Leonie and Lola's impending baby arrivals. Especially since this is Lola and Baz's first child.

Two: The Big Four are only just getting used to Lachlan and me as a couple.

Three: I don't want U.K. society to think we rushed into marriage or have an excuse to ostracize me for not inviting them. I got a taste of it from some guests as an American interloper at our introduction weekend…

I voice my concerns, and Lachlan narrows his eyes at me. Emerald fire sparks.

"No. Fuck. No!" He states. "You are my wife. I do not give a bloody rat's ass what anyone says, Haley!"

I bite the corner of my lower lip as I think of how I can persuade him to go along with me on this. I flick my gaze back to him, ready to pursue my case. But the hurt in his eyes stops me.

My seatbelt clinks open, and I launch myself onto his lap. I wrap my arms around his neck and press my forehead to his. I close my eyes, and we breathe each other's air.

"I'm sorry, Lachlan. Please forgive me, my love. I just don't want to mess up," I whisper.

He squeezes my hips to ground me.

"Tell you what. As far as your brothers go, they'll get over it, and I truly doubt your girls want you to make less of your happiness than theirs. So we *will* tell our families. Non-negotiable, Haley," he says. Then squeezes my hips again when I open my mouth. He continues.

"We will ask my mother—the Society Queen—what's best. If she agrees with you, I will concede. Do you understand?"

I consider my options and conclude he's right. I tell him as much, and he carries me to the bedroom of his Gulfstream G650 to seal our deal.

By the time we arrive at his Paris penthouse, we decide to wait until Labor Day at Steele Southampton Village to announce our marriage. Lachlan admits it's best, since our families will be together at the same time.

In exchange for the two-month delay, I agree to move to London—not quite Aberdeen as Lachlan wanted, but close—and work out of STEELE London. I'll move into his Hyde Park penthouse. In reality, we'll spend most of our time between Lachlan's Aberdeen penthouse and Jackson

Castle. When we visit Baz and Lola next week, I'll let everyone know and pack my necessities.

My initial reaction to Lachlan's request I move was, why can't he???

He makes two excellent points: he runs Jackson Corporation for that side of the globe while Lydie—who's based in New York City—handles the other; Harris can do the same for our subsidiary, and I can work anywhere in the world. I relent.

Besides, Lachlan and I can be newlyweds without The Big Four breathing down our necks. Plus, it'll give me time to acclimate to living in the U.K. as we decide Aberdeen will be our primary residence. We'll also ask Leonie—using her interior designer hat—to convert Lachlan's full-floor flat and my penthouse in The STEELE Tower into a duplex.

We're excited about the new phase of our love affair. As Sade says, nothing can come between us!

HALEY

"So, what project requires you to move all the way to London, Haley? Asking for a friend..."

Harris sits back and crosses his muscular arms over his chest while he cocks his eyebrow. We're seated at the conference room table in my suite of offices at STEELE International, Inc.

Lachlan and I arrived last night after two weeks in Paris with Leonie, Roger, The Twins, and now baby Daphne. She's absolutely adorable and has the Steele family traits of gray eyes and ebony hair, just like her older brothers. Leonie can't believe not one of them has her amber eyes and mahogany mane. Roger is beyond himself with his little family. Such a proud Papa!

Lola and Baz went to Steele Southampton Village shortly after she gave birth to baby Slade. The video to introduce him to the family was too cute! We've had Face-

Time calls since he was born. But I can't wait to hold Slade in person and to see his elated parents.

Lachlan and I will fly out in two days and stay for a few. He has meetings in Aberdeen he can't reschedule, and I want to get settled in London. Besides, we'll be back in three weeks for Labor Day.

While we're in New York City, he'll take care of business at Jackson Corporation's offices, and I'll meet with my team. First, I had to tell Harris about my decision to work in London…

I roll my eyes at my twin. I know he knows my real reason—not the married part—and wants to give me a hard time. We've never been able to keep things from each other. I give in.

"Oh, fine… I want to be closer to Lachlan. Okay?" I respond, then continue with a sigh. "We've been apart long enough. He can't move here because he's the only Jackson in Aberdeen. Also, both you and I don't need to be based here. I'd like to make it a permanent move. Do you mind?"

Harris studies me in silence.

"No, I don't mind you relocating. We can work anywhere in the world. With the number of clients we have overseas, you'll be closer to them in London," he responds.

Then he reaches across the table and takes my left hand, lifting it in the air.

"What I *do* mind is you not telling me you're married to Lachlan," Harris states as he rubs his thumb over my ring finger.

I glance down and realize my wedding band left a tan

line. In my haste to remove it this morning, I didn't notice the mark. Duh!

As I stare dumbfounded at Harris, I wonder if anyone noticed Lachlan's mark. If so, we're totally busted. I'll send him a text message just in case.

Harris—trained by our father, too—stares at me, awaiting my response.

Independent-Woman-up, Haley Jackson!

"Lachlan and I married while in Sorrento last month. We came across an en masse ceremony, and he proposed," I respond, chin held high. "However, we prefer to tell everyone when we're all together for Labor Day. So, promise not to tell, Harris."

He narrows his dove gray eyes as his nostrils flare.

"That fucker denied you a wedding with your family!" He roars as he slaps his hands on the table and stands. "Is that what you wanted? Or did you go along with his idea so you can finally have your *dream* come true?"

My jaw hits the floor. I've never seen my twin so angry. His typical jokester, easygoing personality flies out the window. WTF?!

"Harris!" I hiss. As I leap to my feet, my chair slides back and bangs against the wall. "How *dare* you?! I have a brain and can think for myself! That's the problem with you and the rest of *your* brothers! I'm not a child nor incapable of adult decisions. And all of you will respect me! Do not say *anything* to *anyone* about *my* marriage! Or else!"

Now his mouth drops open.

"Do. You. Understand?" I snap.

Harris raises his hands, palms out in surrender. The condescending sneer wiped from his face replaced with a hangdog floppy grin.

"Sorry, Haley. I was way out of line," he says contritely. "It's just that you and I are so close. But since Lachlan, you keep things from me. I respect you and know you have a mind. We are twins, so since I'm smart, you must be, too."

His joke makes me smile.

But I can't deny it. The secrets with Lachlan have put a divider between my twin and me—not to mention our families. Only those who guessed—including Harris both times—knew. So I can understand his frustration. He just has to express himself better.

"I forgive you. However, you're right. I won't keep anything from you just as long as you keep it to yourself. Okay?" I say pinky out.

He rolls his eyes and links his finger with mine to swear on it. Then he sits down.

"When have I ever, Miss I'm Going to Natasha's House But Really Went to a Club?" He deadpans.

I throw my hands up and roll my chair back to the table.

"That was like how many years ago, Mr. Marlboro Man?" I retort.

We laugh. Our world is right again.

After we figure out which projects I should take because of the clients' locations, have a status update on all projects, and review prospects, we meet with our team. Surprisingly, a few members of our staff ask about relocating to London. Harris and I exchange glances and tell them we'll consider expansion. Not a bad idea, actually.

We break in time for lunch. Harris and I go to Nobu Fifty Seven for bento boxes. As usual, we can't resist the Whisky Cappuccino for dessert. The espresso gelato is divine!

"I think we should increase the number of people in our satellite office at STEELE London. With you being there full time, it makes sense. Or do you intend to make Aberdeen your base?" Harris asks between bites.

I consider the logistics. STEELE doesn't have an office in Aberdeen, only a hotel. We could look for office space somewhere. On the other hand, when I spend time in Aberdeen, I could commute via helicopter to London since it's only an hour-long flight.

When I share my thoughts with Harris, he agrees it's best to stick with the existing infrastructure in London and to commute. It won't differ from a car ride—the hotel rooftop helipad to the office one.

With the number of clients and projects I'll manage, we decide to offer my administrative assistant—Douglas Washington—and four staffers from Technology and Cyber Security each to relocate. We'll hire two reception-ists and two admins from within STEELE London to join our team. Another lesson from our father: build loyalty by promoting from within.

We decide to get final approval from Baz when we get to our beach compound before we share the news with our staff and call for relocation requests. Not to mention I need to tell our family about my move first…

The rest of the day blurs as I lose myself in the work I love. It's not until Douglas knocks on my door do I realize it's after six in the evening. I tell him good night and shut down my systems.

"Hey! I'm heading out for drinks with Laurent. Do you want to come, or do you have plans?"

I glance up at Harris in the doorway.

It's been a while since we hung out, so I tell him to give me a minute.

"Oh, and you can invite Little Lord Fauntleroy. We don't want hubby to feel left out of all the fun…" he adds with a smirk.

I throw a pad of yellow stickies at him, and he laughs as he scoops it up and drops into the leather guest chair.

I call Lachlan, and he agrees to meet us at Salon de Ning. It's a perfect summer evening for cocktails at the chic rooftop bar on Fifth Avenue.

Before we leave, I slip into my en suite bathroom to freshen up my hair and makeup, plus a spritz of the perfume Lachlan loves. Harris, of course, has a smart comment when I re-emerge. I loop my arm through his, and we head out. Instead of taking a car, we opt to walk the two blocks.

When we arrive, Laurent waves us over to a sofa seating area in a corner above Fifth Avenue. Harris and I weave our way past tables and chairs with umbrellas. Other guests chat as they enjoy the atmosphere and decadent drinks.

"Hey, Haley! Glad you could make it, lass!" Laurent says as he pulls me in for a hug and double kisses. "I hear Lachlan is joining us. How lovey-dovey."

He and Harris guffaw.

"Don't hate, brother."

We turn to find Lachlan grinning. He slips his arm around my waist and pulls me to his side for a kiss.

"Wait until you meet the love of your life, and you'll be as mushy as me, Baz, Malcolm, and Roger!" He adds with a chuckle. "You, too, Harris!"

The boys glance at each other and double over with laughter.

"A right-now woman will do!" Harris cackles.

Lachlan and I settle onto the sofa while the boys take the chairs on either side. A server appears, and her eyes widen at the sight of the three sexy as sin Alpha males who ooze power and wealth. For a moment, I feel as though I need to wave my hand in front of her face to get her attention. But she pulls it together. They, however, don't notice.

"I'll have the Ning Sling, thank you," I tell her.

They give the rest of the drinks, along with a selection of shared plates, before she leaves our group with a wistful glance at Laurent.

He's too busy scanning the rooftop for a potential hookup to see it. Harris coughs—the signal he spotted someone. Laurent swings his head around, and his collar-length sable brown hair brushes his five o'clock stubble.

"They'll learn," Lachlan whispers in my ear. He nuzzles his nose to my neck as he slips his arm around my hip.

"Haley?"

No…

Yes.

Natasha Bond.

My former best friend from high school. The one who lusted after Lachlan and kissed him the summer I realized I loved him and not as a cousin. Now, she stands in front of the coffee table, flicking her big baby blue eyes between my husband and me. With a smile, she tosses her long blonde hair over her shoulder. A white silk, knee-length, strapless dress highlights her willowy figure. Yup, she's still gorgeous.

Her smile widens as she latches onto my man with a predatory gleam in her eyes.

"And Lachlan. Lachlan Jackson! We met years ago. So good to see you!" She gushes.

I swallow down a gag.

"Natasha?" I feign ignorance. Two can play that game.

She nods but stays locked on Lachlan.

He pulls me onto his lap practically and glances at her.

"Yes. However, I do not recall you," he responds coolly.

She flinches as though struck. I suppress a laugh. Lachlan grips my hip.

Fortunately, the server returns and maneuvers between Natasha and the table to place our cocktails on it. Lachlan takes advantage and buries his face in my hair. His soft chuckle blows tendrils that tickle my neck. I giggle and wrap my arms around his shoulders.

With a partial glance over my shoulder, I say, "Nice to see you, Natasha. Enjoy your evening."

Harris and Laurent chuckle when she huffs and stalks away.

"Your possessiveness makes me hard as fuck, Mrs. Jackson. What are you going to do about it?" Lachlan murmurs in my ear huskily.

"Take you to LEVELS New York, and ravish you," I purr.

"Oh, bloody hell! Cut it out already!"

Laurent's exclamation makes all of us laugh.

Once again, the hotties don't notice several heads turn —female and a few males—to gawk at them. I grin knowingly and sip my Ning Fling.

"HELLO, my sweet little nephew! You know I'm your favorite auntie! Yes, indeed, Slade. I love you, too, handsome boy!"

I croon as we sit on the deck at Lola and Baz's beachfront mansion within Steele Southampton Village. Lachlan, our parents, Harris, Roger, and Leonie—who holds Daphne—laugh. Rodolphe and Gaspard play on the beach with their dogs and Nanny Grace. We left Malcolm and Starr in the City after we had a meeting regarding their stalker problem…

"Here, let me hold him," Lachlan says. "Baz, you lucked up. Slade looks just like Lola."

"Whatever, Lach!" Baz retorts.

Everyone laughs since Slade looks exactly like his father. Lachlan chuckles.

"Seriously, you did well," he smiles.

The best friends grin as Baz puffs up his chest. Another proud Papa!

As I glance around, I realize now is as good a time as any to break the news of my move and approval to expand STEELE Technology and Cyber Security to STEELE London. I nod at Lachlan and Harris. Lachlan hands Slade back to Lola as Harris leans forward.

"Let me get Malcolm on FaceTime. I want to tell you at the same time," I say as my fingers fly across the screen of my mobile.

When he's connected, I take a deep breath.

"I'm moving to London after this visit. I want to be closer to Lachlan, and it's easier for me to relocate there than for him to move here. Also, Baz, Harris and I split projects and clients based on locations. We want to expand STCS's satellite office at STEELE London with my admin, two others, two receptionists, and eight staff members— four from Tech and Cyber each. We need your final approval to move forward logistically."

Silence descends.

I hold my breath.

Baz glances from our father to Lachlan to me. My mother looks like she's holding her breath, too.

"Haley…"

"Move to London?!"

"For real, Lachlan?!"

Our father clears his throat. Everyone turns their gazes to him. He pins me with his intense stare. I sit taller and raise my chin. Show no weakness. He switches his gaze to Lachlan, who also remains steadfast. Morgan finishes his appraisal with Harris. He doesn't waiver. Our father sits back and steeples his fingers.

"Those are significant undertakings, personally and professionally. True commitments. I take it you thought them through to the most minute detail?" He asks, then continues when we respond affirmatively. "Then you have my blessing. However, Sebastian—as CEO—decides on the expansion."

Our father turns his platinum gray gaze to Baz. He studies us, then nods.

"Fine. Coordinate with New York and London's human resources and operations teams," he says. He narrows his eyes at Lachlan. "I know I do not have to tell you to respect Haley, nor what will happen if you do not, Lachlan."

"No, to both. And know she is and always will be well taken care of by me," he responds as he clasps my left hand. Unconsciously, his thumb rubs over my bare ring finger.

Morgan and Baz nod.

"Excellent news! Now, let's celebrate!"

The tension abates with our mother's declaration.

Indeed, time to celebrate!

LACHLAN

"You're rusty, *dhuine*. Judging by your tan, you've spent too many days lounging on a beach in the sun. Did you come to fight or to paint your toenails, pretty boy? Oh, I know… The Earl does not deign to get his hands dirty!"

I glare at Ewan Kerr and raise my Highland broadsword as I leap in the air for an overhead strike. Being a world-renowned master of Historical European Martial Arts, he dodges the attack with his targe and pivots for a counterblow. The loud metal clang of my sword hitting his shield rings out in the open-air courtyard of the Scottish Arts Center With Ewan Kerr.

We parry forcefully as we move about the space until he calls for a stop.

"Much better, Jackson. Now you've got some energy, let's burn it off in the ring," Ewan says as he heads for the door to the center's interior.

I follow him and hand my weapons to the assistant, then head to the ring for a bout of bare-knuckle fighting. On the way, I strip my t-shirt off and remove my fencing footwear before I climb into the ring.

Ewan grins devilishly and waggles his fingers at me.

"Come on, pretty boy. Show me what you got," he taunts.

I snort and circle him.

We spar and finish with stretches before I go to the locker room to steam my sore muscles and to shower.

"You ended better than you started, Jackson," Ewan says as we leave the mats. "You're on my calendar for your usual sessions or what?"

"Not quite. I'm in London next week. So, I'll see you next month," I respond as I slap him on the shoulder. "But trust I'll be ready for you."

Before I get in the steam room, I check my mobile for calls and messages. A grin spreads across my face at a text message from My Baby Girl.

Hi! I'm heading to the helipad. I'll see you at the castle. xoxo Your Wife

I chuckle and type a quick response to confirm.

We're spending the weekend at Jackson Castle. Now that Haley settled in our Hyde Park penthouse, she flies to Banff for the weekends. Aberdeen is muggy this time of year. So we escape to the countryside for horseback riding, sailing, and just relaxing.

My parents are more than thrilled she moved. They're in Positano at their villa and will see us in Southampton

Village for Labor Day. Which leaves the estate to My Baby Girl and me.

After I leave the center, I go to Truffelos for a box of her favorite handmade truffles. The shopgirl offers more than chocolates. But I ignore her unwanted advances. I have a sweet little thing on her way to see me, I muse as I stride out of the shop.

"Lachlan?"

Hmmm. Not the sweet little thing I was thinking about…

"Hello, Fiona," I respond as I turn to face her. Then groan inwardly as I greet her mother, Maisie. She raises an eyebrow at me. Wonderful.

"Oh, Lachlan, how nice to see you. It's been a while. All well?" Maisie asks, then spies my package. "That's a big box of chocolates! I thought the Marchioness was on the Amalfi Coast."

Deep breath, Lachlan…

"Yes, everything is great, thank you. And your family?" I ask, ignoring her last remark.

She doesn't skip a beat.

"We're doing well, thank you. It's good to know the Marchioness enjoys Truffelos' chocolates. We'll send her some for the holidays," Maisie says pointedly.

Fiona glances from me to the bag.

"Since you're in town, perhaps you'd like to have dinner. It would be nice to catch up," she says. "As friends, of course. Or stop by the gallery. I have some new pieces you may prefer."

"Actually, the chocolates are for Haley, Baroness," I respond, then turn to Fiona. "As far as dinner, no. But Haley and I may stop by the gallery if she wants to add some artwork to our penthouse or to the castle. Thank you for letting me know."

She nods slowly, and Maisie blinks.

"Now, if you will excuse me. Good evening, ladies," I add and stride away. The bag of truffles for My Baby Girl tucked under my arm.

"I MISSED YOU!"

She jumps into my arms and kisses me silly as I carry her to the Range Rover. Settled on her seat, I stride around the back to the driver's side. Another kiss to her sweet lips, and I drive to the castle.

"Did you get all the items on the list?" My Baby Girl asks.

"Yes. I can't wait to see you barefoot and—"

"Don't you dare, Lachlan Jackson!" She warns, then smirks. "Or you'll sleep on the couch."

I chuckle at our corny clichés. I'm worse than Baz, I muse with a shake of the head.

"Anyway… I'll take a quick shower and get to dinner. If you'll let the wine breathe, I'd appreciate it, hubby," she says with a grin.

When we pull up to the door, the butler takes Haley's bags to our suite. She follows while I go to the wine cellar to select a couple of bottles. Once they're on the kitchen island next to the bag of truffles, I hurry to our suite. Time for a shower and a bit of loving from my sweet little thing.

"Here, you chop the vegetables for the salad and toss it with the balsamic vinaigrette and olive oil. The chicken is almost ready. I'll set the table."

I stare after my wife. The apron strings around her narrow waist emphasize her hips as they sway and her round ass. Whomever invented yoga pants gets my thanks.

"And stop staring at my ass…" she says with a giggle.

I chuckle and get to tossing the salad.

During dinner we talk about our plans for the weekend, then I bring up my run-in with Fiona and her mother. Haley raises an eyebrow and purses her lips.

"Well, I'm glad you told her no about dinner. But to avoid appearing insecure in our relationship, let's go to her gallery. You and I can fly back to London in the afternoon on Monday after we stop by Aberdeen. Sounds good?"

I grin at my brilliant wife.

"Definitely. That's a good point. Whether or not we purchase anything, we show we're not uncomfortable around her," I respond with a wink.

Haley winks back and raises her wine glass filled with Jackson Chardonnay.

"*Gun eagal!*"

I raise my glass with a chuckle at my wife declaring the Jackson clan's *no fear* clan motto

"Gun eagal, Mo Nighean Leanaibh!" I repeat heartily in agreement with *My Baby Girl*.

She made a vow to learn Scottish Gaelic, just as my mother did when she married my father. Haley curls up on the window seat in the library—her favorite room—and reads the books and journals written about and by my ancestors.

I love how she immerses herself in my family's history and Scottish culture. When she tells me tidbits about the ancestors' portraits or an antique's provenance as we pass them, I laugh, impressed with her knowledge. She's taught me quite a few things! As proud of our heritage as my father is, he will be pleased.

After Haley and I straighten the kitchen, we retire to the media room to watch *Whisky Galore*—one on a list of Scottish movies she found on Google. I enjoy feeding her truffles with some Champagne as we make out like teenagers at the back of a theater.

"RACE YOU TO THE RUINS!"

I shout over the wind as I urge my stallion into a gallop across the open field towards a former watchtower on the coast. The sun shines brightly overhead in a cloudless, cerulean blue sky. On the horizon, the North Sea stretches endlessly. We're fortunate to have a glorious day for a ride through the estate.

My Baby Girl whoops behind me as I hear her mare's hooves thunder.

More boxes checked for being an excellent equestrian and knowing her way around a sailboat. Therefore, I push my stallion to the tower, or else she'll accuse me of letting her win. Four older Alpha male brothers make her competitive and not some shrinking violet. Just the way I love her!

She doesn't even glance at me as she comes abreast of us. Completely focused on her goal.

We ride hard and fast—no pun.

I give my stallion his head, and he flies like the wind. We reach the ruins moments later with a triumphant shout.

She concedes as she dismounts gracefully.

"Well done, My Lord!" She says with a bow of her head.

I grin and thank her.

"Not easily achieved, My Lady!"

We tend to the horses, then walk around the tower. I notice a faraway look in My Baby Girl's eyes as she stares out to sea.

"What's on your mind, lass?" I ask.

Her cheeks pinken prettily, and she lowers her head in embarrassment. The tip of a boot kicks a pebble as she removes her gloves.

I wait until she brings her gaze to me.

"Promise you won't laugh," she says, then continues when I raise my hand. "Well, years ago when Laurent showed the watchtower to Harris and me, I became enchanted by it. I would come out here and pretend I was a princess in her tower—it wasn't a ruin at all. Sometimes the bad duke captured her, and her love had to save her. Other times, she was a new bride awaiting the return of her husband from fighting abroad."

She pauses and bites the corner of her lower lip.

I raise an eyebrow.

She sighs and continues.

"The fairytale always had a different theme. But the princess and her hero were always the same. Me... and you," she ends on a whisper.

My heart soars at this new info. I always knew Haley loved her fairytales. She would recreate scenes from plays she wrote and enlisted Harris and Laurent to enact them for our families. But I never realized I was the hero.

I cup her face in my hands and kiss her deeply. All of my love fills the kiss better than words can ever express. She moans softly, and I allow our bodies to talk even more when I make love to my wife on the grass beside her tower. Her hero comes home with a passionate roar.

* * *

"Hello, Lachlan, Haley. I'm glad you could make it. The artist happens to be here and can answer your questions."

"Hello, Fiona, and thank you for telling us about the new collection," my wife responds, accepting double kisses.

I return Fiona's greeting, but with a nod. No contact for me, thanks.

Her violet eyes appraise me without comment at my

denial. Then she loops arms with Haley to lead her through the installation. As Fiona takes us to the first area, the artist joins us.

She's a young woman in her early twenties with large expressive hazel eyes that twinkle as she tells us about her inspiration. Her paintings feature landscapes as mystical interpretations of Banff's forests, moors, and coastlines.

One glance at my wife, and I can sense she's taken by the artwork. There's even one of a watchtower. We smile at one another and tell Fiona we'll purchase it. A few more paintings draw Haley to them, so we add them to the tower. By the time we leave, we accumulate five extraordinary pieces: two for our suite at the castle and the others for Aberdeen, London, and New York City. Fiona will ship all except for the London one since Haley and I will bring it with us.

The artist thanks us profusely while Fiona stares on with a smile that doesn't meet her eyes.

We bid them farewell and head to the rooftop helipad at STEELE Aberdeen. I'll work in Jackson's London offices for the week. After which, we'll fly to Southampton Village for Labor Day.

"That was worth it, don't you think?" My Baby Girl asks as we ride in the back of my Rolls-Royce Phantom Extended, our driver Theodore Doyle at the wheel.

I squeeze her hand and smile.

"Yes, it was. As soon as I saw her style, I knew you'd want at least one. Now you have five!" I respond with a chuckle.

"Ha, ha, ha. They're way too dreamy to not have one in each of our homes. Delightful reminders of the Scottish countryside," she says. "So, don't tease me!"

Once we land in London, Theodore—who joined us on the helicopter—puts the painting and our luggage in the trunk of the Range Rover SVAutobiography. I help my wife into the SUV and get in beside her.

On the way to our penthouse, we pick up some Thai takeaway. After dinner, we select a spot for the new painting. I make a reminder to contact the concierge to arrange for an installer to hang the new piece tomorrow, so My Baby Girl can enjoy it right away.

We spend the rest of the evening getting ready for our work week. Haley jokes we're like an old married couple as we sit in the study on our laptops.

But when I whisper all the filthy things I'll do to her to prove we're not old, she takes it back immediately. Then I live up to my every word.

LACHLAN

"Either you're up to no good, or you're nervous about something. So spill it, bro."

Lucien cocks his head to the side as he studies my face.

Both clans gathered on the deck of my parents' beachfront mansion at Jackson Southampton Village. He and Laurent took a golf cart over from the third property—The Bachelors' Nest the three of us share—within the family compound. It's a six bedroom, eight bathroom, three-story beachfront classic Hamptons-style mansion. Our parent's sprawling residence has twelve bedrooms and sixteen bathrooms over two stories with a two-bedroom guest house and a pool cabana. The private beach spans all three properties minutes away from Steele Southampton Village.

My Baby Girl and I flew in from London late last night and asked everyone to meet us here for breakfast. She and the rest of the Steeles arrived moments ago. She turns to me and smiles encouragingly as her hand squeezes mine resting on my thigh.

I return her smile and face our families.

"Haley and I married in Sorrento two months ago."

Silence followed by exchanged glances, then…

"WHAAAT?!?!?!"

"Oh, Haley, *félicitations, chérie!*"

"NO fucking way, man!!!"

"Whoohoo! Go, girl!!!"

"For real???"

The one I watch is my father.

Connor scowls and stares at me. He shifts his gaze to Haley and back to me. His frown deepens when he looks at our bare left hands. Then he stands.

Fuck! If he walks away.

Instead, he strides toward us, and I rise. Haley stands beside me, gripping my hand in a white-knuckle hold.

"Dad, we—"

"Congratulations, son! I wondered when you would step up and marry the lass!"

He pulls me into a hug, then embraces Haley and double kisses her cheeks.

"Welcome to the Jackson clan, lass!" He bellows.

Haley grins and hugs him back.

"Thank you, Uncle—"

"Oh, no! No more 'Uncle,' lass. *Athair* Scottish Gaelic for—"

"*Father!* I know! I've been studying with a tutor, *Athair*," Haley cuts in, bouncing on the balls of her feet.

Morgan clears his throat, and we turn to him. He closes the distance between us in a few strides thanks to the long legs of his six-feet-four-inch frame. He stops in front of me and raises his eyebrow.

"I suppose you assumed you had my blessings when I gave it to you to date Haley and for her move to London. However, you never asked me for my daughter's hand in marriage," he says.

Fuck! I can't deny he's right.

"I apologize, Uncle—"

"Do you really think that's appropriate?" He cuts in with his head cocked to the side.

This is just getting worse. He's beyond pissed.

"No disrespect—"

"Dad will do, son."

My mouth falls open, and Haley gasps beside me as my father chuckles.

Morgan grasps my shoulders and pulls me in for a hug.

"I agree with Connor. I thought we'd have to sit you down for a talk," he says with a smirk, then turns serious again. "However, you should have asked for my blessing before you actually married my daughter. And in Sorrento with no family? I know my daughter has always dreamed of a fairytale wedding since the time she was a child. Lachlan, how will you make it up to her and our families?"

"I agree!"

"Me, too!"

We glance up to find Aunt Shelley—well, Mom—and my mother glaring at me standing akimbo.

Now we pissed off The Moms.

I turn to my wife and clasp her hands.

"Haley, they're right. I know you were more than happy to marry in our spur-of-the-moment ceremony. But you deserve the wedding of your dreams, and I will give it to you. I promise," I say sincerely.

The most glorious smile spreads across her face as tears fill her eyes. Her lower lip trembles with emotion.

I lean over and kiss her tenderly.

Everyone claps and whistles.

My Baby Girl rests her head on my chest and wraps her arms around my waist as we face our family—the combined clans of Jacksons and Steeles.

The first to approach are our mothers. Tears now fill their eyes as they croon soothing words to my wife. Lydie, Lola, Leonie, and Starr join them, and they move over to the outdoor living room with giggles.

"So you really did it, huh?"

My gaze leaves my wife to settle on Baz. His platinum gray eyes narrow on me.

Here we go…

"Yes, I did. I told you I'd keep Haley happy. We saw the couples going to Chiostro di San Francesco. I proposed, and Haley said yes," I respond.

"Why didn't you tell us then?" Malcolm growls, arms folded across his muscular chest, feet planted apart. *The Enforcer* is ready for action.

I don't want to start our marriage with a battle, so I nod.

"You're within your right to be upset. However, Haley asked we wait to tell everyone until now since both families would be together in person for the STEELE Foundation's Annual White Party. She also didn't want to take any shine away from Lola and Leonie's births. But most importantly, she didn't want to upset her older brothers because you're just getting used to us as a couple."

Roger extends his hand and pulls me in for a bro hug as he claps my back—always *The Responsible*.

"Welcome to the family as a brother, Lach!" He says, then continues. "You better not hurt our little sister or it's over for you."

"Well, you guys are slow on the uptake."

Heads turn to Harris, who stares back smugly.

"I figured it out the moment I saw my twin," he continues as he waggles his left ring finger.

"She's not wearing a ring, genius," Laurent says as he rolls his eyes.

Harris elbows him, and they tussle before he goes on.

"No, but she had a tan line from one!" He says triumphantly. "And none of you losers noticed."

Lucien throws his head back and laughs.

"Leave it to the twin connection," he says.

"Well, as long as Haley is happy, and she gets her fairy-tale wedding, you're welcome as a brother," Baz adds as he gives me a bro hug.

The Big Four engulf me with hugs and punches good-naturedly. Suddenly a spray of Champagne descends on us.

Laurent holds two bottles spurting their contents in the air as he whoops and hollers. Harris grabs another, pops the cork, and takes a swig before passing the bottle to me. With a nod of thanks, I gulp some of the elixir and pass it to Baz. He grins.

We pass the bottle until it's empty, and another takes its place. The girls clink Waterford Crystal flutes as their laughter and chatter fills the air.

My wife glances at me and winks as she raises her glass. I return the gesture with a fresh bottle.

"Aaw… Look at you, Lord Googly Eyes!"

"I'll say it again: wait until you meet the love of your life, Harris. And I'll be the first one in line to say I told you so, bro!" I say with a chuckle and a slap on his back.

"Exactly! I told his ass the very same thing," Baz chimes in as he takes another swig and tips the bottle in Harris' direction, then at Laurent. "And you, too, cuz!"

They glance at one another and double over with guffaws and snorts. Tears pop from their eyes at the hilarity of our statements. Wankers. They'll learn one day.

"Okay, gentlemen, we hate to interrupt your bro fest. But we have a serious matter to discuss."

All laughter stops at my mother's words.

"Is Haley pregnant?!" Morgan asks, mouth agape.

I've never seen him in shock before. To save him, I shake my head with a smile. He takes a breath and smiles back.

Everyone settles in their seats and turns to Lucie.

"Social propriety requires a wedding worthy of an earl and a countess. You married secretly with no announcement of an engagement, let alone a wedding invitation to our friends, royal and noble peers, social circle, and colleagues," she says with an arched eyebrow.

"Lachlan, you may not use your title or interact with others—as you should, especially as the heir apparent. But I raised you better, and Haley will not make a faux pas before she can establish herself in our world," my mother continues pointedly.

She turns to my father, who nods in agreement, then she goes on.

"I recommend we announce you are engaged with a party upon your return to Scotland. Then have your wedding in six months at Jackson Castle's chapel with the reception in the ballroom, as tradition dictates. Afterwards, you can admit it's a vow renewal ceremony and you wanted to have your family and friends with you for the momentous occasion. Haley will be the Countess of Aboyne, and no one can say she's the outsider American not following protocol."

My mother pauses to glance at me, my father, and Dad Morgan.

"I agree. That's the best solution. You can keep your original wedding date, but get the full regalia as expected of our station," Connor states.

"That sounds best," Dad Morgan says. "We want the best for both of you. Haley, Lachlan, tell us your thoughts."

My Baby Girl walks over and slips her arm around my waist with a hand on my chest as she stares up at me.

"I think it's a brilliant solution. The last thing I want is to ruffle anyone's kilts or knock anyone's coronet askew…" she replies.

We laugh at her joke—my father the heartiest.

I drop to one knee and slip a navy blue velvet box from my trousers pocket.

"Haley Jackson, you are my wife. Now, wear the first of my rings—The Jackson Emerald."

I press the diamond closure to reveal our most important family's heirloom. The thirty-three carat, flawless, pure green, Colombian emerald has an octagonal step-cut set on a diamond platinum band.

"Emerald is as the stone of successful love. It brings loyalty and provides for domestic bliss by enhancing unconditional love and unity. Partnerships remain in balance. However, emerald can signal unfaithfulness if it changes color… And I vow that will never, ever happen, my love," I state.

She drops to her knees in front of me and cups my face.

"I love you, Lachlan Jackson—always have and forever will. I wear your rings with pride," she says before she kisses me breathlessly.

"Put a ring on it!"

We part to laughter at Lola's phrase in honor of her favorite singer, Beyoncé.

I slip the exceptional emerald ring on my Haley's finger and kiss her palm before I rise and lift my wife to her feet.

"Let's see it!" Starr calls out and the other girls chant.

My wife blushes as she holds up her hand. The gigantic emerald and diamond band sparkle in the morning sun.

They oh and ah over the ring. Her sisters-in-law's engagement rings are just as phenomenal with flawless nearly thirty-carat and twenty-five-carat diamond stones, respectively.

I notice how Malcolm watches Starr keenly. She's unaware and giggles at something Lydie says. He must sense my stare and glances at me. I grin like the Cheshire Cat at witnessing *The Enforcer* fall in love. He smirks back. Another one gives up being a playboy Dom!

"Well, get ready for Sergeant Shelley and I assume Lieutenant Lucie to handle your wedding plans, *chérie!*" Leonie exclaims.

Lola giggles and adds, "Absolutely! And you can use the app you created for me to track my wedding."

My Baby Girl clasps her hands and turns to her Moms.

"Will you help me, pretty please?" Haley asks with puppy-dog eyes. "I'd appreciate it truly!"

My mother looks at Mom Shelley, whose brown eyes shine with happiness. They whisper together as they gesture at Haley. Then they turn to face her.

"We believe that can happen!" They respond in unison and laugh at Haley's audible sigh of relief.

"Excellent! Now for breakfast—"

"And more Champagne!"

* * *

THE EARLY MORNING sun glints across the Atlantic Ocean as the wind catches the colorful kite floating high above me. I race with the waves, using my core strength and leg muscles to control the kite and the board beneath me.

I throw my head back and roar with the wind as I overtake Roger.

We're out kitesurfing with the rest of the guys. It was Malcolm's idea, since he and Lucien are the thrill seekers of our bunch. They lead the pack as we race across the water.

"Yeah, baby!" Lucien shouts, as he does aerial acrobatics with ease.

Malcolm follows with midair front and back rolls.

Oh, and the show-offs…

I have to admit they are masters of the waves as they harness control of the wind with incredible agility and speed.

"Out of the way, Lord Googly Eyes!"

A glance over my shoulder reveals Harris gaining on me. The nut job comes so close our kites and cords nearly tangle. I shift my hold and slip to the left. The wind catches my kite and sails me further ahead.

"So long, sucker!" I shout over my shoulder.

We spend over ninety minutes on the water before we head for the beach. While we gather our equipment, male ribbing ensues, along with jokes and taunts. Afterwards, we strip out of our wet suits down to our neoprene diving shorts. A quick dip under the outdoor showers before we head up to the deck of The Bachelors' Nest for a hearty breakfast.

"Well, I hate to break it to you, brother. But The Nest is for bachelors only… And you're no longer one of us. So you gotta go, bro!" Lucien announces as he slaps five with Laurent.

I throw a grape at him, and he catches it in his mouth —show-off.

"Hey! I know. I move in here, and you and Haley take over my suite of rooms, plus hers in our wing. Problem solved, Lord Googly Eyes!" Harris proclaims.

Laurent and Lucien tackle him from his chair, and they wrestle on the floor.

"Okay! You pass the test. Welcome home, cuz!" Laurent says.

I glance from one to the other and back again.

"Bugger off, you wankers!"

They guffaw until all of us join in.

"The beachfront property on the other side of Mom and Dad's and two away from here is up for sale. I know the agent with the pocket listing," Roger says. "It's in good condition. My Residential Properties Division can get the remodel together for you in no time. My gift to both of you."

I call My Baby Girl to ask her if she wants to see the property. She shrieks and tells me she's always loved it. I tell Roger, and he arranges for a showing in an hour since the owners left for the season.

The single guys give me a hard time for skipping out on our breakfast. But the attached ones have my back.

Either way, I chuckle and leave them to their meal. I have a house to buy for my woman. And nothing else matters.

HALEY

"**O**h, Haley! Congratulations! Your ring is phenomenal!"

I grin at my gym buddy, Maribelle Hayes. She claps her hands and grabs me in a hug.

As always, the matchmaker called to invite me on a double date with her husband and his friend. This time, I surprised her with my engagement news. She insisted we meet in Southampton Village right away. I invited her to join me and the girls for our Girls' Day Out of shopping, lunch, and mani/pedis.

"I'm so happy for you, Haley! Now show me a picture of that mystery man of yours!" Maribelle continues.

She pretends to swoon when I take out my mobile and pull up a photo of Lachlan in board shorts, jogging along the beach. Sweat shines on his tan skin as muscles ripple beneath with each step. A grin plays on his face as he waves at me.

"OMG! Of course you'd marry a movie star, Haley Steele!" She says as she fans her face. "He's super hot."

I grin like the Cheshire Cat.

"Lachlan is, isn't he," I respond with a giggle. "And Calvin is hunkalicious, too!"

Maribelle beams at the mention of her husband—a successful Wall Street hedge fund manager. Her ten-carat, brilliant-cut diamond engagement ring and diamond eternity band glitter in the sun. Her man did well by her, too.

In fact, all of our men lavish us with the best. I can't wait to see what ring Malcolm will give to Starr. I side glance at her as she chats with Lola by the accessories section of the boutique we're in. Each of us will pair up soon. Harris is bound to find his life partner. Despite his bravado, I know he's no different from my other brothers and me.

"And my brother is lucky to have Haley!" Lydie adds as she passes us on her way to the dressing rooms with an armful of clothes.

"Indeed, he is a lucky lad and a bonny one to boot!" Billie says, switching her Savannah accent for a Scottish lilt.

I laugh at her perfect execution.

"We're having an engagement party in Banff at his family's seat next month. I don't have the final date, yet. But it'll be over a weekend. You can stay at the castle or at the village's bed-and-breakfast, if you prefer. Do you think you and Calvin can make it?" I ask hopefully. The more friendly faces around me, the better I think.

Maribelle's eyes widen.

"A castle? For real?" She asks, flabbergasted. "Are they royals or something?"

"Nobles. His parents are the Marquis and Marchioness of Huntly. Lachlan is the heir apparent with the title Earl of Aboyne. His siblings have titles, too," I respond with a grin.

Her mouth drops.

"You're speaking to the future Countess of Aboyne," Blair says.

The daughter of a wealthy manufacturing tycoon from a prominent London family, she's well acquainted with the U.K. social scene. She giggles at Maribelle's reaction and motions for her to close her mouth.

"Haley, you are a girl's dream come true!" She says. "You couldn't keep Calvin and me from your party! Hopefully, we'll score a wedding invitation, too…"

"Most certainly!" I respond. "No way would I leave Mrs. Matchmaker out of my nuptials!"

Maribelle laughs and hugs me again.

"Whether or not he's an earl, I'm so thrilled for you, Haley!" She says.

"Thanks, Mari!" I respond gleefully.

"I don't see you for years. Now, I see you every day."

Maribelle and I turn around to find Natasha.

Oh, great…

"Hello, Natasha. It would seem so," I say. "How are you?"

Her baby blue eyes darken to denim at the sight of my engagement ring. They lift to my face. An expression somewhere between shock and annoyance mars her beauty. She raises an elegantly arched eyebrow and purses her full lips.

"Obviously not as well as you, Haley," Natasha states with a scowl.

Caught between us, Maribelle's gaze flits between my former best friend and me. With a smile that doesn't reach her eyes, Maribelle extends her hand to Natasha.

"Hello, I'm Maribelle Hayes, a friend of Haley's," she says coolly. "Isn't it so exciting. Our girl is engaged to a fantastic hottie, Lachlan Jackson."

Natasha's nose wrinkles as though she's smelled a skunk.

"You said he's your cousin," she says, ignoring Maribelle's hand and comment.

Take a breath, Haley, I tell myself before I snap. Highly un-countess-like behavior, I hear Mom Lucie whisper in my ear.

"I did say we're cousins," I begin. Maribelle gasps, and I smile at her. "Only because our mothers have been best friends for their entire adult lives. So our families are a very close-knit clan. Hence, no blood connection."

Turning to Natasha, I continue, "I know you had a crush on Lachlan, and you kissed. So I can understand your dismay. Pity for you, your pretend friendship with me didn't garner a relationship—or a ring—for you with my brothers or my *cousins.*"

While Natasha's mouth gapes, I loop arms with Maribelle.

"Bye, Natasha," I call over my shoulder.

Maribelle waggles her fingers for a wave without a backwards glance.

"Good for you, Haley! She's not worth your time or invitations… *Obviously!*" Maribelle snickers.

"Who is that woman?"

I glance up into narrowed amber eyes. Golden flecks spark fire. *The Lion* is on the hunt.

"Natasha Bond. In high school, she and her clique befriended me. I should have known the most popular seniors didn't want to be friends with a sophomore. She wanted to date one of my brothers or cousins. Typical gold digger, even at eighteen," I respond with an eye roll.

Leonie snorts in derision as she glares over her shoulder at Natasha. Then my sister raises her left hand and wiggles her ring finger.

"None for you," she says. "Buh-bye, now."

Natasha huffs and spins on her heel to stalk from the boutique.

"Oh, good, Leonie. I thought I'd have to get involved. And that woman would not appreciate what I'd tell her," Lydie says as she appears beside me. "It's like swatting flies, keeping the disreputable ones away from my brothers. Thank God for you, Haley."

Our laughter fills the boutique. Other shoppers glance in our direction, and it makes us laugh even louder.

"Okay, ladies, let's move on to the next shop." Lola says as she—along with Starr, Blair, and Billie—join us. "I want to check out the baby boutique next door."

Leonie's eyes soften at the mention of babies. The Hot *Maman* claps.

"*Oui, Chérie!* Let's go. Rodolphe and Gaspard need some sweaters for the fall and Daphne can use a few more onesies," Leonie says. She loops arms with Lola and sashays out the door.

Starr, Maribelle, and I go to the crystal shop for new malas and geodes. Starr says I need the power of quartz to amplify the energy of my new homes. We'll meet Lydie, Billie, and Blair at Carbon 38 for new workout clothes and athleisure wear.

The shopgirl at the crystal store tells Starr about a new shipment that has the types of crystals she suggests for me. Impressed with the stones and raw geodes, Starr explains each one and their benefits. But she steps back to let me pick the ones that speak to me. I scan the selection. Their natural beauty and vibrations call to me. I opt for some rose quartz for love, carnelian for passion, selenite to cleanse, and amethyst for peace.

"Excellent. You'll sit them out in the sun to purify them when you return to the compound. Now, I saw a red jasper bracelet for Malcolm. It increases sexual vibrancy, you know," Starr says. Then adds with a wink, "Not that he needs any help—"

I cover my ears and whistle.

Her laughter tinkles past my fingers.

Maribelle goes with Starr, saying she needs one for Calvin.

Afterwards, we go to Carbon 38 and other shops before

we stop for lunch at Lucien's restaurant. The staff greets us and leads the way to our table on the deck overlooking the Atlantic Ocean. We give our cocktails and appetizers orders to the server.

"Leonie, I have a huge favor to ask you," I say as we sip our drinks.

She shifts her gaze to me and smiles.

"Anything for you, *chérie*! What is it?" She asks as she sips her iced lemon ginger tea.

"Lachlan and I are making Aberdeen our permanent residence with London as the secondary since I'll work from the STEELE offices as my base. We want to combine my penthouse with his full-floor flat into a duplex pent-house at The STEELE Tower in New York City. The beach house we just bought needs a complete renovation to match our style. Roger said his division will handle both with the beach house as a wedding gift. So… Lachlan and I want to ask you to oversee both projects. I love your designs for your and our parents' Paris residences and the nurseries you did for Lola and you. Please!!!"

Leonie bites her lower lip and shakes her head.

"I'm so sorry, Haley. I cannot believe this. *Je suis désolé, chérie*," she responds.

My heart drops, and I sit back as disappointment hits me. Damn. Her work is so phenomenal. I wish she could do them.

Laughter rouses me from my pity party. I glance up to find Lola cracking up and nudging Leonie.

"I was right, Leonie! You owe me dinner," Lola crows.

Then she turns to me, hazel eyes glowing with mirth. "Of course she'll help you, Haley! What you don't know is I bet you'd ask her, and she bet you wouldn't."

Leonie joins in with Lola's infectious laughter.

"It's true. I figured you'd want to do them yourself," she says. "I'm excited to help you. Roger told me about the beach house. I'll make it fabulous for you and Lachlan. And the penthouse, wonderful. Plus, I'm glad to have a sister on the other side of the Atlantic with me. We can see one another regularly."

I jump up from my seat and give her a big hug.

"Thank you, sis! You are the *absolute* best, Leonie!" I exclaim.

"*De rien, chérie!*" She giggles.

We talk about the properties and timelines. They can do them simultaneously with completion before the new year. Leonie and I decide to sit down with Lachlan to discuss our wants. Then she'll show us some designs and meet with the STEELE team to finalize the schedules and staff. Her excitement matches mine!

When lunch ends, we go to the spa for manis and pedis. A manager calls for bottles of Veuve Clicquot Champagne and crystal flutes when Billie tells her my good news. The Moms—including Josy—join us as a surprise. The rest of the afternoon passes in pampering amongst loved ones.

I couldn't have wished for a better way to celebrate my engagement.

LACHLAN

"Well, son, I will say it again. I am extremely proud of you. And not only because of your marriage—uh, engagement—but also also how you beat Stewart Scotch to acquire Ainsley Scotch successfully. It's time for you to take over more responsibility at our company. I plan to retire in a couple of years, and you need to be ready for the helm."

The smile on my face wavers as once again my father brings up me being the one to succeed him at Jackson Corporation.

Lydie wants it, and she can have it. Despite our father's desire, I will not destroy my sister. And me assuming the head of Jackson would do it. She'd also see the move as a betrayal. I doubt our relationship would ever recover. So not worth it. At. All.

As though sensing the discussion, Lydie walks into my office at Jackson Town House in Aberdeen. Her stride falters when she sees our father and me at the conference room table. She flicks her gaze between us. The surprise in her eyes morphs into suspicion when she notices the Champagne bottle and two flutes.

With an arched eyebrow, Lydie approaches the table.

"A celebration? What did I miss?" She asks as she pins me with emerald fire.

I cock my head to the side and meet her stare until her gaze drops.

True, I won't hurt her. But I won't allow her to pull an Alpha move on me. We're both natural dominants and I won't hesitate to show my force.

When she lowers herself onto a chair beside our father, I rise and stride to the bar. Returning to the table with another flute, I respond.

"I bested Stewart Scotch to close on the Ainsley Scotch deal. The signed contracts arrived, and our legal team approved the paperwork. Here, have a glass to celebrate."

Lydie takes the proffered Champagne, and we raise our flutes with a nod.

"Congratulations, Lach. Well done," she says. "I will inform the board."

"Lachlan will send the message, Lydie. No need for you to do it," Connor interjects.

She schools her face, but not before I see a flash of hurt.

"Thanks for the offer, Lydie. However, I already have the message done with details to answer questions they may have. Let's get started on our weekly update meeting. I plan to leave for Banff afterwards. Haley landed there this morning, and we have stuff to do," I say.

Connor claps and nods.

"Yes, the celebration continues with your engagement party," he says. Then he turns to Lydie. "And when do you suppose we will have one for you? As I said before, it is time you settled down with a husband and children, Lydie."

She purses her lips in response as she opens her laptop.

"Here's the chart of—"

Deftly, she ignores Connor and moves into the meeting. He doesn't pursue an answer. The question was more rhetorical to make his point.

I shake my head. Not for me to worry about.

"HELLO, sweetheart! You're just in time. Come, we're in the salon."

My mother greets me with double kisses and a big hug. She grins like the Cheshire Cat as she loops her arm through mine to lead the way.

"We *must* complete the seating chart for dinner. Then there's the—"

I nod as my mother—Lieutenant Lucie—rattles out the to-do list. My mind is on my woman, who I haven't seen in a week. A client in Japan needed her on site. Business called…

When my mother and I enter the salon, My Baby Girl sits next to an attractive man in a well-tailored three-piece suit. His blonde hair contrasts with her ebony mane as their heads lean too close together over a laptop. She giggles about something he says too low for me to pick up.

A growl rumbles deep in my chest.

MINE!

My mother stops walking and stares up at me. I ignore her shocked expression and stride into the room.

"Haley," I say. My tunnel vision excludes Sergeant Shelley, my sisters-in-law, and Starr, along with an unfamiliar woman.

All heads turn to me.

My Baby Girl jumps up from the sofa and rushes towards me, arms out as she smiles.

"Hi, my love! I missed you so much!" She exclaims. "Are you as excited as me?"

I lift my woman off of her feet and slant my mouth over hers for a kiss that leaves no doubt she is mine, all mine. Once I set her back down, she clutches my biceps through my suit jacket to steady herself. Swollen lips tinged bright pink part as she catches her breath.

A smirk spreads across my face as I glance over her head at the offensive male who dares to flirt with my woman.

He meets my stare and licks his lips. A flicker of lust fills his chestnut brown eyes.

What the fuck?!

"Lachlan, let me introduce Bailey to you. He's the new event planner I hired," my mother cuts in with a knowing smirk of her own. "Bailey, this is my son and Haley's fiancé —Lachlan."

He crosses the room and extends his hand to me. It's as soft as his yellow patterned silk tie and matching pocket square. His delicate grip a touch longer than necessary.

Okay, so now, I'm at a loss. This wanker is flirting with me, not with my woman!

"A pleasure to meet you, Lachlan," Bailey says. "The Marchioness tells me you're the genius behind your family's Scotch blends. I enjoy them immensely. Such flavorful tastes you offer, Lachlan."

My Baby Girl giggles and squeezes my waist.

"Okay, Bails, stop flirting with my man, or you and I will have a major problem!" She says as she leads me to the sofa.

Her girls titter, and Mom Shelley laughs out loud.

"Lachlan, sweetheart, your face is priceless!" She says.

"And what a handsome face indeed"—Bailey raises both hands palms out—"But I heard you loud and clear, Haley, honey. Off limits!"

They laugh, and I snort.

Bailey picks up the laptop and sits on the other side of My Baby Girl. The screen displays a schematic of the ballroom with numbered tables. A seating chart lists guest names and their table numbers. He goes through the room by table while The Moms make comments.

It's not until I hear the Ridels do I pay attention.

"Wait, who of the Ridels will attend?" I ask as I glance between My Baby Girl and my mother. "You don't mean all of them, do you?"

My mother looks at Bailey and the woman who works with him.

"Kindly excuse us a moment," she says as she gestures to the salon's door. Once they leave and shut it behind them, she turns to me. "We invited all of them, and they accepted. Beside the Baron and the Baroness, Heath, Fiona, and Gwyn have a plus one each. We don't want them—or anyone else for that matter—to think we cannot interact just because Fiona isn't the bride."

"Is that wise?" I ask, concerned Fiona may make a scene or put us in an uncomfortable situation. I express my thoughts to them.

My Baby Girl answers.

"I won't give Fiona the slightest glimmer of a notion she's gotten to me in any way whatsoever. You and I need to make it clear we are solid in our relationship," she states emphatically. "We invited Callum. But he RSVP'd no."

When my eyes narrow, she rubs my thigh to calm me.

"For the same reason as Fiona. It's all right. Okay?" My Baby Girl beseeches me.

I grunt in agreement. She giggles and kisses my cheek.

"But understand my warning. If Callum so much as breathes the wrong way, I will finish him. *Okay?*" I respond.

"Yes, My Lord," she says, eyes downcast and head bowed.

Oh, the Little Temptress will pay for playing to my Alpha Dom…

"Now that's squared away, let's get finished," my mother says as she rises to open the door for the event planners.

They return, and with the utmost discretion, they make no reference to the conversation. We complete the seating arrangements, along with other tasks related to the dinner and the weekend activities, before I can steal my wife away. I take her hand and rise from the sofa.

"Thank you, Moms, ladies, Bailey. Now, if you will kindly excuse us," I say with a nod.

My Baby Girl mimics my words of gratitude and waves as I lead her from the salon.

With each step, my cock lengthens and thickens down my trousers leg. It's been way too long since I had her writhing beneath me and calling my name in ecstasy. Plus, she needs to be punished. A hungry growl slips past my lips. She gasps and shudders. My pace quickens.

Once the door shuts on the sitting area of our suite, I grip her hips and toss her over my shoulder. The Little Temptress yelps when I swat her ass—the jiggling flesh warm through the silk of her wrap dress. I smack the other cheek. She gasps.

By the time we reach the bedroom, her ass is hot. But I've only just begun.

With ease, I sit on the edge of the king-size bed and shift her from my shoulder to drape over my thighs. I untie the belt of her dress and use it to bind her wrists at the base of her back before I flip her dress over her head.

Her muffled cry of surprise and the sight of her pinkened skin make my cock twitch.

As I stroke her ass cheeks, I lean over to croon in her ear. My warm breath flutters across the delicate shell, and she trembles.

"You are a naughty girl, Little Temptress. You did not tell me you invited Fiona and Callum. How do you think that made me feel?" I ask.

She shifts her hips, and the delicious aroma of her arousal wafts around us. My mouth waters.

"It was the right thing to do," she says in a feisty tone.

THWACK!

The Little Temptress squeals as her legs flail. I top them with one of mine to hold her in place firmly. Then I trace the tip of my finger along her seam. A satisfied purr makes her shiver.

"So wet for me already, Little Temptress"—I slip the digit to the first knuckle into her wet pussy—"You and I know it isn't the pain from the actual spanking that turns you on. Rather, my display of dominance that makes you want me to possess you sexually. Did you not tell me on purpose to warrant your punishment?"

THWACK! THWACK! THWACK!

"Too slow to answer, Little Temptress, or is that defiance?" I croon as I palm one cheek to squeeze the sensitive skin between my fingers.

"Oooh… Yes, My Lord! I didn't tell you because I didn't want you to say no. Mom Lucie agreed!" The Little Temptress wails.

I snicker wickedly and sit up. I rain a pattern of smacks from the top curve of her ass to the round center, below at the juncture where it meets her thighs, then her upper legs. Each cry and jerk she makes causes my cock to weep, tormented by the confines of my trousers. It aches to bury itself to the balls inside of her tight, soaking pussy.

Not until she relaxes across my thighs with only whimpers do I slow down. A few more smacks, and I position the Little Temptress on her knees with her chest and cheek on the mattress. The sight of her inflamed ass and dripping pussy make me groan low and guttural.

I don't bother to remove my suit, merely unzip my turgid cock and slam inside of her with one brutal thrust. Then chase my release with stroke after pistoning stroke. Her juices a natural lubricant to ease my way.

She keens from the unrelenting invasion, and the sensation of her punished backside slapping against my groin. Despite the pain, she meets each powerful thrust with one of her own.

I ride her like a wild stallion between more spanks to her ass as my balls smack her engorged clit.

The tightening of her inner walls harkens her orgasm. I will demand at least three before I blow my load. A pinch to her clit, and she spirals into carnal bliss.

"You will give me two more, Naughty Girl," I rasp against her ear.

A strangled cry precedes flutters along my cock. I bend my knees and grip her hips to change the angle of entry. The bulbous tip of my dick grinds against her G-spot. She yowls and climaxes again.

Fuck. Me.

I squeeze my eyes shut and flex my ass to stave off my release, spurred by her luscious body and soft cries.

"One. More." I grit between my clenched teeth.

My right knee lifts to the mattress, bringing her leg with it. Fully opened to me, I snap my hips to drive deep. My tip hits her cervix, and she wails. Her pussy convulses around me, and I can hold back no longer.

I lower my torso over her back and pound her pussy until I can no longer stand, and stars dance before my closed eyes.

With a primal roar, I release a torrent of my seed inside of my woman.

No Bailey. No Fiona. No Callum.

MINE! ALL. MINE.

HALEY

"You take my breath away."

My heart leaps at the sound of Lachlan's deep baritone voice from behind me in my dressing room at Jackson Castle. I spin around to face him.

"Simply gorgeous, Mrs. Jackson," he says. His eyes darkened to forest green with passion as he strides towards me.

He captures my face in his palms and leans down to press his lips to mine. He sucks in my breath through my parted mouth as I gasp.

"I'm an extremely lucky man to have you as my wife. I wish I could shout it from the rooftop, Haley Jackson," Lachlan murmurs, with his forehead against mine.

I wrap my arms around his waist and meld into him with a contented sigh.

"I wish you could, too, Mr. Jackson. But not yet," I say and step back with a deep breath to decrease the rate of my racing pulse. "With the way you're looking at me, we won't make it to our engagement party."

He brings his fist to his lips and chuckles. Emerald eyes glitter with mischief.

I try to sidestep him. But he reaches out an arm and wraps it around my waist. He pulls my back to his front before the mirrored wall. His lips trail open-mouthed kisses from behind my ear, down my neck to the sensitive spot where it meets my shoulder. I purr with need as I press my ass back against his burgeoning erection.

His grip tightens on my waist.

"Baby Girl," he moans.

It's nearly my undoing until my mobile chimes with the ringtone for Mom Lucie.

Lachlan sighs and loosens his hold enough for me to reach the mobile on the center island behind him.

"Hi, Lieutenant Lucie, reporting for duty. We're on our way," I say once I accept the call. Then bite back a squeal from a pinch to my pebbled nipple by Lachlan.

Our gazes meet in the mirror. His narrows on me. My lips part on a breath.

"Oh, sorry! Yes… Will do… See you in a moment," I say into the mobile. I end the call and glance back in the mirror at my husband, who slowly lowers himself behind me.

"Lachlan? What are you—"

The question gets swallowed up by my gasp.

The naughty boy slips beneath the train of my floor-length gown and nips my inner thigh as he nudges my legs apart with his shoulders. I lean forward at the waist to press my palms on the mirror. My mobile squeezed between my fingers.

"Oh, God, Lachlan… Aaah baby… Mmmm mmm," I moan, and my warm breath fogs the mirror. My hips grind my pussy onto his face as he fucks me with his talented tongue and long fingers. In seconds, I come undone with a cry.

"Irresistible, Mrs. Jackson," Lachlan purrs in my ear before he nips it between his front teeth.

I yelp and jolt as he chuckles.

"The peek-a-boo skin proved too much for me," he murmurs against my heated neck. "Not to mention my collar and my ring you wear."

A smile tugs at the corners of my lips. I knew he'd get the symbolism behind my choice of jewelry, not to mention like my gown.

The white Swiss-dot tulle and crepe dress has a nude underlay behind the vee-neck wrap top with sheer sleeves that end in long, flared cuffs that draw the eye to my stunning engagement ring. A layer of the tulle falls behind the full-leg split in the crepe skirt. The gown reveals just enough without the skin exposed too much. One of my platinum strappy sandals peeks from behind the sheer dotted fabric.

I kept my makeup minimal, and my hair cascades down my back. The only other jewelry I wear are my diamond drop earrings and Cartier Love bracelet—all gifts from my husband.

"All for you, Mr. Jackson," I purr as I wrap my arms around his neck. "But we must go, or else. First, I have to freshen up my lipstick, and you wipe your lips of it."

He darts his tongue out to lick his lips in a slow circle while his darkened eyes fill with heat.

"I can still taste you, Mrs. Jackson," he murmurs seductively.

My pussy quivers with an erotic flashback. It takes all of my strength, but I manage to move away from my sexy as sin husband.

Time to announce our engagement to the world.

"Baron, so good of you to come. You know Haley. I'd like to introduce her as my fiancée now."

My heart flutters each time as Lachlan and I stand on the receiving line to welcome our guests—his parents before him and mine after me. Now, my pulse rate increases as Piper Ridel engulfs my hand in his larger one.

His violet eyes stare into my very soul.

"Congratulations, Lachlan, Haley," he says as the Baroness peers over his shoulder at me.

"Yes, congratulations to you. May I?" She asks with her hand extended to my left one.

Naturally, she wants to see my engagement ring.

Proudly, I raise my hand. The enormous emerald glitters in the light of the reception hall.

She gasps.

"The Jackson Emerald... I've only ever seen it in magazines and the society columns of the newspapers. It is truly extraordinary," Maisie utters in awe.

"Thank you," I respond and lower my hand as I turn to my father. "Baron, Baroness, you know my father, Morgan."

They move down the line, and I hear Lachlan greet Heath. I smile at his witty remark as he introduces his date. But my heart stutters when I come face to face with Fiona. And Callum. Together.

"Good evening, Lachlan, Haley," Fiona says with a smirk. "Congratulations on your engagement."

In my periphery, I see Lachlan's jaw tighten as he grinds his molars to bite back a retort. Quickly, I recover and respond.

"Good evening, Fiona, Callum. Thank you. How nice of you to join in our celebration."

Callum's emerald green eyes scan my face for any sign of our past connection. Finding none, he nods.

"Fiona and I wouldn't want to miss the opportunity to offer you our best wishes," he says.

"How kind of you," Lachlan states tersely. Then he turns to Fiona's younger sister, Gwyn, and re-introduces me.

Although Fiona and Callum move down the line, I sense him watching me. I refuse to acknowledge his intense gaze.

By the time the receiving line ends, I'm ready for a cocktail. Pronto.

"You said Callum declined the invitation," Lachlan says

with a frown as he snags two glasses from a passing server and hands one to me.

I take a sip to soothe my parched throat and nod.

"He did," I say once replenished. "What's more odd is him and Fiona arriving as a couple. What do you think that's about?"

Lachlan shrugs and tosses back the rest of his drink. He scans the crowd of two hundred guests, then his eyes narrow, and his jaw works.

"I don't know what the fuck they're up to. But I doubt it's any good. This is exactly why I said you shouldn't have invited them," he growls. "I'm telling you now, Haley, if he starts some shit—"

"Lachlan, sweetheart, time for the announcement," Mom Lucie says with our dads and my mom next to her. "And no, I don't know what happened with Callum. But you will remain calm, Lachlan Jackson. Haley is your wife. She is yours, and you are hers."

"Absolutely! Do not allow them to mess with your head," my mother adds.

"Piper knows better than to allow his daughter to misbehave," Dad Connor states.

My father nods, "You are a Jackson now, Haley. But I did not raise a sheep."

I smile at my father's reference to super wolves and sheep. Steeles are powerful wolves who eat sheep, not cower like one. My back straightens, and I take my husband's proffered hand. I tilt my head up, and he kisses my lips.

"Let's do this, Mrs. Jackson," he murmurs in my ear.

I grin from one to the other.

MINE!

We gather on the stage before the seven-piece band. The leader hands the microphone to Dad Connor, who beams at our guests.

"Once again, the Marchioness and I welcome you to our home. Along with our close family friends, Morgan and Michelle Steele, we have the pleasure to announce the engagement of our children—the Earl of Aboyne Lachlan Jackson and the future Countess of Aboyne Haley Steele. *Slàinte mhath!*"

The guests raise their Champagne flutes to our good health and cheer.

Beyond where our families stand—including Luc, Guy, Josy, and Patrick—my gaze catches Callum and Fiona. The expression of longing in his eyes is the direct opposite of fury in hers. A shiver races down my spine, and I glance away.

Lachlan must sense my unease. He smiles down at me and raises my left hand to his lips. The three emeralds glitter, his eyes even more than the stone. His love envelopes me as it shuts out the negativity that threatened to upset our joyous moment.

"I love you, Mrs. Jackson," he mouths.

My heart explodes with jubilation.

"I love you more, Mr. Jackson," I whisper.

When the guests quiet down, my father speaks.

"Thank you for your well wishes! The couple asks

instead of gifts for them, kindly make donations to the STEELE Foundation and the Jackson Foundation. Shortly, we will gather in the ballroom for dinner and dancing. Enjoy this spectacular evening!"

The guests murmur their appreciation for our philanthropy and the evening ahead.

Lachlan and I spend the rest of the cocktail hour milling with everyone. My girls corner me, and we make our way to a quiet corner.

"Nice collar, Haley… I take it you understand all about it now," Starr grins. "I had to hold Malcolm back from throttling your Alpha Dom!"

"Ha! Me, too! Baz nearly burst a blood vessel when he saw you," Lola chortles.

I stare pointedly at their necks adorned with their fancy evening collars covered in diamonds. Then huff.

"Well, they're the biggest hypocrites!" I pout.

"*Absolument, chérie!* Roger was no better than his brothers," Leonie giggles.

Billie covers her mouth and says, "Incoming."

We turn to see my husband striding towards me. Guests greet him, and he smiles briefly before he continues on his direct path.

"Hi, my love," I say as the girls part for him. "Everything all right?"

He grins and slips his arm around my waist, pulling me into his side. He leans down and brushes his nose against the side of my neck as he inhales deeply.

"Now it is," he murmurs. "You were away for far too long."

Lachlan lifts his gaze to my girls and continues, "Do you mind if I steal my fiancée from you?"

Blair grins and shakes her head.

"We wouldn't want to keep you apart for far too long," she mimics his words.

"Well done, mate!"

Patrick extends one hand to Lachlan while the other wraps around Billie's side. The petite beauty barely reaches his shoulder even in her five-inch heels. She snuggles against his side with a sigh.

Lachlan thanks his fellow Scotsman. As they chat, my brothers and Luc appear to claim their women, too. Except Harris.

He raises his eyebrow at my collar, and I lift my chin. He rolls his eyes, and I giggle. My twin won't push the issue, and I love him for it.

After a while, the butler announces dinner.

On our way to the ballroom, Lachlan and I catch up with Maribelle and her husband, Calvin. She and I excuse ourselves for the ladies' room while the men continue to our table.

"Haley! This is the best weekend ever! I cannot believe I'm in a castle filled with royals and nobles. Calvin has to keep reminding me to lift my jaw off the ground!" She exclaims as we enter the anteroom. "I'm so excited for you!"

"Aren't we all…"

Fiona and Gwyn. Great.

Their violet eyes spark fire as they glare at me.

"Yes, we are. And as guests, you shouldn't be here, if you're not," Maribelle says defensively as she stands akimbo in her couture Valentino gown.

They scowl at her and leave the anteroom without another word.

Maribelle and I watch them retreat. Then she turns to me and shakes her head.

"Damn, girl, what is it with you and women salivating over your man?!"

We burst out laughing as I shrug.

The evening goes on without further issue. Lachlan twirls me around the dance floor between the delectable dishes Lucien created in our honor. *The Sexy Chef* surpassed his greatest achievements for the event.

"Are you happy, Mrs. Jackson?" My husband asks as he dips me.

When he lifts me back up, I bite the corner of my lower lip and respond, "Yes, My Lord."

He growls as lust flares in his eyes.

"I cannot wait to finish what I started in your dressing room earlier, Little Temptress," he says.

I lean up to whisper in his ear, "Neither can I, Sir."

"Don't tempt me to take you aside now," he threatens.

I bite my lip to keep from giggling.

"May I?"

A glance over my shoulder reveals Baz. My oldest brother extends Lola's hand to Lachlan and takes mine.

As he leads me away, I suddenly feel like a little girl again.

"Relax, little sis. I promised Lola I won't say a word about a certain piece of jewelry around your neck, a certain someone should know better than to give to my little sister no matter what I or her brothers do," he says with a straight face. Although the mirth shining in his platinum gray orbs belie his attempt at sternness. "I wouldn't think to mention a single thing about it."

By the time he finishes, we crack up, and guests turn toward the commotion. Which only makes it worse.

"Oh, dear, have I made a terrible impression for the future Countess of Aboyne?" He jokes. "My bad!"

I shake my head as another giggle bubbles out.

"Baz, you're the worse! And don't worry, Lachlan didn't force his collar on me. I'm proud to wear it, just as Lola is to wear yours, and Starr to wear Malcolm's," I respond. "And thank you for not saying a single thing…"

He smirks.

"Well, you look good. So in the end, that's all we care about—your happiness, Haley," he says seriously. "We love our little sister."

Tears fill my eyes, and I duck my head against his powerful chest.

"I love my brothers, too," I whisper.

We dance on in comfortable silence until the music switches.

"Ah, well, here comes Little Lord Fauntleroy now," Baz

says with a chuckle. He kisses the top of my head. "Be good, little sis."

I smile up at him just as Lachlan pulls me into his arms, and Baz slips his arms around his wife. We dance beside each other. Best friends and their women who are also besties.

My life is beyond good. And I am grateful.

"Hello, Little Lass."

The unexpected sound of Callum's voice from behind startles me as I leave the ladies' room.

I joined Lachlan for a business dinner in Aberdeen he has with the former owner of Ainsley Scotch, but I needed to step away to take a client's call. Little did I know Callum would waylay me in the corridor.

It's been a month since the engagement party, and I haven't seen Callum since. Although I've heard from him quite often. His frequent text messages and voicemails, not to mention bouquets of flowers, border on stalker behavior. And Steeles are more than familiar with those types—Roger and Malcolm can attest to them.

At first, I responded via text to let Callum know it's best to move on, and I wish him well. I didn't even bother to ask what's up with him and Fiona. Ugh.

Then he kept reaching out.

Now, rather than answering his communications, I ignore them. I ask my administrative assistant to send the flowers to the local hospital for critical care patients. Let the beautiful arrangements brighten their day. I have my husband to make me smile. Thank you very much.

And he does so all the time.

We're married for four months, and we couldn't be happier. The relief of not having to keep our relationship a secret—at least from our family—makes a world of difference compared to the first time. The worry of ruining Lachlan and Baz's friendship compounded with upsetting The Big Four took its toll on us before. This time, we're free.

Even to the point where we went to LEVELS London for a date night of dinner and fun with them and my girls, including Lucien and Laurent. Of course, I didn't wear a scandalous outfit, nor did Lola, Leonie, and Starr. A nude-colored lace-trimmed silk chemise with marabou feather mules and my collar did the trick. Lachlan was more than pleased with my attire, and Baz didn't have a conniption. Small miracles…

My move into Lachlan's Mayfair and Aberdeen penthouses plus his suite at Jackson Castle happened easily. The best part was buying new clothes more suitable for the climates and more riding gear. Leonie stayed in London to help me pick out my new wardrobe, then we flew to Paris for Fashion Week for even more clothes. Lola had her Paris atelier do a private showing of her new collections for me while she sat in via video conference.

Nothing beats having a megamodel as a sister-in-law and another as a luxury lingerie and evening wear designer!

Mom Lucie helped me to select which invitations to accept from society in Scotland and abroad. Lachlan and I received a crazy amount of requests for lunch, dinner, galas, receptions, charity polo matches, and appearances as a couple and separately. Mom Lucie says it's best to remain a tad unreachable. It leaves them clamoring to gain access to us. So our calendar filled up with the most choice ones only.

We laugh at the society chess games and agree they're a bit much. Having grown up a regular person without wealth or a title, Mom Lucie understands both perspectives. Her introduction to that side of the spectrum was a doozy, but her mother-in-law made it easier for her. And she's determined to do the same for me, although I'm more than familiar with the wealth part. I still appreciate her tales. I joked she should write a tell-all autobiography turned television series. She just shook her head and laughed.

Lachlan, on the other hand, grumbled about all the hoopla—except for the polo matches, his favorite sport after sailing. He's taken me out on *Gorm Domhainn* a few times. I know my way around a full-rigged sailing yacht from summers in the Hamptons. But the waters of the North Sea can be treacherous and demand total focus. The thrill of it exhilarates me.

Other times we go riding through the estate. He told me we can't visit the watchtower ruins because the caretaker deemed them unsafe. I wanted to go by to see for myself. But Lachlan wouldn't budge. But with over one hundred acres, we have more than enough places to explore. As a consolation, he bought me a gorgeous Arabian mare with a silvery gray coat. She's perfect for the trails, as an elegant breed made for endurance to cover a long distance at a good speed. Perfect to outrace Lachlan and his stallion! One look into her intelligent black eyes and I fell in love. I named her Moonbeam for her coloring and enigmatic beauty.

When we go to the castle, we're usually the only Jacksons in residence since everyone besides Lucien—who stays in Paris—is in New York City. It's like my fairytale come true to roam within the castle and the lands all alone with My Lord. We take advantage of no other eyes while we make love in a field beneath the open sky or against a wall in a corridor. My pussy clenches hard and weeps whenever I think about our illicit trysts.

Then there's our times in London.

Lachlan gave me free rein to redecorate all of our homes, so I started with Mayfair, since I'm there most often. Leonie gave me some pointers and hooked me up with furniture and decor contacts along with access to her family's warehouses of fine antiques, antiquities, and fabrics. She even offered a representative to assist me. Josy volunteered to help me find the best pieces. Guy told me if I don't see what I want to let him know and his staff will source it out. I won't change much in any of our homes. Just add a touch of me and us to them.

I had to find a new personal trainer since New York serves as Borya's base. Fortunately, Norm has an Elite Training Facility in Mayfair close to the penthouse. He and Anita flew over to help select the best trainer and yogi for me. Norman had to explain to Lachlan the male trainer is not interested in me; he has a boyfriend. We turned it into a weekend where the four of us hung out.

All in all, I've settled into my new life with my husband. Lachlan will grumble about no one else knowing we're married, especially when he introduces me to someone as his fiancée. But I think Mom Lucie is correct in the way we present ourselves as engaged. And sure, we're still getting used to living together—*You left the toilet seat up!* to *That's my side of the bed.* and my favorite *Haley, put your shit away!* However, I'll never tire of the mornings I awake to Lachlan feasting on my pussy or watching him as he sleeps. Just this morning I thought about how it's only getting better.

Now this. Callum and his shenanigans.

I take a calming breath and arch my eyebrow.

"Hello, Callum. Funny seeing you here. If I didn't know you're not crazy, I'd think you were stalking me," I respond. "Do tell me I'm correct."

He chuckles and slips his hands into his suit trousers' pockets.

"You're correct, Little Lass," he says with a smirk. "I'm actually here with Fiona for dinner. So purely coincidental."

Okay, I have to know.

"Interesting how the two of you spend time together," I throw out the bait.

Again Callum chuckles and raises to the balls of his feet and back.

"Well, we've known each other for some time, being in the same social circle and all. Now that I'm back in Aberdeen to run my family's business, we've reconnected," he says. Then looks at me pointedly. "Are you jealous, Little Lass?"

I choke and cough to clear my throat. The absolute audacity!

"Actually, no. I'm just not a believer in coincidences. Particularly combined with your incessant calls, texts, and flowers. It makes me wonder your point," I respond.

His emerald green eyes scan my face, then my body, from head to toe and back. He cocks his head to the side and pins me with an intense stare.

"I am not a man to give up on what I want so easily, Little Lass," Callum says, then strides past me for the dining room.

My jaw drops as I watch him disappear around the corner.

Fuck. Me. No, he didn't.

I duck back into the ladies' room to clear my head and to school my face before I return to the table. Lachlan jokes I could never play poker. And right now, he'd have no trouble reading me.

I replay the conversation in my head. Questions swirl in

my mind. What role does Fiona play in Callum's scheme to win me back? Is she even aware he wants me and not her? What the fuck do I tell Lachlan, if anything? This can't amount to anything good.

A cool cloth to my neck relaxes me, and I leave. Surreptitiously, I glance around the dining room to spy Callum and Fiona. Bingo! They're at a table out of Lachlan's line of sight. She's holding Callum's hand and laughing. Anyone would believe they're a couple in love. For a moment, I feel sorry for her. Not!

Lachlan stands when I near the table and helps me into my chair.

"Everything all right?" He asks.

My eyes widen. Damn, he knows.

When he frowns at my reaction, I realize he's referring to my business call. I plant a smile on my face and nod.

He studies me briefly, then turns back to the Ainsley Scotch former owner and his wife. We continue our meal with small talk about sports, shopping, and upcoming holiday plans. I don't allow Callum and Fiona's presence to distract me.

By the end of the evening, I relax and decide to let it go. Callum is just an Alpha Dom who's not used to being told no. I highly doubt he'll continue to pursue me, especially with Fiona clinging to him. I'm thankful she's moved on from Lachlan, even if Callum thinks he still wants me. He'll get over it.

And I'm damn sure not mentioning it to Lachlan. He'll go berserk…

When we get back to our penthouse off Union Street near Jackson Town House, the private elevator doors open to the entry foyer of our full-floor flat. Lachlan places his palm on the plate by the front door to unlock it. Thanks to Harris and his technology developed in our subsidiary, none of us use keys to enter our residences.

The ambient lighting increases from dim to bright gently as we walk through to the living room. The decor leans towards tufted cognac leather sofas, dark hardwood floors, and Jackson clan tartan accents—Old World charm at its most sumptuous. Lachlan let Mom Lucie decorate for him since he couldn't care less as long as he had a large flat-screen television somewhere, an office, and a king-size bed.

I pulled a face when he mentioned the bed. But he made it clear he never had a woman at any of his homes or on his yacht. I'm still not sure if it made me feel any better, since the mere thought of him with someone else makes me physically ill.

He managed to make me feel better when we christened every room and every surface in each of our U.K. residences. It was one marathon I'd do again and again!

As much as I don't mind the style of the penthouse, I want to lighten it up with a jewel-toned color palette and honey- and copper-toned hardwood. I love his clan's tartan, and it will work well with the new theme.

Each of the four-bedroom suites will have a unique look but blend seamlessly with the rest of the flat. The entertainment rooms—except for Lachlan's TV/game room—will get makeovers, too. The library, I took over as my office since I love to curl up with a good book. I asked Lucien to help turn the kitchen into a chef's dream—even if I don't like to cook, I'm trying. My goal: keep my man well sated in all ways. Yaaasss, honey!

Leonie and her team drew up the plans, and work started a couple of weeks ago. It's not disruptive since we only had a few structural changes. Most of the pieces are on order or on the watch list. It won't be long before we complete this penthouse. Meanwhile, work continues on the beach house and our New York City duplex. Being heavy duty, they'll take a bit more time.

I follow Lachlan into the living room. He goes to the bar for his evening Jackson Special Blend Scotch. I drop to a sofa and take off my stilettos with a groan. I flew straight from STEELE London to Aberdeen—a long day and evening in heels.

"Here, have some," Lachlan says as he sits beside me and offers his drink. He tsks. "And give me your foot. You and these fuck-me shoes. They're sexy, but deadly."

Oh, did I mention foot massages on the regular as another form of marital bliss? Mmmmhmmmm…

Lachlan's powerful hands and fingers work my tired feet and sore calves while I sip his Scotch and hold the Waterford Crystal snifter to his lips. Wouldn't want him to get parched as he pampers his pet. No, Sir!

I groan in pleasure and writhe when he kneads a particularly achy spot. My knee brushes his crotch.

"Damn, Baby Girl, you're making me hard as fuck," he

mutters. "Unless you want my cock filling your open mouth, tone down your moans…"

I bite my lower lip to stifle another deeply satisfying groan and close my eyes. My leg twitches again.

"Fuck it," Lachlan growls.

My eyes pop open when I'm bounced onto his lap. The back split of my Chanel skirt rips to make space for my thighs to straddle Lachlan's hips.

"Babe! I just got this skirt," I pout as I reach around to feel for the tear.

He growls and rips open my silk pussy bow blouse. Button scatter every which way. He shows no mercy to my custom Lola's Coterie pink lace balconette bra, either. The matching G-string shredded. Lachlan bares me before him.

His lust-filled eyes rake over my heaving chest, nipples pebbled by the sudden air. He cups each breast and kneads it like my foot massage with deep strokes. A pinch to my nipples, and I groan in ecstasy.

Warmth blows across the peaks, followed by wetness as he engulfs one, nearly swallowing my heavy breast.

Not to be outdone, I yank his Hermès tie off and pull open his Saville Row dress shirt. My palms on his firm pecs mimic his movements. He groans when I squeeze his nipples between my fingernails. I squeal from a bite to my breast. He sucks to mark me, and I grind down on his thighs, pressing my pelvis along his burgeoning length.

"My Baby Girl…" he moans huskily.

I crash my mouth onto his and reach down to release

his dick. It thumps free to stand tall. He sighs into my mouth as I fist him and tug. Hard.

My only thought: get Lachlan inside of me.

With a guttural groan, my pussy stretches around his bulbous head and ridged shaft as I impale myself on his massive ten-inch cock. Fully seated, I roll my hips. I sing his praises as his cock grinds into my G-spot. Breaths turn into pants as I increase my pace to ride Lachlan to oblivion.

He sinks back into the buttery leather and holds my hips to maintain my balance. He watches where our bodies connect intimately. His girth stretches my hole as my pussy sucks him inside greedily. Mesmerized, his mouth hangs open.

I give it my all, relishing the power I have over my Alpha Dom-cum-husband. My breasts jiggle as I raise and lower myself again and again, followed by circles of my hips.

"Cum for me, Mrs. Jackson," he commands with a pinch to my engorged clit.

I fall apart. For him. Only for him.

No one else or what they do matter in our lives.

LACHLAN

The ringing of my mobile jolts me awake. At five in the morning, it takes me a moment to register the ringtone for My Baby Girl. Then I spring into action. My hand shoots out to grab the device from the nightstand. My heart races as questions form in my mind.

She's in New York City for business meetings. What the hell happened to make her call me so early?

Is she all right?

Did I miss the tracker app alert?

My finger jabs the accept button on the mobile's screen.

"Haley! What—"

"MALCOLM!!!!"

Her plaintive wail chills me to the bone.

Fuck. Me. Something bad happened to him.

Between her sobs, she explains the app Harris created to track all the Steeles, Starr, and the Jacksons showed Malcolm's vitals as yellow, not green.

Should the person's vitals change from green to yellow or to red, Harris programmed the app to alert the Steeles for their relatives and the Jacksons for our family. The app automatically dials the local police and medics and provides them with the GPS coordinates.

The GPS showed Malcolm somewhere along Benedict Canyon Drive, close to Starr's home in Beverly Hills. Harris called Starr, and they tracked him down. They airlifted him to Cedars-Sinai Spine Center because of a horrific motorcycle accident.

Morgan arranged for everyone in New York City to fly on his Gulfstream G650 to LAX. Haley calls me on her way down to the lobby to meet her parents, Baz, Lola, and Harris. Roger, Leonie, The Twins, Daphne, and Nanny Grace are en route from Paris on their private jet.

"Baby Girl, I'm on my way. Let everyone know. I'll tell the rest of the clan. We'll pray for Malcolm. I love you," I tell her earnestly.

"OH, LACHLAN!"

My Baby Girl races across to me and crumbles in my arms as soon as I enter the private waiting room at the hospital. I pull her close and bury my face in her hair. The delicate yet intense floral scent of her elegant perfume blends with her natural aroma. It centers me immediately.

The entire plane ride I worried and didn't sleep at all. I spoke with her only when she called so as not to interrupt news from the doctors. The thirteen-hour flight and jet lag combined with the stress have me bleary-eyed. But I set myself aside to care for my wife.

She looks worn out. Puffy darkened skin circle red eyes. Her face swollen and tear stained. Ebony locks thrown into a topknot with wild strands bursting from the hair tie. A velour tracksuit and Converse sneakers cover her curvy frame and feet. So opposite to her usual well-kept self.

I push a loose tendril behind her ear.

"What's the latest?" I ask.

She covers her mouth and sobs.

Fuck.

"He made it out of surgery. But he's paralyzed and in a coma. The doctors don't know when—" Baz chokes, then clears his throat as he wipes a tear from his eye—"Or if he'll wake up."

No. Fucking. Way.

Tears fill my eyes as I glance around the room. My gaze settles on Starr as she sits inconsolable between Lola and Leonie. They have their arms around her. But she hangs her head and sobs. Next, I spot Mom Shelley, and she's beside herself, clinging to Dad Morgan. Roger and Harris approach, and I hug them with one arm. I won't let my wife go.

I send a silent prayer asking for Malcolm's recovery and for the healing of our family, come what may.

AFTER TWO WEEKS of staying in suites at STEELE Beverly Hills, Sebastian, Lola, Haley, and I returned to New York City. Since Lola is pregnant with their twins and needs to see her OB-GYN regularly, they didn't move to the West Coast.

Dad Morgan and Mom Shelley took up permanent residence in the President's Suite at the hotel. Roger and Leonie moved in to a long-term mansion rental next to Starr's home. Harris moved into Malcolm's Sunset Strip penthouse.

The siblings divided STEELE International responsibilities, too.

Sebastian claimed the East Coast since he needs to be in New York City as CEO and head of his Retail Division. Roger took over Malcolm's Entertainment Division and the West Coast operations in addition to his Residential Division. Haley chose the East for her and Harris' Technology and Cyber Security.

The other half of the Dynamic Duo remained in LA. Besides his STEELE duties, Harris is working with the police. He has shared little information with us, but we know he and Haley are wizzes and will solve any problem.

We skipped Thanksgiving in Bougainvillea Cay, opting instead for a quiet meal in the private waiting area turned office and living room at the hospital. No one wanted to be far from a still comatose Malcolm, especially during the holiday.

My parents and siblings came out to stay and to offer comfort. Not only are our mothers best friends, but Lucien and Malcolm are super close. It broke my heart to see my strong younger brother sick with grief. No one can imagine life without Malcolm.

Lydie switched places with me so I could stay in New York City with My Baby Girl and not leave Jackson Corporation's headquarters empty of a Jackson for an indefinite amount of time. I figure I can return in a month or so. Until then, I'm staying put to support my wife and to offer any help I can to my best friend and STEELE.

"There you are, babe. I was looking for you," I say as my arms slip around her waist from behind. My hands slip along the silk of her kimono where my fingers brush her ribcage. She has eaten little, and it's beginning to show.

She leans into me and puts her hands on top of mine.

"I couldn't sleep. Too much shit going on and buzzing in my head. I can't stop thinking about Malcolm. That damn Ducati and all the other motorcycles he rides! I hate them so much! All the time, I beg him to be careful. And now—"

Her voice catches as sobs wrack her body.

I lift her from the stool at the island and carry her to the sofa in the sitting area of the kitchen. Cuddled on my lap, she buries her tear-stained face in my neck as I rub her back, murmuring soothing words.

There's not much I can say since none of us have ever faced a tragedy such as this one with Malcolm. I can't tell her I understand or don't worry. What's best is to comfort her and be the strength she needs.

I love Malcolm like my siblings and cannot believe this

shit happened. What I do understand is her frustration with him and his thrill-seeker obsession—him and Lucien. Countless times I've expressed my concerns for their daredevil antics doing extreme sports only for them to laugh. Now, I pray Malcolm recovers.

"Shit is crazy right now. But I know Malcolm would want everyone to take care of themselves. Did you eat breakfast, yet? I can make an omelet and freshly squeezed orange juice for you," I say encouragingly.

My Baby Girl stays quiet. But her tears stop as her breath returns to normal.

I give her some time to consider my words. When she doesn't respond, I rise and carry her back to the stool.

"I'll get started. How's bacon, red and yellow peppers, chives, and tomatoes? There's a fresh loaf of multigrain bread," I say as I maneuver around the newly redesigned chef's kitchen.

Fortunately, the reconstruction of our duplex penthouse completed the kitchen first. Every tool, accessory, and top-of-the-line Wolf and Sub-Zero appliances chosen by Lucien make it a chef's dream. I smile as I place the omelet skillet on one of the six burners at the memory of My Baby Girl going into minute detail with him about the options. Meanwhile, she barely boils water to cook spaghetti.

Her weary eyes follow my progress as I chatter on about tips *The Sexy Chef* gave me to prepare a five-star omelet. When I recall my horrible first attempt and the ensuing mini fire, a slight spark gleams in her dove gray orbs.

A good beginning.

By the time I plate our gourmet breakfast, her stomach growls hungrily. She covers her mouth with her hand to stifle a giggle. I smirk.

"You can't resist the appeal of your husband cooking for you. Can you, Baby Girl?" I tease.

She huffs and rolls her eyes as she reaches for her fork.

"Ah, ah, ah. I will feed you," I admonish.

When she opens her mouth to protest, I pop a forkful of the fluffy eggs into it. The scowl morphs into a smile as she hums her pleasure. Like a baby bird, her mouth pops open for more as her eyes twinkle.

Her sounds of delight and the intimacy of the act of feeding my wife make me content.

After she gets her fill, I eat the rest of the four-egg omelet, then use the crust of the bread to gather the remnants.

"Here, one last bite, Baby Girl," I command.

Obediently, she opens her mouth as her eyes darken. My little sub can't deny her Alpha Dom. Her tongue flicks out to lick the corner of her mouth where a pepper left a bit of olive oil.

Erotic tension flares between us. But I know she's not quite ready to play. Although there's no better way to take her mind off of her brother. I won't take advantage of her distress. Even if she's willing.

"Now that your belly is full, go take a shower and dress

warmly. We'll go for a walk to see the Christmas tree at Rockefeller Center and the store windows," I tell her.

"Lachlan, I'm not in the mood for festivities," she whispers, eyes downcast.

I cup her face to level our gazes.

"Haley Jackson, I will not allow you to waste away or not live your life. Malcolm certainly would agree with me. Do you understand?" I say in my most Alpha Dom tone.

Her nostrils flare as her pupils dilate.

I cock my eyebrow.

"Yes, My Lord," she responds breathily.

"Good, girl," I say and brush my lips over hers. "I'll be up in ten minutes. I expect you showered and getting dressed."

I watch as she slides off of the stool and leave the kitchen. My fingers fly across the screen of my mobile as I unlock it to send a text message to my mother. She's still in LA, so it's way too early to call.

Plan in place, I head to our temporary bedroom.

AS WE STEP out of The STEELE Tower onto Fifth Avenue, our gazes rise to the giant crystal snowflake star above Fifty-seventh Street. The stones sparkle in the sun and stand out against the clear blue sky. The snowflake star is one of the many highlights of Manhattan during the holiday season.

I glance down and squeeze My Baby Girl's gloved hand.

She shifts her eyes to mine. A small smile tugs at the corners of her full mouth. I lean over and kiss it.

"Let's start with Bergdorf's, then make our way down the avenue. You can make wishes at each window like you did as a kid. Sounds good?" I say with a smile.

Tears glisten in her eyes.

"I only have one wish. For my brother to wake up and be whole again," she whispers sadly.

My arms wrap around her, and I snuggle her close to my chest as I agree. She buries her face into my Moncler down jacket and hugs me tightly. My lips brush the top of her head.

Tourists and native New Yorkers bustle around us. They fade as my focus homes in on my wife and easing her sorrow. I rock her gently, then give her a squeeze.

"Come, we have much to see, Baby Girl."

We move with the crowd to cross Fifty-seventh Street. The scent of roasted chestnuts fills the brisk air around us. I make a mental note to get some before we return home. Or order fresh ones from Whole Foods at Columbus Circle and roast them on our professional range...

As expected, the luxury retailers go full throttle. Fantasy worlds draw you past the windowpanes filled with glamorous gowns. Extraordinary jewels at Van Cleef & Arpels, Tiffany's, Bulgari, and Cartier make my wife's eyes shine. What woman can withstand their dazzle? A necklace at Harry Winston brings a gasp from her lips as her eyes widen.

"Oh! It resembles the snowflake star," she says, awed by the beauty.

I flick my gaze between the necklace and my wife's face, more gorgeous than any piece of jewelry or anything else. My hand squeezes hers as I give a tug to uproot her from the spot. I nod at the doorman as he welcomes us inside the salon.

"Good morning," a salesperson greets us.

"Good morning," I reply. "The snowflake star necklace in the window interests my wife. Kindly show it to her."

Haley begins to protest. But I silence her with my finger to her lips and a shake of my head.

"It's a happy reminder of today. Don't deny me the chance to make you smile, Baby Girl," I tell her.

A beatific one blossoms on her face.

"I won't. Thank you, my love," she whispers.

The salesperson settles us at a table, then leaves to bring a tray with several versions of the necklace and watches resting on the navy blue velvet. He explains they're a part of the Winston Kaleidoscope Collection. The colorful gems take center stage to mimic the endless beauty found through the ever-changing lens of a kaleidoscope. Each pendant set in symmetrical patterns and precisely crafted with minimum platinum to maximize the brilliance of every stone.

"Oh, this one with the aquamarine center," my wife breathes. "May I?"

The salesperson smiles and unclasps the catch. She unbelts her Brunello Cucinelli quilted cashmere down coat and leans forward, lifting her hair from her neck. The pendant rests against her black cashmere turtleneck sweater.

The greenish-blue aquamarine center stone, along with various shapes of diamonds, blue and pink sapphires, rubellites, and more aquamarines glitter against the dark background. The pendant won't outdo the platinum chain with more gemstones along its links.

"Beautiful, Baby Girl," I murmur in her ear.

She grins at our reflection in the table-top mirror.

"We'll take it, thank you," I tell the salesperson as I hand my AMEX Centurion Card to him. Then I grin when my wife throws her arms around my neck and kisses me silly.

"Is Malcolm all right?!"

My Baby Girl stares at me panicked as we eat lunch at Harry Cipriani. She sags with relief a moment later. Then nods as someone on the other end speaks.

"Oh! Thank God! What's happening? Well… I couldn't possibly think about the wedding now"—She glances at me and bites her lower lip—"What? Mom… How? Hmmm… I… If you think so… No, Malcolm wouldn't… Perhaps you're right. Let me talk to Lachlan, and we'll call you back, okay?"

She ends the call and sets her mobile on the table. A frown mars her forehead as she spins the device. I reach over and place my hand on hers. She glances up at me and sighs.

"That was The Moms. They said we need to continue on our wedding plans, and I have to select my gowns and the bridesmaids' dresses like yesterday. They said Malcolm wouldn't want us to stop and by the time the date comes around, he may be able to—"

She breaks off with a sob. I clasp her hand.

"Baby Girl, listen. They're right. It would piss Malcolm off if you didn't continue on account of him. You know your brother as well as I do. He wants you happy and not worried about him all day. We have to have faith he'll pull through. Understand?" I tell her.

She takes a deep breath and dabs her eyes with the linen napkin.

"You're right. They're right. So, fine," she responds. "They're flying back to New York tonight with Dad Connor. My dad will stay in LA and promises to not keep anything from us."

"Good idea. Now, why don't you go rinse your face off. Your dessert will be out soon," I say with a smile.

She nods and I help her from the chair.

When she's out of sight, I open my mobile and send a thank you text to my mom.

Plan in motion!

HALEY

"NASA Control to Haley. Come in, Haley. We need your head out of the clouds. We're trying to get work done here."

I swing my gaze from the floor-to-ceiling windows and the pearl gray sky as puffy snowflakes swirl about. This high above Fifth Avenue feels as though we float in the clouds. I stop fidgeting with my engagement ring and face everyone at the large double pedestal table and the flat-screen television mounted on the wall.

Lydie, Starr, Leonie, Billie, Bailey, and his assistant via video conference, along with Sergeant Shelley, Lieutenant Lucie, Lola, Blair, and I, sit in my mom's home office. It's set in my parents' STEELE Tower duplex penthouse on the fifty-seventh and fifty-sixth floors.

Most people wouldn't consider the three generously sized rooms a home office. But then, my mother isn't most people. An anteroom for two assistants' desks, a sitting

245

area, and a bathroom, a conference room, and her inner sanctum with en suite bathroom comprise her version of a home office. She runs her private activities—including personal parties, gatherings, and events—from here and her STEELE Foundation work from her offices on the executive floor of the corporate headquarters below.

We'll put the space to good use since it's all hands on deck to plan our wedding. We originally set the date for 3 months from now. But with Malcolm's accident, I told them the only way I would go forward would be to delay it a couple of months. I want to give him more time to wake up and be able to come. I refuse to have my wedding all the way in Scotland with my brother all the way in LA paralyzed and in a coma. Lachlan agreed despite his increasing desire to tell everyone we're married—the caveman. So we pushed the date back.

Five months may seem like a long enough time to plan. But not really.

As Sergeant Shelley and Lieutenant Lucie pointed out, the time for my dresses alone would normally take a year to create—couture, of course. Not to mention ensuring time for guests to plan to attend. The events will occur over five days—rehearsal and dinner, bridesmaid luncheon, wedding ceremony and reception, morning after brunch with activities in between. Hence, two planners to help coordinate everything.

My mother added how time and money go hand in hand. So we can more than afford to request priority treatment from designers, florists, engravers, decorators, and other vendors as needed. And with two major destination weddings for Baz and Roger under her belt, she has the experience to make it happen for me.

Lieutenant Lucie reminded us the venue and the catering are no problem. The Jackson Castle chapel, reception hall, and ballroom need no reservation, and Lucien and his team will handle the food and cake. Lachlan's team will partner with Lucien's for pairing the Jackson labels with the menus.

It's good to be a Steele-Jackson!

"Oh, so now a grin brightens your glum face. I would grin from ear to ear!"

Billie's giggles and ours join to fill the room.

"Well, then, let's get down to business," Sergeant Shelley announces. Then raises her wrist to emphasize her Chopard Happy Diamonds Joaillerie watch. Set against rose gold, the diamonds and colored sapphires sparkle in the light. "Time is still of the essence, ladies, gentleman."

Lieutenant Lucie opens her Hermès black matte alligator portfolio and lifts her Montblanc champagne gold rollerball pen. She scans through the pages, then glances at me.

"While the theme colors are yours to choose, I recommend shades from the Jackson clan tartan since the men will wear kilts and the women sashes. Lachlan will pin you with one during the ceremony. But it's your decision, darling," she says with a smile as she holds up a piece of the cloth.

I smile back as I take it in my hand.

It's handloomed in luxurious eight-ply cashmere. Lachlan explained the colors represent Aberdeenshire and the family: emerald green for the rolling lands; navy blue for the Don and Dee Rivers and the North Sea; silver for the mica in the gray granite; amber for Jackson Scotch.

I flip the tartan around my fingers as I consider the options. Lachlan and I represent the blending of both families. It's serendipitous the Jackson tartan includes silver, like the name Steele and our signature gray eyes. Plus emerald green for the Jacksons' eye trait.

"I love that idea, Mom Lucie. How about emerald green and platinum as the primary colors and amber as the accent? It's the blending of Steele and Jackson," I respond. My gaze flicks between The Moms to gauge their reaction.

Both grin wider than the Cheshire Cat and clap.

"Fabulous, sweetheart!" My mother gushes.

"How absolutely perfect, darling! I couldn't agree more," Mom Lucie exclaims.

"I'll send a note to the florist to put together some sample bouquets and boutonnieres. We'll have the decor options ready by the end of the week," Bailey says.

I turn to my girls and smile.

"Now for the bridal party. Lachlan and I like the closeness of our loved ones to stand with us. So we'd like to ask you, Lola, to be my matron of honor with Baz as the best man. Leonie paired with Roger. Lydie with Harris. Blair and Billie paired with Lucien and Laurent, respectively," I pause to lean towards Starr on the television screen.

"Starr, our prayer is for Malcolm awake and paired with

you. It'll be seven months since the accident, so it's a definite possibility. Okay?" I ask. Tears shimmer in my eyes. But I won't allow them to fall. Like Lachlan says, we must have faith.

Ever the yogi, she clasps her hands at her heart center and bows her head. But not before I see the same tears in her sorrel brown eyes. She takes a deep, cleansing breath and nods.

"Yes, Haley. Although Malcolm or I would ever ask you, I am grateful you delayed your wedding for your brother. I am honored you asked me to be a part of your celebration and pray Malcolm and I will stand with you," she says.

Leonie puts her arm around Starr as they sit in the private room at the hospital.

Everyone is quiet for a moment, lost in their thoughts.

My mother clears her throat.

We turn to her, and she smiles. Tears shine in her rich brown eyes, too.

"Never forget. We are one big family, and family comes first," she says firmly. "We stand together in all things, at all times."

We express our agreement before she goes on.

"Now, the gowns and dresses…" she says, with one elegantly arched eyebrow raised. Back to Sergeant Shelley in a blink.

"Oh, *chérie*! Whichever atelier—Paris, London, Milan, New York—you want to create your gowns. Let me know, and it will happen! They owe me many favors," Leonie says.

Lola claps and shimmies as much as her pregnant belly allows.

"Ooohhh! And your lingerie trousseau! Hmmm. Perhaps one of your evening wear outfits. Leave it to me, Billie, and Blair. Right, girls?" Lola exclaims.

They agree and giggle about the new naughty collection inspired by BDSM.

My face flushes scarlet as I drop my eyes to avoid The Moms' gazes.

"Well, in that case, send a selection to me, too!"

My head snaps back up.

"Me, three!" My mother says as she high fives Mom Lucie.

They giggle more than Billie and Blair. No denying The Moms are subs to The Alpha Dom Dads…

"Can we get back to the gowns and dresses, please?" I ask to change the subject.

"Yes, of course, sweetheart," my mother replies. "First, your wedding gown. What are you thinking?"

My eyes light up as I sit up taller.

"A princess ballgown! Sweetheart neckline. Wisps of sleeves fall off my shoulders. Narrow, corseted bodice. Layers of tulle topped by appliqués make a full skirt. Long train with matching veil. Face covered. Coronet," I ramble on about the fairytale gown of my dreams.

Since I was a child, I collected photos of various ballgowns. Over the years, I digitized them and access the files on a secure cloud. When I created the wedding planning app for Lola, I updated everything. After Lachlan and I married, I customized the app for myself and uploaded my inspirations.

With a grin, I type on my laptop and pull the app up on the other television screen.

Everyone shifts to face it.

"Here. Let me show you," I say as I click the tab labeled Haley's Wedding Gowns.

Bailey leans closer on the television screen and asks me about the app. I tell him it's my creation, and I can sell a license to his company. He agrees immediately without even asking the cost. My mother winks at me. Years ago, she predicted it could be profitable. I grin back.

After we review the photos and my notes with sketches, Leonie speaks up.

"That is amazing, Haley. I can only think of one designer to bring your fairytale princess ballgown to life... The Master of Couture, Monsieur Valentino."

Lola nods and reminds us he created her wedding gown. As if we could ever forget the exquisite piece.

I sigh wistfully.

"Do you think he can fit me in?" I ask Leonie.

She whips out her mobile and taps on the screen. In no time, she's speaking in rapid French. I'm fluent and have no trouble understanding her conversation. With Monsieur Valentino himself!

We sit in silent anticipation while they speak. When her feline amber eyes glitter and her megawatt smile spreads across her face, we know it's all set.

She puts the call on speaker, and we thank him wholeheartedly. I send the file to his assistant while he's on the call and they confirm receipt. He promises to have sketches and fabric swatches by the end of the week. The Moms and I will fly to Paris the day before to decide and to take measurements. He'll also create my rehearsal and reception dresses.

When we end the call, I squeal with delight as I dance around the office. Leonie laughs when I thank her and promise I owe her big time. She waves me off and repeats Shelley's phrase about family. My heart overflows with love.

We discuss my thoughts on my girls' dresses. Since each has a unique style and figure, we decide to let them choose their designs with floor-length dresses and with each in one of the wedding colors. Lola as wife to the eldest Steele and Blair, with her cerulean blue eyes, choose platinum. Starr and Leonie choose amber, and Lydie and Billie claim green to match their eyes, respectively.

"Oh, and Leonie, we'd like Rodolphe and Gaspard as the ring bearers. Okay?" I ask.

She claps her hands and agrees.

We move on to the guests. Between The Moms, Lachlan and I decided to let them have full rein. We gave them our list of must attends. Other than that, they know best who to invite from amongst the family, friends, royals, nobles, society members, business associates, and political figures from around the globe. The Moms confirm they'll have the approved list by this evening.

Right on time, my mother's assistant announces the

invitation company rep's arrival. They're the best with their incomparable designs. We spend the next hour discussing my preferences and reviewing several options, from classic parchment to miniature carousels. As much as I adore the miniature castle, we forgo it for elegant hand-calligraphed vellum. The rep leaves with the promise to have a sample the next morning.

Sergeant Shelley sits back and grins.

"Well, ladies and gentleman, we're off to a splendid start. Everyone has their assignments. Haley, you, Lucie, and I will fly to Paris, then go to Aberdeen. If Lachlan's schedule allows, he may join us. His input matters, too. Any questions?" She asks as she glances at each of us.

When no one responds, I rise.

"I was uncertain at first. But now I feel a whole lot better. Thank you so much!" I exclaim, then hug those at the table and blow kisses to the ones on the television screen.

A chorus of you're welcome and we love you makes my heart soar.

Nothing can stop Lachlan's and my fairytale wedding!

* * *

Hi, Little Lass. I see you are back in town.

I nearly hurl my mobile against the wall after I read Callum's text message. The absolute stalker audacity of the man! Had I known he was a nutter, I wouldn't have become friends with him at Harvard B-School. And what about Princess Fiona the Fair?

Asshole!

He really needs to quit already.

The only thing that stops me from tossing my mobile is Lachlan lying on his side with his head in my lap. We're watching a movie in the media room of our Aberdeen penthouse. I'd rather not disrupt our downtime after a hectic week of wedding planning and work.

We only have a few days here before we fly back to LA for Christmas. Our family opted not to go to Verbier since Malcolm is still unresponsive and there's no way Starr would ever leave his side. Nor would we for the holidays.

I close my eyes and count to ten.

When I open them, I'm still livid. I have to do something.

"Hold up, babe, I have to clear something up at work. Can you pause the movie?" I say.

He scoots up and presses the remote. Then he swings his questioning gaze at me.

"Was it the text message?" He asks.

I nod.

"Your phone has been blowing up at the oddest times. Where the hell are your clients?" He grumbles.

A kiss to his full lips, and he leans back into the sofa, arms crossed over his firm chest. Pecs and biceps pop behind his long-sleeved t-shirt.

"I'll be right back. Think of what I can do to make it up to you… My Lord," I say as I bite the corner of my lower lip and lower my gaze. I peek up at him through my eyelashes. "Whatever would make you feel better, Sir."

His nostrils flare, and his pupils dilate with lust. A frisson of erotic energy zaps between us. He reaches for me. But I squeak and dart away. He growls at the loss and more at the exaggerated sway of my hips as I sashay from the room.

Once I take care of Callum, I'll take care of my man.

LACHLAN

"So, brother, you're a married man who's about to get married again. First a secret crush, then a period of secret lusting after, followed by a secret relationship, now a secret marriage. Damn, it's too hilarious!"

"This is better than those reality TV shows. Oh, wait, I know call it *Lachlan's Love.* Can he give his beloved the red rose? Tune in four months from now for the season finale!"

I roll my eyes and take a much-needed sip from my Waterford Crystal snifter. I refuse to allow Lucien and Laurent's incessant teasing to irritate me. It's bad enough I haven't held My Baby Girl in almost two weeks.

She stayed in New York after the holidays in LA. I flew on to Paris for business before I return to Aberdeen.

Why I decided it would be a good idea to hang out with my annoying as fuck wanker brothers, I do not know. Guys' Night Out… Yeah right. More like Guys' Nightmare.

They get a kick out of rubbing in my face the facts of

Lachlan's Love with My Baby Girl. If I didn't love them, I'd drop kick them real quick. The thought of it gives me a moment of satisfaction.

"What the bloody hell has you grinning? Or is it your blue balls making you squirm?" Laurent asks gleefully.

I'm tempted to throw a handful of salty nuts in his face. But we're at Jackson Smoke&Scotch Paris. The lounge Lucien opened a few years ago on Rue Saint-Honoré—the first of several, London, New York, and Los Angeles. More hot properties for the Jackson Corporation to add to our list of luxury establishments created by *The Sexy Chef.*

The original lounge in the legendary Place Vendôme/St. Honoré area is the place to see and be seen. Where money is no object for the people it attracts. Old society, fashionistas, and celebrities frequent the nearby high-chic spots to shop, drink, and dine.

If we had been in one of the glass-enclosed tasting rooms instead of out in the open at a cluster of vintage leather club chairs, I would have tossed nuts at the tosser. Instead, I take another sip of my Scotch and shake my head.

"Don't hate little bro, or you *Sexy Chef.* And I suggest you concern yourselves with your own balls and not mine. You see, I don't need to find a different hook up each night. I've got a hands down, hot as fuck wife who more than takes care of my needs—sexual and otherwise," I respond with a smug smirk.

They eye each other. Lucien nods his head and turns to me with a serious expression.

"You are right, oh sage older brother. The love lives of us lowlies cannot compare to your illustrious—albeit clandestine—marriage. Perhaps one day we may rise to your level. Right, Lowly Laurent?" Lucien says.

"Oh, most definitely, Lowly Lucien. We aspire to *Lachlan's Love...* NOT!!!" Laurent replies before he howls with laughter, clutching his sides as he doubles over. He glances up with tears in his bottle green eyes and laughs some more at my stoic expression.

His laughter comes to an abrupt stop when the salty nuts land on his head.

"Bloody wankers," I mutter, pushed to my limit.

He shakes his mane of sable brown hair and dusts the nuts from his Saville Row three-piece suit, then smirks.

"Aaawww... We love you too, Lach!" He says as he and Lucien jump up and grab me in a headlock.

The other patrons turn to stare. But when they recognize The Jackson Trio—dubbed by the media as the most sought-after of the world's most eligible billionaires—they smile at our antics. A couple of women sashay over and ask for *The Sexy Chef* for his autograph.

He obliges and asks them to join us. He winks at me over their heads. I roll my eyes and down the last of my drink. Time to go.

I bid my brothers good night and leave for a FaceTime tryst with my fiancée... my wife. Those two got to me, but so what, I chuckle as I slip into my Aston Martin DB7 Vantage. I'll have the last laugh. Especially when they meet their love matches.

The City of Lights flies past me as I navigate through the streets, headed to my penthouse in the *seizième*. The arrondissement is renowned for the ornate nineteenth-century buildings, wide avenues, prestigious schools, museums, and spacious parks. French high society has flocked here for their places of residence for years. The *seizième* is comparable to the luxurious Kensington and Chelsea neighborhoods in London. French popular culture has coined the phrase *le 16e* as association with great wealth.

I park in the garage and stride to my private elevator. By the time the doors open, I'm hard as fuck. The thought of seeing My Baby Girl's curvy body and dripping wet pink pussy drives me wild. The double ornate glass and wrought-iron doors glide open silently at the touch of my palm to the plate. I hasten through them.

On my way to my bedroom, I shrug out of my coat and suit jacket and loosen my tie. I leave a trail of discarded clothes in my wake. Without hesitation, I grab my iPad and climb onto my king-size, four-poster, lattice-canopy bed. The cloud of fluffy white silk linens and pillows billow around me. Their soft caress does nothing to compare to my woman.

"Hi, Baby Girl. Or should I say, Little Temptress?" I purr when the FaceTime connects.

She's a vision.

Flushed cheeks and pouty baby pink lips with glossy ebony waves cascading over her shoulders down her back to her waist. Soulful dove gray eyes peer at me from behind the thick fringe of her lashes.

Just as stunning and arousing is the way her pebbled nipples poke through the black lace thigh-skimming kimono. Also visible through the lace are a pair of matching panties and suspenders attached by garters to sheer black silk stockings. When she crosses her long, toned legs, a pair of black suede fuck-me stilettos appear on the screen.

My collar and ring glimmer in the glow of candlelight.

My wife personifies perfection.

MINE!

A growl rumbles in my chest when her lips part on a pant.

"You're earlier than I expected, My Lord," she says breathlessly. "I just finished changing."

I flick my eyes to the time and frown. It's midnight in New York City. Where could she have been out so late? Before I can voice my question, she repositions her iPad.

Crotchless panties… Fuck. Me.

Her little pink pussy winks at me. The folds swollen and moist already—succulent.

I lick my lips greedily as my mouth waters for her taste. My eyes close for a moment to recall her sweet, musky nectar on my tongue. I can almost smell her natural fragrance.

"Bend your knees. Heels flat on the bed. Thighs spread wide. I want to feast on the sight of your creamy pussy, Little Temptress," I growl.

She bites her lush lower lip and repositions herself.

"Untie the sash, but leave the kimono draped over your tits," I command. "Now, put your arms overhead and hold the headboard."

My fist grips the base of my turgid length. With slow, deliberately long strokes, I imagine my cock slipping into her tight, juicy pussy. A groan falls from my lips as a bead of pre-cum eases from my mushroom head. I use my thumb to coat it with my jizz. Needing more lube, I lick the palm of my hand and fist my cock again.

I hum in carnal satisfaction.

"My Lord?"

My gaze flicks to My Little Temptress' face. She licks her lips and rolls her hips.

"May I touch myself, Sir?" She asks. "Show you more of my pussy?"

My eyes narrow, and I growl.

"For me or for you, Naughty Girl?" I demand.

Her eyes widen as though busted, then close to slits as she raises her chin and gazes at me with hooded eyes.

"For both of us, My Lord," she purrs.

Fuck. Me.

I grunt and nod my approval.

"Leave one hand on the headboard and use the fingers of the other to part your folds. I want to see that hidden gem," I command.

Open for me, her swollen clit reveals itself. I want to nip and suck it until she gushes in my mouth. My strokes increase. My balls grow heavy. I use my other hand to knead the achy sac.

Her plaintive moan draws my attention to her face again. Now crimson with the exertion to control herself, she pants through parted lips.

"One finger inside. Only to the first knuckle," I instruct the vixen. Knowing not to disobey me—even long distance—she complies with a soft moan. "Good, girl. Now, slide it in all the way. Curl the tip and stroke your G-spot."

She hisses with erotic pleasure and lifts her hips to drive her finger deeper.

I allow it.

"Add another finger," I instruct through gritted teeth. The sight of her writhing gets to me. "Add a third finger. Keep your eyes on my cock and follow my strokes. Good, girl…"

The sounds of her slippery pussy as it grips and releases her fingers and her cries of pleasure spur me on. My pace increases. The base of my spine tingles. But I need her to cum. Now.

"Use your other hand to pinch your clit. Now," I command.

Her hand drops to her glistening gem. Thumb and fore-finger capture it. She throws her head back and screams my name as the first wave of her orgasm breaks over her.

"Keep moving your fingers," I growl. The tingle moves to my balls. "Do not stop and look at my cock!"

She mewls and opens her obsidian eyes—the pupils overtake the gray irises. Beads of sweat form on her upper lip. She pokes the tip of her little pink tongue out to lick the moisture.

FUCK!

My balls tighten as my ass clenches and my heels dig into the white silk.

"Cum for me… Cum. For. Me. Now!" I roar as the first spurt of my seed jumps from the slit of my cock. Like a geyser, it goes off again and again with ropes of creamy cum in the air to dribble down my still hard shaft and coat my abs and thighs.

My hooded gaze shifts to My Little Temptress. Her mouth a perfect O as she cums at the sight of my intense release. The kimono falls open to reveal her jiggling D-cups. Nipples so hard they look like they hurt and beg for my mouth to suckle them for relief. Her body writhes so much, she kicks one heel off her stockinged foot. Her toes curl as her foot points.

Her hands still work her pretty pussy.

"Good, girl," I praise huskily awed by her as my fist strokes my cock. "Cum for me once more."

She breaks beautifully with a surprised cry.

I groan along with her.

As one, we slump back against our beds, lost to the carnal bliss. The sound of our breathing the only thing to be heard. The heaving of our chests the only movement.

Slowly, I return and blink to clear my vision. I scan the bed for the iPad. My Baby Girl snores softly curled on her side in a fetal position. I ache to wrap her body with mine.

"Good night and sweet dreams, Mrs. Jackson. I love

you," I whisper as I trace her face with my fingertip on the screen.

So worn out from the multiple orgasms and the late hour, she doesn't hear me.

I end the FaceTime and rise from the bed to pad into the en suite bathroom. In the shower, I press my palms against the marble wall and hang my head as the warm water washes over me.

My mind replays my brothers' words then my tryst.

Yeah, Haley and I may not have a traditional love affair, but she is mine now. No matter whether the world believes we're only engaged. We know she is mine, and I am hers, as fate always meant us to be. Forever.

I grab the bodywash and clean myself. I shake my head at my partially erect cock. Down, boy...

Also true, FaceTime with your woman thousands of miles away doesn't compare to her underneath you. Undoubtedly, Lucien and Laurent are fucking some women right now at LEVELS Paris. In the flesh.

With a sigh, I dry off and don a pair of black sweatpants. No way will I be able to sleep. So I might as well get some work done. We'll go on a two-month honeymoon. So all the shit I can get done now, the better.

I leave the bedroom with my mobile and head to the home office. While my laptop powers up, I pour two fingers of Jackson Special Blend Scotch. I stare sightlessly out the window, lost in thought.

The vibration of my mobile in my pocket rouses me.

A smile spreads across my face.

"Hello, Mrs. Jackson," I say when the call connects.

"Hello, Mr. Jackson. I'm sorry to have fallen asleep on you," she says sheepishly.

"No worries. But why were you just getting in? It's late there," I ask.

I take another sip and lean my butt against the window frame. The sight of My Baby Girl in all that black lace and silk blew the question out of my head. I'm glad I remembered.

She hesitates.

I hear rustling in the background. Then she's back on the line.

"Sorry, I had to take the lingerie off," she says.

I wait for her to answer my question. A twinge of concern pokes at the edges of my mind. I shake my head to clear it and ask again.

"Why were you just getting in?"

She mutters something as she yawns.

"Haley, why won't you answer me?" I ask as the hairs on the back of my neck rise.

Even though I don't believe she would cheat on me, the only answer that comes to mind is she was out with someone and doesn't want me to know.

"Maribelle and I went out to dinner after a late day at the office," she responds. "Lachlan, I have an early meeting. Can we say good night now?"

I sag in relief. That's plausible. Plus, Maribelle is married too, so she wouldn't get up to no good. This is all Lucien and Laurent's fault. Putting doubt in my mind.

Bloody wankers.

"Lachlan?" My Baby Girl calls to me.

I nod, then remember she can't see me.

"Sure. I hope you had fun. Next time give my regards to her and to Calvin. Good night, Mrs. Jackson. I love you," I respond.

"Good night, Mr. Jackson. I love you more," she whispers.

I end the call and plop down on my desk chair. I roll my eyes at my overreaction and foolishness for listening to my brothers.

My Baby Girl... My wife loves me, and I love her.

All is right in our world.

achlan, I need to see you. You won't answer my calls or texts. It's really urgent. I can meet you at your office. Please.

I sigh at the second text message from Fiona today—the second of many in the past few days. Plus, the phone calls and voicemails. Hell, she even got a hold of my Jackson Corporation email address yesterday and sent a round of emails.

What the fuck could be so important she would need to see *me*? And urgently?

I shake my head and click the phone icon on my mobile screen. Another sigh and I lean back in my leather desk chair. It's bad enough I have jet lag. Now to contend with Fiona's bullshit. I do not have the patience for it.

But the jet lag is well worth it.

Malcolm awoke from the coma. Thank fuck!

I flew to LA to see him. My Baby Girl arrived before me since the family in New York City flew in hours earlier. Everyone is so elated he's back—well, not fully. None the less, it's a positive start.

I have meetings I can't reschedule. So I left everyone and returned to Aberdeen in the wee hours this morning. No time to stop at our penthouse flat, I showered and dressed on my Gulfstream G650. Doyle met me at the airport and drove me to Jackson Town House. Only minutes ago. Fiona must have a super sense to know I'm already here.

"Lachlan, what's wrong, darling? How was your flight?"

My mother's voice brings me back from my musings when she answers my call. It's ten at night in Beverly Hills where she's staying at the STEELE hotel with my father. Normally, I'll send her a text message when I land. The call throws her.

"Nothing, Mom. I don't mean to upset you," I say, and she murmurs thanks for my safety. We're all on edge since Malcolm's accident. "Question, have you heard about anything being wrong with the Ridels? I've gotten a lot of calls and texts, even emails, from Fiona stating she and I need to speak. I ignore them, figuring she wants to see me for other reasons. But this morning she texted it was urgent we meet today. I don't want to disregard her if something is amiss truly."

Silence on the other end of the line, then muffled talking, followed by rustling.

"I'm at a late dinner with Shelley, Morgan, and your father and had to excuse myself. It's doubtful this is a conversation we want them to hear before you and I figure Fiona out," my mother says, then continues. "I have not heard of anything about the Ridels. The only news on Fiona is her dating Callum. I find it interesting both of your exes—well, not in Fiona's case—are a couple. But then, we are in the same social circle, so it makes sense."

My mother pauses, then adds, "Why she would need to speak with you? I do not know. Have you told Haley about the communications?"

I shift in my chair. Guilt makes me squirm.

I'm the main one asking for trust and honesty. Yet, I haven't told my wife about the woman who wanted to marry me, contacting me incessantly. The main reason: I don't want to upset My Baby Girl. Especially with Malcolm's situation, the wedding planning, and her work weighing on her. She's as determined as I am to get shit done before our honeymoon. The long hours at the office and dinner meetings prove it.

"No, Mom, I haven't told Haley. I didn't want to add any more to her plate. She'd worry about it, especially since I'm here in Aberdeen where Fiona is and Haley is all the way in New York," I respond. "I'll see Fiona today and get it over with. If something comes of it, I'll tell Haley."

"Fine. But you do not want lies of any kind in your marriage—even ones of omission. How would you feel if the roles were reversed where Haley failed to tell you something about Callum? Remember, your marriage vows are sacred, Lachlan," my mother says.

Her words hit me hard as we end our call. She's absolutely right. I'd be pissed as fuck!

I'll tell My Baby Girl everything regardless of the outcome of my conversation with Fiona. I won't allow anyone or anything to come between my wife and me.

A glance at the time shows it's six-thirty. The first meeting starts at seven and no break until three and a business dinner at seven. Well, it's best I get my work done before I deal with Fiona, anyway.

I shoot her a text to meet me at my office at three-thirty. She responds immediately. I toss my mobile onto my desk and power up my laptop. Time to start my day.

"THE HONORABLE FIONA RIDEL has arrived, Mr. Jackson."

"Kindly see her in, Isla," I ask my administrative assistant over the intercom. I rise from my chair and put on my suit jacket as I remain standing behind my desk. It'll block any unwanted greeting from Fiona.

A knock on the door precedes Isla, ushering Fiona inside my office. I thank my assistant and gesture towards a guest chair.

"Hello, Fiona," I say.

She walks in hesitantly and perches on the edge of the chair. Delicate hands smooth invisible wrinkles from her silk skirt as she crosses her ankles. Her lower lip trembles when she removes a pair of large-frame sunglasses.

Uncovered, puffy and red eyes peer at me from beneath pale blonde eyelashes. The violet irises darkened to navy blue.

"Hello, Lachlan. Thank you for seeing me," she says. Her voice wavers at the end.

I school my face to stop a frown from forming. Something is definitely wrong. What?

Instead of asking, I fold my hands on the desk's surface and wait for her to state her business. She requested we speak. Let her go first. My gaze remains neutral as her eyes scan my face.

Fiona sighs and removes a handkerchief from her handbag to dab a tear from the corner of her eye. Then she takes a deep breath and clears her throat.

"Lachlan, I—I apologize for calling and texting you. I—I tried to ignore the ill sense. At first, I thought I was mistaken. Everything seemed to go so well between us—"

I rise from my chair and glower at her.

"Fiona, we had this conversation a long time ago. There is nothing *between us*. Kindly leave. I have work to do," I grit out.

She clutches her chest as her eyes widen and more tears fill them.

I shake my head and round my desk headed for the door.

She grips my forearm.

"No, you misunderstand, Lachlan!" She cries out.

I pause and stare down at her. Confused, I can't help the frown on my face. What the fuck?

Her tongue darts out to moisten her lips, and her eyes skitter around the room to avoid my questioning look.

I pull my arm from her hand, and she places it in her lap. Head bowed, her fingers fidget.

"Fiona, I have a very busy day. Finish or leave," I demand. The jet lag, back-to-back meetings, and her reticent behavior finish me off. And my work isn't even over yet.

She blinks at my curt tone, then fishes into her handbag to withdraw a yellow legal envelope.

What now?!

"I do not refer to you, Lachlan," she says as her fingers toy with the envelope. Then she nods towards my chair. "Give me a moment, and I will explain. I promise not to keep you any longer than necessary."

She continues when I sit.

"Callum Graham and I have been dating for months now since he moved back to Aberdeen. He even asked me to marry him," she says and lifts her left hand where a substantial diamond ring flashes.

"Recently, he's been spending more time in New York City. At first, I thought his late nights and frequent business dinners were true. But then"—She pauses to unclasp the closure on the envelope—"I became suspicious and hired an investigator. My father says as an heiress, I can never be too careful."

She pulls color photos from the envelope and holds them at an angle where I can't decipher the images. A sob catches in her throat when she glances down at them.

Curious, I lean forward.

"I don't want to hurt you, as Callum has hurt me," Fiona says as she lifts the stack of photos to her chest. Her lower lip trembles as she goes on. "But I believe you should know."

With a sigh, she hands the photos to me image side down across my desk.

The hairs on the back of my neck rise. Not certain I want to know what or who's in the photos and how they can possibly relate to me, I shake my head.

"I should know what, Fiona? Just say it already," I snap.

Tears and timidness disappear as violet sparks shoot from her eyes. Her chest heaves, and her face flushes scarlet.

"Her ex-boyfriend still wants her, even though we're engaged! You want her! I gave my best to Callum and to you! Now, what about me?! Your *fiancée* wants every man to want her! See for yourself, Lachlan!"

Fiona shouts and throws the photos onto my desk as she glares at me.

I freeze.

Images of Haley and Callum together scatter across my desk. His hand on Haley's elbow next to Central Park. Them laughing in a restaurant. The most damning ones of them standing outside of The STEELE Tower's residential entrance. At night.

It takes only a moment for me to realize the photos capture separate encounters based on the different clothes they wear.

My brain short circuits.

I swallow past the bile in my throat.

Fiona sits with her arms crossed over her chest, a smug expression on her face.

"I knew Haley was no good. You fell for her instead of asking me to marry you. Your precious *fiancée*! I'm the one who—"

"Enough."

I take a deep breath. As much as I want to punch a hole through these bloody photos into my desk, there is no way I will allow her to see me upset. But she has to go.

I gather the photos and toss them into the trash can beneath my desk, then meet her narrowed gaze.

"As I said, I have a busy day, Fiona. Now if you will take your leave," I say as I rise and stride to my door. I open it and call to Isla. "Kindly escort the *Honorable* Fiona Ridel to the lobby. I have a meeting now."

Isla doesn't blink at my mention of a non-existent meeting. She nods and hurries to my door.

"Right this way," she tells Fiona as she holds out Fiona's coat.

"Lachlan—"

"Good day, Fiona," I cut her off.

Taking her time, she puts her sunglasses on and grips her handbag. Without a glance at me, she snatches her coat from Isla and sweeps from my office with her head held high and her back straight.

I shut the door and clench my fists. The urge to punch something still strong. Instead, I jab the screen of my mobile to send a text message to my flight crew. I storm to my desk and gather my shit.

"Gladys, I'm flying to LA now. Kindly let Isla know to cancel all of my appointments until further notice," I speak into the intercom to my personal assistant.

It's nine at night in LA. Fourteen hours to get here, and I'm still fuming from my conversation and the fucked-up photos. I cannot believe Haley cheated on me!

The doorbell chimes to for her suite at STEELE Beverly Hills. Seconds later, I jab again and hold it. My mother confirmed Haley was at the hotel. So, I know she's in there. And she better be alone!

"Who is it?!"

She hisses through the shut door.

"Me!" I shout.

The door opens, and I barge past her into the living room. I glance around for evidence of Graham being here. Her laptop sits open on the coffee table next to a plate of hamburger and fries, with a bottle of red wine and a single glass.

My stomach growls at the sight and aroma. Lunch was so long ago. Fueled by anger, I ignore the hunger.

I put my laptop case on the chair, and my bags fall to the floor. I pivot to face Haley, a scowl on my face.

"Lachlan! What the hell? Why are you here and

frowning at me?!" She asks as she follows me into the living room.

"You tell me, Haley!" I snarl.

I toss the envelope, and the photos fall out at her feet. Naturally, I fished them from the trash when Fiona left and put them in a fresh envelope.

Haley growls and stoops to pick them up. Her eyes widen.

I cross my arms over my chest to stop from rampaging around the room.

"How did you… Did you have me followed?" She murmurs as she flips through one photo after the next.

"Oh, so that's your greatest concern, Haley? Whether I had you followed? What the FUCK?!" I end in a roar. "My wife sees photos of herself cavorting around New York—hell, maybe even here, or all over the world—cheating on me with her ex-boyfriend, and that's her only response?!"

I shake with fury as my hands fist at my sides. I swear, if that bastard was here, I'd rip his fucking face off.

Haley's mouth drops, and her face turns crimson.

"How *dare* you?! That's your conclusion? I *cheated* on you? Without even asking me one fucking thing or giving me a chance to explain?! That's my response, Lachlan Jackson!" She roars right back.

As warped as it might be—or maybe it's the lack of sleep depriving my brain to think logically—my cock hardens and my palm itches. Haley's defiance turns me on.

I shake my head to clear it and glare right back at her.

"Answer me, Haley," I growl.

She shudders but stands fast.

"Did. You. Have. Me. Followed."

I stalk towards her.

She takes steps back until her ass bumps against the wall. Her eyes widen, and she glances over her shoulder to find she's trapped.

My hands bracket her face as I lean down.

"Answer me, Haley," I growl.

She pushes against my chest with her small hands. Dove gray eyes narrowed to slits as her lip curls.

"Fuck you, Lachlan!" She snarls.

My nostrils flare as I inhale to gain control of my rage.

"One last time. Tell me why you were with Graham," I grit out through clenched teeth. "Are you cheating on me?"

Tears fill her eyes.

She hangs her head. The hair forms a curtain—a barrier —between us.

"You don't trust me. After all we've been through. You do not trust me, Lachlan," she whispers. "You didn't have to hire an investigator. That's low."

Haley raises her face. Her teeth dig into her lower lip to hold back more tears from slipping down her cheeks. She swipes them away.

"No, I am not cheating on you. Photos don't always tell the full story," she says, then sighs. "For some time now, Callum has left voicemails, sent text messages, flowers, made comments when our paths crossed. I ignored them all. Until one night he sent a text that creeped me out.

Somehow, he knew I was back in Aberdeen. You and I were watching a movie, and I said it was work related."

She pauses to take a breath.

I hold mine, unsure of what to think.

"I called him, and he asked to have dinner with me when I was in New York. I agreed only to tell him it was enough," she says and points her chin towards the photos behind me. "That's the restaurant. The others are times he ambushed me. What they don't show is me pushing him off and yelling at him."

Haley glares again and continues.

"Your guy should have told you that part instead of making it appear as though Callum and I were all lovey-dovey!"

I open my mouth to speak. But she holds up her hand.

"However, I will apologize for keeping it all from you. I thought I could handle Callum, and I didn't want to upset you for something that was so stupid. Besides, he's supposedly dating Fiona. Which makes it even worse," Haley says, shaking her head.

Fuck!

I get it now.

This shit is all a setup. Graham and Fiona want to sabotage Haley and me. Bloody wankers!

My forehead drops to rest against hers. She stiffens but relaxes when I lower my hands to her hips to lift her up. I carry her to the sofa and sit with her on my lap.

"I didn't hire an investigator. Fiona gave them to me today—rather yesterday afternoon. She'd been contacting me too, and I ignored her until then. She insisted it was urgent. I wanted to get it over with," I admit.

Haley's eyebrows shoot up and her mouth drops open again.

I shake my head and continue.

"So she met me at my office. First, she put on a sob-story show about being engaged to Graham and being suspicious about his behavior and time in New York. When I told her to get on with it, she got pissed and blathered on about Graham and I both wanting you and you happy about it. Leaving Fiona without either man," I say and pause. "Then she showed the photos to me. I didn't let her see they bothered me. But I've been furious ever since. Think about it from my perspective."

Haley sighs and nods.

"I, too, apologize for not telling you about Fiona's communications. Especially since I want our marriage built on trust and honesty. I forgive you. Do you forgive me?" I end.

Haley straddles my thighs and cups my face with her palms.

"I forgive you, too, Lachlan," she says and presses her lips to mine.

She opens to me on a soft moan when my tongue licks the seam of her lips. Our tongues dance slowly, then build.

My already aroused cock thickens and lengthens in my sweatpants. I groan when her fingertip traces the outline of my erection. Without hesitation, my hand slides beneath her shorts to find her wet for me.

My Little Temptress is as turned on by our argument as I am. Her hips roll as she rides my fingers to her first orgasm.

As her pussy walls clench around my fingers, I use my other hand to free my aching cock. She rises to her knees and pulls the seat of her shorts to the side. Both of us groan in satisfaction as her tight little pussy stretches around my girth.

I grip her hips and slam up into her wet heat.

"Oh... Fuck!" She cries.

Between pistoning strokes, I tell her she is mine. Only mine.

Her body convulses with two more orgasms before I flip her onto her knees, ass out, hands on the back of the sofa. I slam into her spasming pussy with a feral growl.

One. Two. Three brutal thrusts.

My head falls back.

I roar my release like a wild animal claiming its mate.

She screams my name as her fingernails claw the silk fabric.

My vision blackens. I collapse against her and roll us on our sides, her back to my front. We're quiet while our bodies return to normal.

My Baby Girl turns her head to look at me over her shoulder.

"They did it on purpose," she states.

I nod and pull her tighter against me.

"I tell you this, if Graham does one thing, it's over for him," I declare.

"Fiona, too," My Baby Girl adds.

We fall back into a comfortable silence as our minds process all that happened.

Yeah, it's fucked up. But as the saying goes, what doesn't kill us makes us stronger. And we've been through a whole lot…

"*A*h, this is a delightful respite, Baby Girl. Thank you for the Valentine's Day surprise, Mrs. Jackson."

Lachlan stretches out beside me on a sunbed at the front of the sixth deck. The sun glistens on his tanned skin, damp with sweat from our bout of lovemaking moments ago. The muscles in his arm flex and ripple as he covers his face with the crook of his elbow and strokes his eight-pack abs. My man is the epitome of hunkalicious. Yum!

We're on board *Serendipity,* the megayacht my father gave to my mother for their thirtieth wedding anniversary. *Serendipity* is a majestic boat. The largest megayacht in the world has a length of six-hundred feet, nine inches. That extra nine just to nudge past the next yacht down. At least for now, *Serendipity* holds the record since everyone competes for the prize of the biggest on the water. There are already rumors that a Russian oligarch contracted a prominent builder specifically to outsize *Serendipity*.

It's definitely a beauty to behold. The all-white, sleek design boasts seven decks. The top for the bridge; the sixth for four palatial suites where my parents, Malcolm, Sebastian, and I stay; the fifth deck for four suites where Roger and Harris and up to four close friends stay, plus our private library, office, family and dining rooms with galley; the remaining decks accommodate twenty-four guests in staterooms, quarters for eighty-eight crew, helicopter pad, submarine and water vehicles and toys garage, swimming pool, spa, gym, barbershop and salon, disco, living and dining areas, and an entertainment deck with a bowling alley, cinema, pool room, cards room, and game room. The open-air decks hold chaises, beds, tables, televisions, and dining spots. *Serendipity* is a floating haven for rest, relaxation, and partying.

After the shock of Callum and Fiona's failed coup d'état, I decided my husband and I needed a break from them and the stress we've been under during these past few months. My mom suggested we take *Serendipity* to cruise along Spain's southern coast. This time of year, the weather is still warm in the low seventies and sunny. We'll anchor off of Málaga, Marabella, and Estepona to take a tender to visit the resort towns and their beaches. A couple of nights dancing at clubs would be fun, too!

We have less than three months before our wedding. The planning is progressing well with everything on schedule. Sergeant Shelley, Lieutenant Lucy, Bailey, and his assistant have been aces. I couldn't be more pleased than I am with all they've accomplished in such a short period of time.

Not wanting to miss the wedding of the year, all two hundred and fifty guests RSVP'd yes and confirmed their participation in the weekend activities. We plan for horseback riding through the estate; a charity polo match; a cooking demonstration with wine pairing; a Jackson Scotch tasting; a tour of the area's heritage houses; shopping in the villages. It's going to be a lovely getaway for our guests as they join us in the celebration of our vow renewal.

I'm so thankful Malcolm will attend. It's rough, but he's strong and determined. We have no doubt he will push through.

On our way back to Aberdeen for a week before I return to New York City, we'll stop by Paris to check in with Monsieur Valentino and his artisans. I'm in awe of his creations for my gowns—including my cathedral-length veil. A grin spreads across my face at the thought of them. I'll be a vision in white for my husband.

Lola, Blair, and Billie refuse to give me even a hint to my lingerie trousseau. They insist I will owe them big time for making me irresistible during the honeymoon. My one request is for an all-white lace set for our first night. I want to recreate our first time when Lachlan claimed my virginity. Tingles ripple through me whenever I think of that special moment.

Leonie has been true to her word. The residences are

nearly complete with a month to go on the beach house and the last pieces being delivered to the duplex penthouse this week. Aberdeen finished a couple of weeks ago. This will be the first time I see the finished penthouse flat. Lachlan remains mum since he's seen it already and wants me to enjoy the surprises he has in store.

Overall, I'm a lucky girl!

"You're more than welcome, Mr. Jackson," I purr as I scoot closer and nuzzle my nose against his neck. My fingertips trail across his firm pecs to tweak a nipple. "I serve to pleasure you in all ways, My Lord."

I squeal.

In an unexpected move, Lachlan rolls over and positions me beneath his sizable frame. His forearms frame my face as his hands cradle the back of my head. My legs part to give way to his narrow hips. Our groins meet. My fingernails drag along his flanks to cup his ass. My legs wrap around his muscular thighs. We're caught up in each other. Now and forever.

"Do you now, Little Temptress?" He purrs.

His emerald green eyes dance as he stares down at me.

I shimmy my hips and bite my lower lip.

"Yes, My Lord," I whisper.

"I love you," he whispers.

"I love you more," I reply.

He dips his head to kiss me as our pelvises roll in an erotic rhythm. My Adonis makes love to me, and I prove just how much I serve to please him.

* * *

THE BASS of the music thumps as we grind on the dance floor of the outdoor beach club in Marbella. Warm bodies writhe around us as a mist floats from above to cool everyone down. It's perfect for the sultry Mediterranean night. The crowd shouts when the celebrity DJ spins Avicii into the mix.

Lachlan and I throw our hands up and yell along with them. We've been dancing for over an hour straight. My white minidress clings to me. The outlines of my puckered nipples and silk G-string clear. I don't give a damn! We're having the best time.

I throw my head back and roar as I gyrate my hips.

Lachlan grips them and yanks me against his chest. He bends his knees to let me feel his excitement. He growls when I swing my leg around his hip and dip backwards, grinding my pussy against his thick girth.

Knowing he'll hold me up, I wrap my other leg around him and let my arms hang to the floor beside my head.

Not deterred by the shift in position, Lachlan increases his grip on my hips and ass. He sways us back and forth with ease.

Others around us cheer.

I yell for more.

Lachlan flips me up and brings one of my legs up against his chest as the other lowers to the floor. The heel of my sandal rests beside his ear. I'm in a complete standing split. He continues to grind into me. His dick pulsates against my core.

We shock no one with our blatant display of mimicking sex. They're too busy fucking or damn near at it.

"You tempt me like no other, Mrs. Jackson!" Lachlan growls in my ear.

I turn my head and nip at his sensitive lobe. Then drag the tip of my tongue along the shell of his ear to soothe the sting.

He growls and spanks my ass through the thin fabric of my mini dress.

I yowl since the sweat makes the smack sting.

He chuckles wickedly.

A quick change, and his front presses to my back. Once again, he bends his knees to grind his dick into my ass. One hand grips my hip while the other slides between my upper thighs to cup my mound beneath the hem of my mini dress. His finger glides along the wetness of my G-string.

I groan and widen my stance as I press down against the thick digit.

Lachlan continues to rock against me while his fingers explore my dripping pussy. My juices drip down my inner thighs, and my legs shake. He draws an orgasm like no other from me. I turn my head for his mouth. He crushes it against mine and swallows my moans of sheer ecstasy.

Now, it's his turn.

I slide my hand up his thigh. My fingers reach between my ass and his groin to unzip his pants. He stills.

"Be very careful, Little Temptress," he warns.

Ignoring him, I reach into his pants and angle my ass. Fine with my determination to have him, Lachlan pulls the string of my panties aside, grips his dick, and slides into my greedy pussy. We groan in unison.

"Fuck, Baby Girl…" he groans when fully seated. He grinds against my butt cheeks as his hold on my hips increases.

I'm sure to have marks in the morning.

My focus returns to the present, and I buck against him. He pulls out to drive in deeper. His thrust lifts me to my toes. My back arches, and I moan silently. Eyes closed, lost in the sensation of his massive cock throbbing deep inside of my core.

His dick gets impossibly bigger. His body tenses.

My hips burn from his unrelenting grip.

When the first pulse of his seed fills my pussy, Lachlan clamps his teeth on the tender juncture where my neck meets my shoulder. It muffles his roar.

I quake, overtaken by another mind-blowing orgasm fueled by his release.

As the beat of the music morphs into a slow, seductive tango, Lachlan wraps his powerful arms around my waist. Still intimately connected, I place my hands atop his on my lower belly. He purrs in my ear. I hum in response.

We're lost in carnal rapture.

* * *

"I know I shouldn't say this with all the things we have to do…. But I hate to leave. Can we stay for another week?"

Lachlan smiles and shakes his head.

I try again.

"Okay, how about a few more days?"

It's early morning, and we're standing on the third deck of *Serendipity*. The crew prepares a tender to take us to the marina, where one of them will drive us to the airport. Lachlan's flight crew scheduled his jet to fly us to Paris in an hour.

We had such an incredible and relaxing time these last four days. I want our trip to go on forever. But he's right. We have loads to do.

I sigh when he takes my hand and helps me to the tender.

"We have the rest of our lives for trips like this one, Baby Girl. No need to worry. Plus, we have our honeymoon to look forward to soon enough," my husband says as he kisses my temple.

I snuggle against him with another sigh.

"Don't you want to see your dresses?" He murmurs in my ear.

Just as he says it, the sun's rays appear on the horizon. A sign of good things to come.

I tip my head back for a kiss as I murmur, "I love you, Mr. Jackson."

He nips my lip and tugs.

"I love you more, Mrs. Jackson," he replies.

Yup, all good things ahead.

LACHLAN

"Get your fucking hands off of my WIFE!!!"

My roar precedes her spinning against the wall as I yank Graham away from her. One hand holds him by the throat while my other arm rises. My fist draws back, and I punch Graham in the mouth.

Bone meets bone with a sickening crunch.

Blood pours from his split lip.

He staggers, caught off guard by my ferocity. The throat hold keeps him locked in place.

I don't let up. The Scotsman in me will never let me stop in war. And this one is a longtime in the making. The bloody wanker refuses to listen.

Another punch skids off his cheek as he ducks his head. His knee misses my balls but hits my thighs. My legs buckle, and my grip loosens.

With a war cry of his own, he takes advantage and elbows me on the side of my face. My ears ring. But I shake it off. Determination to end this wanker urges me on.

"Lachlan! Callum! Stop it!" Haley yells.

I ignore her as my opponent and I circle one another. Two Alpha males face off. Equally trained in Historical European Martial Arts.

This may not be a duel with Highland broadswords, as I imagined in the past. But I will end the competition and reclaim my woman once and for all.

We arrived at the charity fundraising gala for Aberdeen and Aberdeenshire's division of the Scottish Wildlife Trust an hour ago. It's a big event on the social calendar. Haley didn't want to miss an opportunity to mingle since many of the guests will attend our wedding. She's hellbent on making a good impression.

I scanned the ballroom for Graham and Fiona.

Of course, they were in the middle of the room chatting with other couples. Fiona ensconced firmly at his side. She made sure her engagement ring was in full view. Her tinkling laughter floated towards us.

Haley stiffened beside me, and I reminded her it was her idea to come out for this event. She nodded, and we moved in the opposite direction of the group.

We successfully avoided Graham and Fiona during the cocktail hour. However, I caught glimpses of them staring at us at separate times. When it happened, I slid my gaze past them without so much as a nod of my head. No need to acknowledge them in any way. Their antics disgust me still.

As Haley and I moved towards the banquet tables, she said she wanted to freshen up before we sat for dinner. I watched as she made her way past other guests. She greeted some she recognized and nodded at those who were unfamiliar to her.

I smiled. She's a natural and will have no problem adjusting to the role of a countess. She's even encouraged me to become more involved. Rightly so since it is a part of my responsibility to my family and to my heirs.

Yeah, heirs. We want a family of our own as soon as possible. The decision will please my father immensely. Hopefully, enough for him to stop with his quest for me to take over Jackson Corporation instead of Lydie.

After some time passed and Haley had not returned, I went in search of her. The red silk satin gown she wore made it easy to spot her. Not amongst the last of the guests to enter the dining area, I headed to the ladies' room.

"—said not to bother me."

"Well, tell me, are you married to Jackson or not, Little Lass? It's a simple yes or no answer."

She hesitated, and her fingers brushed the bridge of her nose. The former tell she did when nervous, and she adjusted her eyeglasses. Now she wears contact lenses and rarely makes the gesture.

Fuck. Me. She was about to lie. About us.

"No."

Her whispered response might as well have gone through a megaphone. It bounced off the walls and knocked me square in the gut.

My wife just denied she's married to me. Denied me to her ex-boyfriend. Of all the people in the world.

Fuck. Me.

A red veil descended over my vision. I rushed forward. Graham and I clashed.

As we circle one another, he smirks.

"You sure about that? My Little Lass answered *no* to being *your wife*, Jackson. She's fair game, mate," he growls.

Haley gasps.

I ignore her. I've heard enough.

"Oh, she's my wife all right," I snarl. "You should worry about *your fiancée* coming to me for *my* ring. First Haley, then Fiona. Seems no woman wants you to claim her, *mate*," I snarl.

He takes the bait and rushes me with a battle cry.

Swiftly, I spin to the side and punch Graham on the back of his neck as he flies by me. He stumbles and drops to his knees, then to the ground with a grunt.

I tempered the force enough to knock him out—not to cause permanent injury. Any harder, and he would suffer whiplash, or worse. I watch him for signs of steady breathing.

The wanker is out cold, but fine.

A scream makes me bring my attention to the rest of my surroundings. Fiona hurries forward and kneels beside Graham. She touches his back tentatively. He groans and moves to sit up. She glares at me.

"Look at what you did, Lachlan!" She shouts. "You attacked him! You—You *monster*!"

"No! He was defending me from Callum!" Haley yells.

The women glare at one another until Graham spits blood from his mouth.

"She still said no, mate," he says with a smirk despite his busted lip.

Haley grabs my hand and tugs.

I glance down at her.

"Let's go, Lachlan. Please," she says with wide eyes.

As we walk away, Graham repeats the phrase and chuckles.

I curl my lip and growl as I turn.

"No! Don't! Please!" Haley begs as she yanks on my arm with both hands. "Let's go…"

The ride in the back of my Rolls-Royce Phantom Extended is tense and silent. Occasionally, Haley flicks her gaze at me as she sits huddled against the opposite door. I ignore her and stare out at the streets of Aberdeen until we reach the garage of our penthouse.

Doyle bids us good night.

The silence continues on the elevator and into the flat.

I go to the bar to pour a Scotch. Hell, maybe I'll drink from the bloody bottle.

"Here, let me put this on your cheek and one on your hand."

Haley looks up at me as she holds ice in two baggies and a tea towel. When I don't answer and continue to stare, she reaches for my hand tentatively.

I shrug her off and take a swig from the bottle.

"Lach—"

I raise my hand.

If she speaks, the last thread holding back my rage will unravel. And it won't be good for either of us. I stalk towards my office, intending to stretch out on the sofa and drink myself to sleep. This night can't end fast enough.

She follows me and squeezes past the door before I can shut it.

Unlike Fiona's accusation, I am not a *monster* and would never slam the door in Haley's face.

I take another swig before I drop on the sofa and lay out with my head on a pillow and the bottle clutched to my chest. My eyes close.

Without opening them, I sense Haley sit on the coffee table. She puts an ice pack on my cheek. I jerk my head away.

"Lachlan, please! Don't ignore me."

She sighs when I do just that.

"I didn't *deny* you. We agreed not to tell anyone until our wedding."

Silence.

She huffs and continues.

"You wanted to keep us dating a secret! Remember? So how is this any different, Lachlan?!"

When she mentions our first relationship during which I wanted to avoid pissing off my best friend—her brother! —the thread pops. My blood pressure rises.

I sit up so abruptly, she scoots back on the coffee table. I slam the bottle down next to her. Amber liquid splashes from the top. Some lands on her dress.

She gapes at me as I tower over her.

"It's completely different, Haley! We're married, not dating. I want to shout to the world you're mine! For all of my rings to sit on your wedding finger. Not only your engagement ring! Making no mistake, you are my woman. Graham and Fiona think we're only engaged! They would have backed the fuck up from the beginning had they known we're married."

My body vibrates as my anger comes to a head. I move around the table to put space between us. Back and forth, I pace as I yank at my hair.

I cannot believe this shit!

"How would you feel if the roles were reversed, and I denied you were my wife to Fiona? Huh?" I shout.

Before she can answer, I continue.

"You would never know because I would never deny you were mine. My wife, Haley."

Suddenly, the fight leaves me, and I sag from the loss of adrenaline. If she doesn't get the difference, there's not a damn thing I can do about it. It's on her. Not me.

I stop pacing and face her.

Her lip trembles as tears stream down her face.

"Haley, you need to figure shit out. I can't do it for you," I say, then stride to the door.

I hear the rustle of her dress as she comes after me.

She grabs my forearm, and I pause to stare down at her.

"Where are you going?" She sobs.

"I don't know. But I can't stay here," I respond with a shake of my head.

She gasps.

"What does that mean?" Haley asks as she squeezes my arm with both hands.

"You need some time… I need some time," I answer as I extricate my arm from her hold.

"What?! What—What about our wedding? It's in less than three months!" She wails.

I open the door and glance at her over my shoulder.

"It will either be a vow renewal or a divorce. The choice is yours, Haley."

* * *

Lachlan & Haley's Story Continues: *Grant My Desires*

**Turn the page for the Steele & Jackson Family Trees,
Author's Note,
and a Preview of *Grant My Desires***

STEELE INTERNATIONAL, INC

Multigenerational, multibillion-dollar business luxury real estate development and management corporation

Headquarters & Family's Primary Residences:

The STEELE Tower, New York City

A modern, gray-tinted glass fifty-seven story mixed-use skyscraper on southwest corner of Fifty-Seventh Street and Fifth Avenue within Billionaires' Row

Global Offices:

- The United States of America (New York City,
  New Jersey, Chicago, California, Miami, Las
  Vegas)
- The Caribbean (St. Maarten, St. Barth's, St.
  Lucia)
- The French & Italian Rivieras (Nice, Cannes,
  Positano, Capri)
- Monaco (Monte Carlo)
- The United Arab Emirates (Abu Dhabi, Dubai)

STEELE FOUNDATION: A STRONG AND SUPPORTIVE HOUSE

Builds and manages attractive, affordable housing for urban,
lower-income families

Available for download at **bit.ly/STEELEFamily**

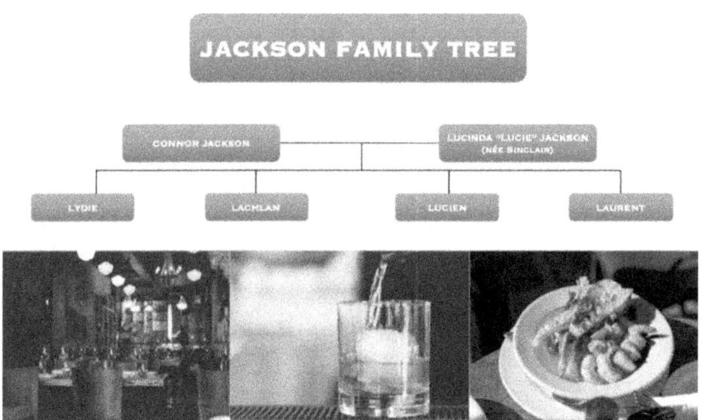

JACKSON CORPORATION

Multigenerational, multibillion-dollar business fine dining, distilleries, and vineyards corporation

Headquarters:

Jackson Town House, Aberdeen, Scotland

A landmark property built by the founders of Aberdeen granite on Union Street; the second largest granite building in the world.

Global Offices:

- The United Kingdom (Aberdeen, Scotland;
  London, England)
- The United States of America (New York City,
  New Orleans, Miami, Chicago, Los Angeles,
  Napa)
- The Caribbean (Puerto Rico)
- France (Paris, Cannes)
- Monaco (Monte Carlo)
- Australia (Sydney)
- The United Arab Emirates (Abu Dhabi, Dubai)

JACKSON FOUNDATION: ENJOY LIFE
RESPONSIBLY

Operates alcohol treatment centers for lower-income individuals
and support for their family members

Available for download at **bit.ly/JacksonFamilyTree**

Author's Note

Thank you for reading Part II of Lachlan and Haley's sexy, sizzling romance! I hope you enjoyed the continuation of their off-limits love affair. If so, I'd love to hear your thoughts, please share a review at **bit.ly/CLBooksSI-JC2Review** and tell your friends.

Click below for what's up next for this darling duo:

Grant My Desires Lachlan & Haley Part III

At **CharmaineLouise.com** take the *Four types of lovers. Which are you?* **Quiz** to match your Sexy Fantasy: sub, Voyeur, Dominatrix, or Dominatrix sub Switch.

Follow me on social media including my CLBooks Coterie Fan Club below or on your favorite channels below and subscribe to my newsletter at **bit.ly/CLBooksNewsletter** for a **Free Book**.

Ready to take it to the next level? Well do not hesitate, Pet… **Click here for Bedroom Kandi by Kandi Burruss Luxury Intimate Toys & Bedroom Accessories and Sensuous Bath & Body Products.** Now.

Fulfill Your Desires.

xoxo

Charmaine Louise

bookbub.com/authors/charmaine-louise-shelton
facebook.com/CharmaineLouiseBooks
instagram.com/charmainelouisebooks
goodreads.com/charmainelouisebooks

**STEELE International, Inc. - Jackson Corporation
A Billionaires Romance Series Crossover Book 3**

Grant My Desires Lachlan & Haley Part III

Click on the link below or visit books2read.com/u/
bz12QD to get your copy.

Grant My Desires Lachlan & Haley Part III

Books in the Series:

Tempt My Desires Lachlan & Haley Part I

Tease My Desires Lachlan & Haley Part II

Grant My Desires Lachlan & Haley Part III

Intrigue My Desires Harris & Kat Part I

Decode My Desires Harris & Kat Part II

Honor My Desires Harris & Kat Patt III

A Trilogy of Desires Lachlan & Haley Parts I-III

A Trilogy of Desires Harris & Kat Parts I-III

Series Extras

Series Playlist

Visit CharmaineLouiseBooks.com for the complete list.

"I never thought I'd say this to you. I always figured it would be Lachlan I'd have to curse out—hell, even beat my best friend's ass—over you. But oh, no… Haley, *you* messed up, didn't you?"

My eyes widen at my brother's declaration.

Sebastian Steele, the eldest of The Big Four—as I nicknamed my overbearing brothers. Or The STEELE Quaternity as the media dubbed the multibillionaires for being the most sought-after of the world's eligible billionaires. Their near-limitless wealth, power, and good looks attract women like bees to honey.

Well, three of them are out of the lineup, including Baz with Lola, then Malcolm *The Enforcer* with Starr, and Roger *The Responsible* with Leonie. My fraternal twin, other half of the Dynamic Duo, and youngest of the four, Harris, still clings to his playboy card like a life preserver in a tsunami.

Baz pins me with his platinum gray eyes—a Steele trait along with ebony hair and olive skin tone. As I stare back at my handsome brother, I can agree with women finding them attractive. At six feet, four inches with a muscular frame, he towers over me, and I'm no petite woman at five-eight. An Alpha Dom who oozes sex appeal with no effort whatsoever, women can't help but to vie for his attention.

However, Lola—his petite spitfire wife—snagged him. Her Independent Woman-cum-sub proved too much for Baz to resist. Their passionate love affair started with a meeting for her luxury lingerie company, Lola's Coterie, then had its fair share of setbacks. So he can speak from experience about relationships with trials.

"You know how I know? Lachlan's been evasive for weeks. At first, his excuses of work made sense to prepare for time away during your honeymoon. But when he didn't have time to see me while I was at STEELE Aberdeen—in your own backyard—I knew shit was fucked up. Even then, I assumed he was at fault. But now, paying more attention to you, I can tell you're the one at fault, Haley. What did you do?"

Effortlessly, Baz shifts between older brother and leader. An ability he's cultivated over the years as the leader of our siblings. Then most recently as the CEO of STEELE International, Inc. It's our family's multigenerational, multibillion dollar luxury real estate development and management company based in New York City with global offices and properties.

After his retirement a few years ago, our father,

Morgan, trusted Baz to carry the legacy into the future. My brothers and I respect him and accept his leadership. Each sibling works at STEELE: Malcolm president of the Entertainment Properties Division; Roger, president of the Residential Properties Division; Harris and I, as the tech wizzes coder and hacker, respectively, co-founders of our subsidiary STEELE Technology and Cyber Security.

Our mother Michelle—known as Shelley by those closest to her—runs STEELE Foundation that builds and manages attractive, affordable housing for urban, lower-income families. The name is a play on the house foundation, being strong and supportive like steel. The annual fundraiser at my parents' beachfront mansion within our family's compound—Steele Southampton Village—marks the end of the summer season. It's a well-attended event that generates millions each year.

She met our father when she was a shopgirl at a STEELE retail property. A native New Yorker with an independent streak and a feisty personality, she captivated our father who's ten years older and an Alpha Dom. Married for almost forty years, my parents have a relationship to strive for.

Baz and Lola, Malcolm and Starr, Roger and Leonie, Lachlan and me.

Lachlan, my teenage crush turned first and only lover now husband. Well, at least for now…

It's been six weeks since Lachlan left our penthouse flat in Aberdeen, Scotland after a major disagreement.

Sixteen years ago, when I was sixteen and he was

twenty, I realized I was in love with Baz's best friend and our cousin. That summer, my mind finally admitted I couldn't deny my attraction to Lachlan.

With gorgeous movie-star looks similar to the debonair Cary Grant, his rugged masculinity and charm leave women breathless. A six-foot-four-inch well-formed frame and blazing emerald green eyes, thick, sable brown hair slicked back from his chiseled cheekbones, and strong jawline with a cleft chin adds to his allure. Not to mention a swoon-worthy Scottish lilt lessened by years spent in the United States. Jackson. Lachlan Jackson.

Best friend or cousin no longer mattered to me.

Cousin since our mothers are best friends who formed a closer bond than they have with their blood siblings and relatives. Blood isn't always stronger. It's those who treat you with respect and love you that count above all.

Lucinda—aka Lucie—as fate would have it, also married a billionaire ten years her senior and an Alpha Dom, Connor Jackson. She ran away from a less than stellar life in New Orleans to New York City and became a bartender in one of their pubs. Jackson Corporation's—their Aberdeen-based, multigenerational, multibillion-dollar global company—repertoire includes fine dining, distilleries, and vineyards worldwide.

The Jackson's Irish and Scottish family created the finest single malt Scotch Whiskey and became billionaires years ago. King James VI titled the Jackson family as Marquess of Huntly with their family seat—Jackson Castle —in Banff, Aberdeenshire.

To go from a regular working girl to the Marchioness of Huntly is just plain ole wow! Another fairytale like my parents' romance.

Aside from Lachlan the first son, and the heir to the family seat with the title Earl of Aboyne, they have Lydie the eldest, Lucien *The Sexy Chef*, and Laurent. All of them take after the Jackson clan with green eyes and dark brown hair. And like The STEELE Quaternity, they refer to the boys as The Jackson Trio for their multibillionaire, power, and bachelor status.

With Connor as the CEO, each sibling works at Jackson Corporation: Lydie, Overall Vice President and Vice President of the Board; Lachlan, President of Liquor and Second Vice President of the Board; Lucien, President of Jackson Corporation Restaurants/Bars/Lounges and Third Vice President of the Board; Laurent, Director of Jackson Corporation Cigars Division and member of the Board.

Lucie runs Jackson Foundation that operates alcohol treatment centers for lower-income individuals and support for their family members. The annual fundraising gala is the highlight of Aberdeen's social calendar. Patrons from across the United Kingdom and the world attend.

The Steele and Jackson Matriarchs being best friends carry beyond us being cousins into our family businesses. STEELE serves and sells Jackson products in STEELE properties around the world, as well as in Jackson restaurants, pubs, stores, and businesses.

Just thinking about how close we are makes my heart clench with sadness.

Before Lachlan left me, he dropped the gauntlet: *"It will either be a vow renewal or a divorce. The choice is yours, Haley."*

Some days it feels like six months. Others six long years. I miss him so much I ache. A hole sits in my chest where my heart belongs. I rub the spot as Sebastian speaks. In hopes the new habit I developed will ease the pain.

Although, as Baz stated, this time I fucked up. Big time.

Despite my teenage crush, neither Lachlan nor I acted on our feelings. It wasn't until three years ago I learned his view of me as Baz's kid sister and a little cousin morphed into an attraction that summer too. He wasn't the one to make the move, though. I did.

After a year of bliss, where he insisted we keep our relationship a secret to prevent Baz from losing his mind and ending their friendship, or worse, I couldn't accept second place and left. Lachlan and I spent a year apart, during which I reconnected with a classmate from Harvard Business School—our family's legacy school, along with Harvard undergrad.

Callum Graham, Duke of Montrose. Another handsome Scottish billionaire with green eyes and long blond hair whose father is grooming him to lead his family's Graham Energy, Oil & Gas Company, based in Aberdeen. He's also an Alpha Dom four years older than me who could have had my heart if it were not for Lachlan.

During our time apart, Fiona Ridel—Princess Fiona the Fair of the enchanted violet eyes and ash blonde waist-length hair—continued her crusade to capture my Lachlan and his ring. The thirty-one-year-old Scottish heiress who his father wanted to make Lachlan's bride and mother to his heirs...

Despite almost a year with Callum, I couldn't help but to go back to Lachlan when he professed his love for me in front of our families. The Big Four were none too pleased. But I could not care less. Lachlan Jackson was mine without hiding from our families.

On a trip to Sorrento, we encountered a crowd of people dressed in white heading to Chiostro di San Francesco. A mass wedding was about to occur. In the spur of the moment, Lachlan dropped to one knee and proposed.

Once again, we shrouded our relationship in secrecy. Only our families knew of our nuptials. At my insistence. This time it was my need to make the perfect impression on Scottish society, nobles, and royals. I agreed with Mom Lucie's suggestion we have an engagement party, then have my fairytale wedding at Jackson Castle and announce it as a vow renewal. Which led to Callum still pursuing me and Fiona sidling up to my Lachlan even though she and Callum claimed to be a couple.

Six months later and three before our public wedding, Lachlan lost his shit when Callum—who trapped me outside of the ladies' room at a fundraising gala in Aberdeen—asked if I was married to Lachlan. I denied it. They fought. We left. We fought. He left.

All of this time, I continue with the wedding preparations and working as though nothing is amiss. I decided not to tell my family—not even my girls Lola, Leonie, and Starr or Blair and Billie Lola's CMO and COO, respectively—because the reality was too painful.

It hurt less not to face the fact Lachlan left and wouldn't answer my calls, text messages, emails, smoke signals with more than one-word responses.

I stayed at our Aberdeen penthouse flat for two weeks. But Lachlan didn't come home and refused to tell me where he was staying. A trip to his office provided the news he was out of the country on business with no return date available.

So I returned to our newly remodeled duplex penthouse in The STEELE Tower on Billionaires Row at Fifty-seventh Street and Fifth Avenue in New York City. Absence makes the heart grow fonder and all that, I suppose. But then again, I guess not since I had no idea Lachlan returned to Aberdeen according to Baz. So my husband doesn't miss me. At. All.

No one found it weird Lachlan and I weren't together since I travel to work with my clients in their offices around the world directly. He's not involved so much in our wedding planning since Sergeant Shelley and Lieutenant Lucie run it with some of my input. Easy peasy…

At least I thought I was doing a pretty good job of being normal. Until now. Obviously my ruse didn't work since Baz all but glares at me. Damn.

"Oh, Baz," I wail as I slump back against the leather sofa in the living room. My dove gray eyes fill with tears.

He moves from the silk-upholstered chair to sit beside me. One arm wraps around my shoulders to pull me to his massive chest while a hand sticks a loose tress of my waist-length ebony hair behind my ear.

Patiently, Baz waits for me to let it all out. I sit back with a hiccup and dab the wet spot on his black cashmere v-neck sweater. He shoos my hand away with a chuckle.

"I don't think that will do it, Hal," he says. Then he goes to the bar and pours two Waterford Crystal snifters of Jackson Special Blend Scotch. "It may be three in the afternoon. But I think this situation requires more than tea. Wouldn't you agree?"

I nod, and he hands a snifter to me.

"Now, fess up," he commands all Alpha Dom.

I take a gulp of the fragrant amber liquid for courage, then cough. It may be smooth, but not a toss-back liquor for my alcohol-consumption level.

Baz laughs and shakes his head.

"Go on," he says. His request not to be denied.

Knowing I can trust my brother to not make me feel like a fool—albeit I am one—I confess the whole sorry tale of that horrible night. As expected, he gives me sage and to-the-point advice.

"Get your ass back to Aberdeen and fix this shit, Haley Jackson! Now."

An hour later, I'm aboard my Gulfstream G650ER private jet bound for my husband.

***

Click the Link Below or Visit books2read.com/u/ bz12QD For Your Copy

Tease My Desires Lachlan & Haley Part II

I dedicate this novel to lovers who refuse to give up on one another. Continue to follow your hearts.

Fulfill Your Desires.

xoxo
Charmaine Louise

WELCOME TO CHARMAINELOUISE — THE SENSUAL LIFESTYLE

GLITZY. GLAMOROUS. STEAMY.

CharmaineLouise New York, Inc. invites you to indulge in *The Sensual Lifestyle* through **CharmaineLouise Books** and **CharmaineLouise Intimates**. CLBrands immerse you in *Sexy Fantasies* with CLBooks contemporary romance novels and give you *Sexy Under Things & Loungewear* with CLIntimates.

Charmaine Louise Shelton the Founder, CEO & Author of CLNY loves all things classic, elegant, feminine, and of course with an erotic edge! Favorite outfit of choice is a cashmere cardigan, leather pencil skirt, and seamed silk stockings with stiletto heels. Sexy Fantasy Type: sub with a dash of Voyeur. When not writing and designing, Charmaine Louise travels and spends time with her Maltese buddies, ZIGGY and Jynger.

CharmaineLouise — *The Sensual Lifestyle*

~ Visit online at **CharmaineLouise.com**

~ Subscribe to **CharmaineLouise Newsletter**

~ Find us on Facebook **@CharmaineLouiseNewYork**

~ Instagram **@CharLouNY**

CharmaineLouise Books *Sexy Fantasies* launched summer 2020. Sizzling, contemporary romance with your soon-to-be favorite Alpha Doms, Powerful Billionaires, and the women they lust after and love for second chances, insta-love, enemies-to-lovers, and more.

Want to chat it up and share your thoughts with other CLBooks Lovers? Read our blog, join our Charmaine-Louise Books Coterie Fan Club and follow us on my author pages and social media to be in the know about the book release dates, exclusive content, giveaways, contests, and more!

~ **Purchase your eBook and paperback novels from my Author Page by clicking here!**

~ Read and subscribe to our blog *The World of Sex*

~ Connect on **Amazon Author Page**

~ **Goodreads Author Profile**

~ <u>**BookBub Author Profile**</u>

CharmaineLouise Intimates *Sexy Under Things &* *Loungewear* debuted in 2003. Inspired by the sensuous sirens and sylph swans of the past and present, the hand crochet cashmere and silk collections are for the sexy: hence, the line names Ginger — Bombshell; Diana — Showstopper; Jackie — Timeless; Lena — Classic. Also known as The Movie-Star from Gilligan's Island; Ms. Ross The Boss; Mrs. Kennedy Onassis; Ms. Horne.

Do you thrive on seduction and being sexy lounging at home? Read our blog and follow us on social media to receive the tips, the latest additions to the collections, private sales, and more!

~ Read and subscribe to our blog *The Art of Seduction*

~ Find us on Facebook **@CharmaineLousieIntimates**

~ Instagram **@CharmaineLouiseIntimates**

Fulfill Your Desires.